MW00438325

HIS
SLAVE

Also by Vonna Harper

Surrender

Roped Heat

"Wild Ride" in *The Cowboy*

"Restraint" in *Bound to Ecstasy*

Night Fire

"Breeding Season" in *Only with a Cowboy*

"Night Scream" in *Sexy Beast V*

Going Down

Night of the Hawk

"Mustang Man" in *Tempted by a Cowboy*

Taming the Cougar

Falcon's Captive

"On the Prowl" *in Sexy Beast 9*

Spirit of the Wolf

Canyon Shadows

His Slave

"Soul of a Cowboy" in *In a Cowboy's Bed*

HIS
SLAVE

VONNA HARPER

APHRODISIA

KENSINGTON PUBLISHING CORP.

www.kensingtonbooks.com

APHRODISIA BOOKS are published by

Kensington Publishing Corp.
119 West 40th Street
New York, NY 10018

Copyright © 2013 by Vonna Harper

All rights reserved. No part of this book may be reproduced in any form or by any means without the prior written consent of the Publisher, excepting brief quotes used in reviews.

All Kensington titles, imprints, and distributed lines are available at special quantity discounts for bulk purchases for sales promotion, premiums, fund-raising, and educational or institutional use.

Special book excerpts or customized printings can also be created to fit specific needs. For details, write or phone the office of the Kensington Special Sales Manager: Kensington Publishing Corp., 119 West 40th Street, New York, NY 10018. Attn. Special Sales Department. Phone: 1-800-221-2647.

Aphrodisia and the A logo Reg. U.S. Pat. & TM Off.

ISBN-13: 978-0-7582-4228-0
ISBN-10: 0-7582-4228-X
First Kensington Trade Paperback Printing: July 2013

eISBN-13: 978-0-7582-8918-6
eISBN-10: 0-7582-8918-9
First Kensington Electronic Edition: July 2013

10 9 8 7 6 5 4 3 2 1

Printed in the United States of America

Incorporating a mystical place called the Blind Spot into this story took me back to my grandfather's time on earth. I never met him. He died at age thirty-six, when my mother was just six. But unlike so many people who are left with little understanding of who their ancestors really were, I was blessed. Homer Eon Flindt wasn't just the father of three children and husband of one wonderful woman, he was also a writer. His stories that appeared in the early pulp magazines are in my possession, as is his one book, *The Blind Spot,* about an alternate and parallel to Earth universe.

I took crazy liberty license when I developed my own Blind Spot. Grandpa's world was benign; mine edgy, erotic, and frightening. Grandma would be shocked by my creation, but I believe Grandpa would understand that at times the muse does what it demands.

Grandpa, I wouldn't be who I am without you.

1

"**I** said, it's past time for you to leave."

"The hell I will! You guys know where that bastard is. Five minutes alone with him, that's all I'm asking."

"It's not going to happen. Now, turn around and walk out of here."

"No!" The fifty-something man's voice rose. "Do you have any idea of the hell I've been through since that monster—he ruined me and my family, and now you're protecting him."

"Look, I'm going to say this only once. *Edge* is a magazine, not law enforcement. We report on lawbreakers. We're not now, nor will we ever be, in the business of hiding or protecting them. You read the Wanted feature, which means you know *Edge* wants those criminals brought to justice as much as you do."

"The hell. All you care about is readership. Damn it, I've stared at that picture of him in Wanted until it makes me sick. It was *just* taken. Where is he!"

Cheyenne Stensen had been standing with her back against *Edge*'s massive glass front door since she'd stepped inside and into the argument between the disheveled man and Mace Brandt, head of security. She should walk through the foyer and enter the elevator leading to her office, but taking her eyes off Mace was easier said than done.

Big as in six-foot-two-plus big with a wrestler's muscles and a bodyguard's stare, the man rattled portions of her she hadn't known were capable of rattling. What, in part, kept her rooted in place was the question of what would happen if the distraught man started a fight with Mace. The outcome was hardly in doubt, but would Mace risk injuring a man much older than himself, someone obviously going through hell? Although she'd seen Mace on an almost daily basis during the two months she'd been working for *Edge,* she didn't know the answer.

"I have no idea where he is," Mace said, pulling her back to the moment. "which is why they're featuring him this month. Go home. Wait for justice."

"Justice?" Tears flooded the man's eyes, aging him even more. "The legal system, you mean? Even if Fergo's found guilty, he'll only get his hand slapped. Me and my family, we have to find a way to start over. We're losing our home, my daughter had to drop out of college, and my wife—"

"Leave." Mace's voice was laced with ice. "This moment."

The man had been flexing and unflexing his fingers. Now he knotted them into fists and stepped toward Mace. Mace had been standing behind his desk, which dominated the foyer, but now he glided more than stepped around it, a seemingly impossible move for someone his size. "Last chance," Mace said in that emotionless way of his. "Either you walk out on your own or I'll do it for you."

One moment after another ticked away as the two men stared at each other, reminding Cheyenne of pit bulls. Then the smaller, weaker pit bull all but dropped to his belly. She half expected the older man to roll onto his back, exposing himself to deadly fangs. Tears burned her eyes at the thought of every-thing the man had endured. If she could get her hands on Fergo, there might not be enough left of him to take to trial.

"Good," Mace said. "And to let you know, if I see you here again, I'll have you arrested."

"Arrested, me? Fergo's the one who needs to be behind bars."

"Which is what *Edge* is trying to make happen. You have two seconds."

The man wasted a whole second gaping at Mace. Then, while Cheyenne tried to remember how to breathe, he spun on his heels, nearly lost his balance, and pushed through the door, jostling her as he did.

"I feel so sorry for him," she finally thought to say when it was just her and Mace in the shining, climate-controlled entry. "According to the charges against him, Charles Fergo has de-frauded investors of millions of dollars, ruined many of them. No wonder that man wants to take things into his own hands."

"His emotions are turning him stupid."

She'd been deliberately keeping her attention off the nerve-unsettling Mace, who'd worked his way into more nighttime fantasies than she'd ever admit. Now, barely believing what she'd just heard, she stared at him. "That's the only thing you're concerned about, that he not act stupid?"

"Yeah." Barely acknowledging her, Mace returned to his desk and settled into the oversized black leather chair designed to ac-commodate his bulk. He fixed his attention on the front door. "I didn't want to start the morning with an incident."

"Incident? You don't feel sorry for him? Empathize?"

"No."

The simple, yet complex response stopped her. It was Mon-day morning. Any moment now, other *Edge* employees would come through the door in preparation for work at the country's most successful monthly publication. She'd spent much of the weekend compiling her research material in preparation for turning it over to *Edge*'s senior reporter and still needed a few minutes to prioritize what she believed were the most important elements. But a man, a sexy as hell man who felt no empathy for someone whose world was falling apart had just spoken.

"I can't believe that," she came up with, wanting to find a core of humanity in him. "He's an innocent victim. Everyone Fergo defrauded was innocent."

"So?"

"So . . . this is unbelievable. I don't know what to say."

"Don't say anything."

He was writing something, maybe an incident report. Although she stared at the solid arm and even more solid body it was attached to, she was hard-pressed to remember what had intrigued her about him. It had to have been the unknown, the macho body and cool silence responsible for keeping the modern *Edge* building safe from the occasional crazy pulled out of the shadows by the publication's hard-hitting articles and exposés. Tall, dark, and mysterious with a mass of rich, black hair and gray eyes was one thing. Emotionally dead was quite another.

About to give him a lungful of what she thought of someone stripped of humanity, a childhood filled with hard lessons silenced her. If anyone should know about keeping one's emotions under lock and key, it was her.

"You're right," she said, keeping her tone neutral. "We're here to earn our keeps, not lead the march for an eye for an eye. As a reporter, I know to remain objective so I can do my job. I hadn't thought about it, but the same must be true for you."

"Hmm."

Giving up on him, she aimed for the elevator. The moment she was inside, she sank into silence. In some respects, she was in the wrong career. If she expected to go through life reserved and remote as her adoptive parents had tried to program her to be, she should have become an engineer or electrician. Instead, she spent her days talking to and writing about people, usually in crises. That, in part, was why she'd accepted her current job at *Edge*. Granted, going from thoroughly researching and then reporting on something as a freelance journalist to simply providing background information had initially felt like a demotion, but it was easier to dismiss a situation because she was no longer the one weaving emotion throughout the written word.

Still, how could Mace callously dismiss a man in pain? Not only that, he obviously had no interest in talking to her. One *good* thing about what had just happened: she'd learned that muscles and a mysterious persona weren't enough. From now on she wouldn't waste time or energy trying to send out sexual vibes to a man without compassion.

The sound of the elevator had ended. Still, Mace continued to stare at the door Cheyenne Stensen had gone through. He knew her name, in part because he'd made it his responsibility to familiarize himself with every *Edge* employee and in part because she'd been giving out messages any red-blooded male would get. She dressed like the majority of the city's young professional women, her wardrobe tailored and expensive, classy. Her hair was short, the style simple. Her makeup, which he knew next to nothing about, probably took a lot more effort than he'd ever guess. At least she didn't hide her chocolate eyes behind gobs of mascara. One thing he hadn't expected, it didn't look as if she got regular manicures.

For reasons he'd never share with another person and didn't fully understand himself, he'd thoroughly checked her out. As a result, he knew she was single and lived alone close enough to work that she could take the bus if she wanted to. She didn't have a criminal record, not so much as a speeding ticket. His search hadn't uncovered any relatives. Neither did she have what could be considered a best friend, which intrigued him almost as much as knowing she didn't have a boyfriend did. That seemed strange for a woman with a healthy, albeit somewhat kinky, sexual appetite.

The front door opened and in walked Robert Walters and Atwood Colby. His investigation of the pair had reinforced what he'd suspected from the day they'd interviewed him for his position: *Edge* wouldn't be the success it was without them.

"Morning, Mace," Robert said as the door closed behind him. "Anything we need to know about?"

"It was quiet over the weekend; I've already seen the surveillance tapes. But I just had to kick out someone who thinks we're hiding Charles Fergo."

Robert and Atwood, dressed in clone suits that cost more than Mace put out in house payments and sporting Rolodex watches, exchanged glances that didn't quite qualify as casual.

"What'd he say?" Atwood asked.

"I'll tell you what," Robert interjected before Mace could respond. "We want to meet with you later today—a request to utilize one of your more *unique* skills. Unless you believe this person constitutes an immediate security risk, why don't you report on what happened then?"

"No, he isn't jeopardizing anyone's safety. What do you mean, my *unique* skill?"

Robert glanced at his watch, then held up a warning finger as the door opened and a trio of women walked in. "We'll explain later, probably right after lunch." That said, they headed for the elevator.

Being in charge of security at a national publication that was the envy of every other magazine in terms of readership, revenue, and what he'd labeled as *presence* might have gone to another man's head, but despite his budget and the decisions he made, Mace accepted that he was just another employee. Robert and Atwood not only wrote his checks, they expected and usually received something akin to reverence from those under them. The two were responsible for *Edge*'s phenomenal success, and it was "off with their heads" for anyone who didn't get that simple fact.

Mace did. He did his job. He was rewarded. The reward gave his life meaning, at least as much meaning as it had ever had.

As for what he did on his own hours, that was no one else's business.

Unless Robert and Atwood had uncovered it.

In the wake of a dismissive shrug, Mace greeted the three women. Instead of hurrying to catch the elevator, they clustered near his desk. One was at least fifteen years older than him, but the other two were around his age, Gina married and Sandi engaged, not that either Gina or Sandi seemed to care when they were around him.

"I'm never going to get to work before you do, Mace," Sandi said, hand on hip. "Do you live here?"

"He couldn't possibly," Gina countered. "Come on, Mace, what'd you do this weekend? What lucky lady got her itches scratched?"

Even as he picked up his pen in preparation for completing the incident report, he wondered how the women would react if they knew the truth, but they never would because whatever their itches, they weren't the kind he had any interest in scratching.

Cheyenne, however, might be a different story.

2

If Robert were the CEO of a business with stockholders, his opulent office might have gotten him fired. However, as a principal owner of *Edge,* Cheyenne figured he had a right to spend the profits as he saw fit. Besides, the mahogany, glass, and chrome furniture was impressive, the original oil paintings beautiful. Even though Robert couldn't be more than five feet ten and 150 pounds, his innate confidence prevented the office from dwarfing him. Obviously professionally decorated, the room was large enough to include a round meeting table with six chairs in addition to his desk. From the looks of the material in front of four of the six chairs, she guessed that's where they'd be sitting. So who beside Robert, Atwood, and she was expected?

Standing in the doorway waiting for Robert to acknowledge her, she added commanding to her assessment of the man. Commanding was a positive label, one given to someone others followed because that person knew what he was doing and led by example. In Robert's case, however, as in Atwood's, healthy doses of arrogance went hand in hand with their self-confidence. She found the arrogance a little off-putting.

"Sorry." Robert put down what he'd been scanning, stood, and headed for the round table. Although he'd left his reading material behind, she recognized what she'd given him this morning. "I wanted to make sure I got the complete picture," he said as he sat. "Excellent job, Cheyenne. I can't think of anything you didn't cover. Now, be honest. Not the most exciting subject you've ever researched, is it?"

Her assignment had been to take a thorough look at the various ways and efficiency or lack of when the VA communicated with those who'd come to the agency for assistance. Robert hadn't said what he needed the information for, but she'd guessed he was planning to write a piece or series of pieces on the bureaucracy's operation.

"At first I wasn't sure how I'd tackle it," she admitted, sitting across from him. "Then I went online. People aren't shy when it comes to speaking their minds, especially if they believe they haven't been treated as they should be."

She might have said more except she sensed Robert wasn't interested in her methodology. Remembering that he and Atwood wanted to talk to her about a project, she glanced at the folder in front of her but didn't open it. She started to cross her legs only to stop because she'd worn a skirt today. Granted, it hit below the knee and wasn't tight, but she had no intention of revealing any more leg around Robert than she had to.

The man had never come on to her, nothing like that, but there'd been an undercurrent to the way he looked at and talked to her that kept her *woman in a risky world* antenna on alert. It was, she'd concluded, as if he was waiting for her to make the first move. Not going to happen.

"You haven't started without me, have you?" Atwood asked, startling her because she had her back to the door and hadn't heard him coming in. Not waiting for a response, Atwood plunked his slightly overweight, albeit well-dressed body in the chair to Robert's right.

Leaning forward, Robert planted his elbows on the gleaming desk, something that made her feel like an outsider passed between the two men. It was as if they shared a silent language and knew things no one else did.

"We'll begin as soon as he gets here," Robert said. "In the meantime ..." He focused his full attention on her. "In the meantime, we want you to know how pleased we are with the work you've done for *Edge*. The freelance pieces you wrote prior to coming on board convinced us that you're the kind of person we want on staff. Frankly, too many journalists are lazy. They don't double-check their facts, and they aren't wordsmiths."

If there were wordsmiths in the room, the label applied to Robert and Atwood. The men's articles were professional and polished. Instead of slanting an exposé, they presented the facts in straightforward prose, leaving it up to readers to draw their own conclusions. At the same time, their use of interviews and personal experiences subtly pulled readers in the direction the two wanted them to go.

Pieces were outwardly balanced with both sides of an argument or position being given equal weight. What probably wasn't obvious to someone who didn't make their living fashioning the written word was that whatever side Robert and Atwood were on came across as the more polished, clear, and direct, while the other was somewhat muddied or defensive.

"I appreciate hearing that my anal tendencies are considered pluses," she said, "especially coming from you. Both of you have earned every award you've received."

Atwood smiled one of his half smiles. "It's just the three of us here, Cheyenne, so you can be honest. Is that your goal, to garner some of those awards for yourself?"

Taken aback by the unexpected question, she retreated behind silence. She'd become a reporter because she was a stickler for accuracy, and the written word intrigued her, but trophies and plaques were hardly her life's goal. The thing was, she wasn't sure she had one.

"You've embarrassed her," Atwood told Robert. "Besides, maybe she's secretly gunning for our positions."

The men chuckled, and although she joined in, she wished she could think of a way to change the subject. Not for the first time, she sensed they were trying to dig deep into her and uncover layers she had no intention of revealing.

"Ah," Atwood said, "there he is."

Swiveling toward the door, Cheyenne found herself looking up at the last person she expected to see in here today, Mace. As he'd done enough times that she should be used to it, he'd entered the room soundlessly. Granted, silence had to play a vital role in security, but she couldn't help but wonder if skill had nothing to do with his career and everything to do with the man himself.

After scanning the room and briefly settling his gaze on Robert, Atwood, and her in turn, he lowered his athletic body in the chair to her right. Granted, that's where the paperwork was, but did he have to sit so close that his body heat flicked out and ran over her arm and side?

"Dispensing with the preliminaries," Atwood said, "let's get to the reason for this meeting. For some time now we"—he nodded at Robert—"have been entertaining a feature article concept with what we believe has tremendous built-in reader appeal, but we needed to have the right personnel in place in order to carry it off."

"I'm not a writer or reporter," Mace said. His posture made her wonder if he'd been in the military. Did the man ever relax? Between his black slacks and body-hugging dark brown turtleneck, he struck her as a creature of the night.

"No, you're not," Atwood said. "But among your *accomplishments* is a certain expertise that has nothing to do with pounding a keyboard, yet is key to the article." Folding his arms, Atwood fixed his full attention on Mace. "We could play twenty questions, but I believe you know what I'm talking about."

Mace remained expressionless. Just the same, she sensed a tension that hadn't been part of him before.

"Why don't you spell it out?" Mace said, and for a moment she wanted nothing more than to jump to her feet and run. Then, maybe because no one was paying her any attention, she forced herself to relax.

"When we hire someone," Robert said, "we conduct background checks on them, or rather we assign you that responsibility. We did the same when we were looking for someone to fill your position."

"I understand."

An insane thought distracted Cheyenne. Was it possible for Mace to pass a lie detector test even if he was lying through his teeth? If he felt no emotion, maybe so.

"It doesn't bother you knowing we were certain to uncover particular *interests* of yours?"

"I figured if that was a problem, you wouldn't have hired me."

"That's one cool customer," Atwood said to Robert. "Nerves of steel. So, Mace, you aren't embarrassed knowing—"

"What I do on my own time doesn't impact my job. If it embarrassed me, as you call it, I wouldn't do it."

"Hmm. No emotional quandary? No asking yourself if there's something sick or unnatural about what you do?"

The conversation swirled around her, shadows confusing and angering her at the same time. Obviously she was the only one who didn't know what they were talking about. Why, then, was she in the room?

"No emotional quandary," Mace said. "As for whether it's unnatural, that's not something I concern myself with."

"Amazing." Atwood shook his head, his fine hair springing free of whatever he'd plastered it in place with. "Has it always been this way? Maybe, when you first ventured into BDSM, you at least had to work at looking yourself in the mirror?"

BDSM! The giving and receiving of physical pain wrapped in a sexual blanket. Suddenly flushed and her mind stuttering, Cheyenne gripped her chair arms. She couldn't have spoken if someone had held a gun to her head.

Much as she would have given anything to fade into the woodwork, it was too late as witnessed by the way Robert and Atwood had turned their attention to her. Mouth numb, she struggled to relax her fingers.

"I've always been able to face myself in the mirror," Mace said. If he was aware of her reaction to what had just been revealed, he showed no sign. "I understand BDSM's parameters, its protocol, if you will. If you're wondering if my activities as a dom might jeopardize my ability to do my job here, they won't. I allow no crossover."

"In other words, no *playing* with the staff?"

With every second, Cheyenne grew more convinced she knew where the conversation was taking them. Mace was a dom, a dominant, someone who understood the rights and responsibilities that came from being a master in a sexual-based relationship.

"Where is this going?" Mace asked. "You're asking questions you already have the answer to."

"And you have ice water in your veins." Atwood made it sound like a compliment. "Is there anything that rattles you?"

"A gun in my face, if I'm unarmed."

"But not having your employers tell you they know you're a fixture at Indulgences."

Still impassive, Mace fixed his gray eyes on Atwood. She

knew about Indulgences. Touted as the most comprehensive BDSM club in the city, it prided itself on offering a full range of experiences for both doms and submissives. According to the subtle promotion, prospective members were carefully screened and activities monitored, which gave the club a clinical feel, at least for those on the outside. Instead of being left alone to engage in whatever turned them on, doms and subs were given a checklist of approved and allowed activities—not that she knew what those activities were because she hadn't worked up the courage to walk in the door.

"What is this about?" Mace asked, emotionless as always.

A moment ago, Cheyenne couldn't have known whether she was hot or cold. Now she felt as if someone had struck a match to her neck. Heat charged through her veins, compelling her to concentrate on her breathing. Her cheeks had become flushed. Thank goodness no one could check between her legs, because they'd encounter a telltale dampness.

Mace was a dom!

"What is this about?" Robert repeated. "Mace, again I have to hand it to you. You've cut through the BS. Bottom line, the lifestyle you've embraced gives us the *in* we need."

"How long have you known?"

"Since before we hired you."

"Then why has it taken this long to—"

"You're only one leg of the operation. You provide the expertise. What we lacked was the journalist to—"

"Wait a minute," Cheyenne blurted. "You're considering assigning me to—"

"Not considering," Atwood interrupted. "The decision has been made. We have every faith in your ability to provide an accurate account of the experience."

"Let me get this straight." For the first time since he'd sat down, Mace angled his body toward her. Damn but the man was big! Big and powerful, a master. "You want her to interview me?"

"That's part of it," Atwood said. "But if we were content to hinge the entire piece on your experience, we could simply ask you to write down what you've observed and participated in. But the dom's role is only part of the scene."

"And the rest is?"

"The sub, of course. Her—I use that pronoun because the majority of submissives are female—experiences both within Indulgences and elsewhere is key. For the article to succeed, it must be comprehensive."

"Wait. You want Cheyenne to go to Indulgences?"

"We want *you* to take her there."

"What?" If she jumped to her feet, would her legs hold her? "Look, I'm sitting right here. I don't appreciate being talked about as if I'm not. What in hell makes you think I have any interest in—"

"That's exactly the point." Atwood's lips curled. "You are interested. In spades."

3

Interest flickered in Mace. Trusting experience to keep his features neutral, he studied Cheyenne. Her eyes had gone wide, and fresh color painted her cheekbones. She needed to learn how to keep her emotions under wrap; otherwise, people would get past her defenses. Maybe he'd offer to give her a few lessons.

Watching her lips thin, he acknowledged that the lessons he'd like to give her had nothing to do with locking up what she felt and too damn much with unpeeling her submissive layers.

"Let me explain." Robert's gentle smile would have done a kindergarten teacher proud. "The Internet is an amazing tool. What too many people don't fully comprehend is how easy it is to break through the so-called security features. I would suggest you upgrade the security on your home computer."

"You're saying what?" Cheyenne spoke through clenched teeth.

"That these two know what's on your computer," Mace supplied. "My guess, they used the same technology I have to protect the integrity of *Edge*'s system, right?"

"Correct you are," Atwood said. "No need to reinvent the wheel when we're already paying for the system, right?" He gave an impatient wave. "Neither Robert nor I have the time or inclination to go into an explanation, Cheyenne. Suffice to say, we know a great deal about your interest in BDSM. Unfortunately, your interest has been limited to observation, not participation."

Mace expected Cheyenne to jump to her feet and stalk out of the room while threatening lawsuit. He wanted to warn her that her checkbook didn't stand a chance against *Edge*'s deep pockets. Warn? Why should he care what she did?

"Tell me." Cheyenne's tone could form lifecycles. "What do you know?"

"That's beyond the point," Robert said. "I'd like to know why you're only an observer. Could it be fear?"

"I can't believe we're having this conversation."

"Believe. Cheyenne, you're anxious to do more than what you've been allowed to at *Edge.* In your previous position, you proved yourself a competent reporter. If you accept the assignment we're offering, the article will be yours to run with, written from a firsthand perspective."

Robert was playing her. Trading on her ambition. Interesting.

"What do you expect from the article?" she asked, surprising Mace because he'd expected her to go off on their unauthorized look into her computer.

"The truth. From your perspective and based on your experience." Robert smiled one of his "no eyes involved" smiles. "We don't know what your experience will reveal both from a personal and reporter perspective, which is why we haven't drawn any conclusions about the finished product. All we ask is that it be authentic and honest."

"Why?"

"I thought we made that clear. Readership. Revenue. Even

the most conservative reader harbors a secret interest in shall we call it fringe sexual practices. Feed that interest and people will be looking for your byline. That one article, done as we know you're capable of, will springboard you to the top here. Maybe put you in line for writing some of the Hunted features."

The wheels were spinning in Cheyenne's mind, he could see that in the way the veins at the sides of her slim neck pulsed, the rise and fall of her full breasts under the damn green jacket.

"You're pressuring me," she said.

"Please don't put it that way. We're offering you an opportunity we wouldn't to *Edge*'s other reporters."

"Because you think I'm interested in what goes on at Indulgences."

"Because we know you are. Don't insult our intelligence."

She leaned forward. "I see through your smokescreen. Bottom line is you had no right doing what you did. My private life is that, private."

"You're not interested in a bonus in exchange for exploring your personal kink? You've written articles, like the one on the emotional damage to children, that demonstrate your courage. Is this so different?"

She shook her hair, the short strands dancing. "You want me to work with him?" She indicated Mace.

Atwood's sigh flared his nostrils. "Frankly, this is getting tiresome. Call our investigation into your potential what you want. We needed assurance that we were right in tapping you for the assignment. Either you're interested or we'll choose someone else."

Robert nodded agreement. "I'm getting the impression that you aren't able to separate the personal from the professional. Quite frankly, we couldn't care less what either of you do in your private time. Cheyenne, we would be remiss to send you alone into Indulgences. Not only isn't it the most sanitary and safe of environments, you might be tagged as a reporter if you suddenly showed up. Mace, as a regular, can provide the perfect, how should we call it, cover. He's your in."

"Interested?" Atwood asked.

"Because if you're not, I'm afraid we'll have to take another look at you in terms of you being a *fit* at *Edge.*"

Cheyenne's jaw ached from clenching it. Her legs felt wooden, and panic nibbled at her nerve endings.

Thank goodness she was no longer in Robert's over-the-top office.

"What's your decision?"

She'd known Mace was behind her; her entire system had been aware of his presence. Drawing on lessons learned as a child, she slowly turned and faced him. Having to look up while responding to the heat radiating from him didn't help. "Do you care?"

He cocked his head, that longish mass of dark as sin hair going with the effort.

"You probably thought it was funny, don't you?" she asked, not giving him time to respond. "They backed me into a corner while ignoring you, but it makes sense. They knew you'd like nothing better than being handed a reason for spending the night at Indulgences."

"That's what you thought? Your privacy wasn't the only one that was breached."

Planting a hand over her mouth, she spoke through the gag her fingers provided. "I didn't think about that. I'm sorry. They had no right."

Instead of agreeing, he latched on to her elbow and dragged her away from the closed door to Robert's office. Yes, oh yes, having his hand on her was a kick in the nether regions, but he was right. Neither of them wanted Robert or Atwood overhearing.

Instead of releasing her once she gave notice that she understood what he was doing, he continued to hold on to her while leading the way to the elevator. Instead of hitting the button to summon the elevator, he tugged on the metal fireproof door leading to the stairs. Her throat closing down, she followed him onto the small landing, waited as the door swung closed.

They were alone in the claustrophobic space, the narrow stairs ahead of her, metal behind, Mace at her side.

"They fed into your ambition," he said. "Are you going to bite?"

Mace took up too much of the space. He was the only spot of life and warmth in here. Most unnerving perhaps was the elephant in the living room in the form of the job assignment that had been offered or maybe forced on them. Wrapping her mind around everything would be easier if he'd release her, but she'd be damned if she'd exude anything except confidence.

Be damned if she'd let him know much he turned her on.

"I'm not a submissive," she said. "Okay, so I'm intrigued by the lifestyle, but if they think I'm dying to have some man put a collar around my neck, they're crazy."

"What do you have against collars? And doms."

Damn him! She'd been played enough for one day. Not caring what he thought, she pulled free. Unfortunately, freedom didn't come close to extinguishing the lingering impact on her elbow, let alone the grinding hunger between her legs. Damn but she needed to get laid!

"Nothing," she said. "As long as it involves other people."

"I don't think so."

What was with Mace? Didn't his eyes ever reveal anything? "What are you talking about?"

"I'm a dom, just like our bosses said. I've been playing with the lifestyle long enough that I know when I see a submissive." He held up a warning hand. "Okay, someone with submissive tendencies. That politically correct enough for you?"

She'd never slapped a man, but for two cents she'd leave her handprints on Mace's lightly shaded jaw. Of course, then she'd be tempted to wrap her limbs around him and press her breasts to his chest.

Shocked by the far from politically correct thought, she willed her hands to remain at her sides. "Playing with the lifestyle? Not ballsy enough for the real thing?" *Shut up. Just shut up.*

There it was, the faintest glimmer of something in his deep eyes. Too bad she didn't know what that something was. "What do you care?"

The words of a man on the defensive? "You're right, it's none of my business, just as what I decide is none of yours."

"Isn't it? If I'm expected to show up with floggers and ropes, I need advance warning."

"Don't worry. I'll give you plenty of notice, if."

"It's going to be interesting." He didn't move a muscle. Just the same, he felt closer somehow. Invading her space. Testing her.

Slouching in his leather chair, Robert studied his nails. His cuticles needed clipping, something his manicurist would do when he saw her later today. Right now he had more important things on his mind.

"I don't trust him," Atwood said. "He's been here, what, nearly a year? I still can't figure him out."

"I was thinking the same thing. He's a bit of a wild animal, a cougar maybe. Got too much of the predator in him."

"Nah, nothing wild about Mace. He's ruled by a lot more than filling his belly. You know what I'm thinking, that man's a pit bull."

Made more uneasy than he'd ever admit by the image of a frenzied mass of muscle and teeth, Robert glanced out his window. In the distance were treetops, proof that the city park was only a couple of blocks away. Unfortunately, the close-up view was of *Edge*'s parking lot.

"Pit bulls need to be kept chained," he said. "But trained right, they're valuable."

"As long as no one turns their backs on them. Are you sure we're making the right choice? Maybe someone we can keep in line?"

Robert shook his head and went back to studying his nails. "Then we'd have someone without balls. Mace has what we're looking for, all the qualities we need at the Blind Spot."

Sighing, Atwood began rubbing his paunch. Damn the man, he was letting himself go, not that he'd ever say anything because Atwood could sink him as quick and deep as the other way around. Like it or not, they needed each other.

Fortunately, there were rewards, specifically the Blind Spot.

"I want to see her there," he admitted. "On her knees. Naked. In chains."

"Not so fast. One step at a time. And most important, the whole time we're getting there, she can't see it coming."

"What about Mace?"

"He'll think he's been given the keys to the city."

"I'm not sure he cares about that, but if those keys work on her chains—that's how we feed our pit bull."

4

Caught. Immobile. Naked. Hot.

Cheyenne's dream relaxed its grip on her by degrees. First she became aware of cotton sheets on her bare skin, then the dawn-cool air coming in the open window. Any moment the alarm would go off, and she needed to pee, but sleep continued to caress her. As long as she kept the day at bay, she could burrow into the fading memories, maybe build and expand those images until they tipped her into a climax.

She'd been in a dark room, perhaps a cave, perhaps a dungeon, albeit a climate-controlled one. Because she couldn't lift her head to a natural position, her back and neck had ached. Harsh bars had pressed at her from all directions, even under her hands and knees.

She was in a cage barely large enough to hold her. Someone had stripped off her clothes and thrust her into the cruel contraption, and now she waited for whomever had done this to her.

Instead of terror, she panted in anticipation, her nipples so hard they hurt, pussy wet and soft and aching. In short, she was a bitch in heat, helpless and ready for—something. She didn't know how long she'd been in the cage, whether this was the first time, or what her captor looked like.

Her captor. A man, of course. With bottomless eyes and an expression that said he had every right to do this. He stood in the shadows, looming over her, turning her into a trapped animal, drawing out the time until he'd taken possession of her.

"It's going to be another hot day, folks, so take advantage of this temperature while you can. The latest on your commute, repairs on the Morris Bridge are still slowing traffic to a single lane. If you can avoid—"

Paying no attention to what else the radio announcer had to say, Cheyenne freed herself from her pale blue sheet and sat up. Not bothering with slippers, she padded into the bathroom and plunked her ass on the toilet. Holding her head in her hands, she tried to recapture her dream, but like ocean fog, it slipped off into nothing. Hopefully it, or one like it, would return tonight. In the meantime, she had to deal with reality.

She was in the shower before resigning herself to decision making. Her first, the easy one, was to use rose-scented shampoo. The other involved her career, or more specifically whether it was going somewhere as opposed to, possibly, the unemployment line.

Turning so her back was to the shower head, she let the spray wash over her hair. Using both hands to get at the suds made the most sense, but the task could still be done with one while the other went between her legs.

Hot up inside, wet and slippery and willing to get even more so with the slightest bit of encouragement, which she wished to hell she had time for.

How long would it take to get off this morning? Hard to say because she didn't make a practice of keeping track. Easy to do when she combined fingers on her clit with chain, blindfold, even gag fantasies.

Mace was a dom!

A sharp shake of her head failed to throw off thoughts of the too damn big and dangerously sexy man. All that served was to make her dizzy, which came between her and finishing what she'd started with her hand job.

What would his hands feel like on her body, between her legs, caressing her breasts, hell, mauling them?

Still light-headed, she straightened and reached for the soap, but it squirted free and landed over the drain. Bemused, she stared through the water sheeting off her head. Being alone was safe, kind of, but she'd feel a hell of a lot safer without the kind of thoughts she'd been having from the first time she'd seen Mace. The man got to her. Worse and better than that, he was the perfect dom poster man.

Sexy. Dangerous.

A pro to her lower than amateur status.

Bending over, she snagged the soap. Then although logic said she should bring it and her washcloth together, she pressed the bar between her breasts.

Decisions. Accept the challenge Robert and Atwood had thrown at her. See if Mace really was what their employers had made him out to be. Play sub to his dom and write the article of her career about the experience.

Or...

There really wasn't an *or*, was there? Not if she wanted to go on paying her bills.

Cheyenne had argued, ad nauseam, that she didn't want to go to Indulgences with Mace. Smart and savvy girls kept their own wheels under them on the first *date*. No way was she going to be beholden to him for getting to and from the club.

He'd shut her up by pointing out that security cameras scanned the parking lot. There was only one way to pull off their act of being a couple of consenting players in the BDSM scene, and that was by playing according to the rules.

And the rules said he dressed in snug black slacks, shiny shoes, a muscle-hugging turtleneck, and drove a black sports car while she huddled beside him sans bra and panties wearing a skirt that kissed the top of her thighs and a see-through blouse unbuttoned to the middle of her breasts.

If her folks could see her now, not that they'd care.

"You come here a lot?" she asked around the knot in her throat. Although she didn't hug the passenger's door, she kept to her own space as much as the small interior allowed. "Would they call you a regular?"

"I was for a while. Not so much lately."

"Why not?"

It was night, the boulevard jammed as befitting a Friday evening. Any driver who valued his life and wheels kept his attention on the traffic. Fortunately, Mace fit that demographic, which meant she could occasionally glance at him without being studied in return.

"Things change. I change."

"What do you mean?" Would he guess that her questions, in part, were designed to try to keep her nervousness tamped down?

"We all change, Cheyenne. At first the new is exciting. Then it becomes familiar and the seeking starts all over again."

She could ask what he meant by *seeking*, but if the condition went as deep as she suspected, he wouldn't open up any more than she would. "I don't know. Sometimes the familiar is the perfect base. For example, I've always loved the written word. To me it's kind of like having a hundred blank canvases and an endless supply of paint. There's no end to the possibilities."

"You're good with the written word."

"I appreciate the compliment, if that's what it is," she said. "There must be something that turns you on the same way diving into a new project does me."

"Sex turns me on. Isn't that enough?"

No, she wanted to yell at him, no! Life in all its forms was to be embraced, celebrated. At least that's what the manual said. But what if no matter what she put into her life, her parents never considered it good enough?

"Sex in general?" She forced the question. "Or the kinky kind like what's going to happen tonight?"

His silence gnawed at her. Should she shut up or, even better, ask for an explanation of what to expect? Cover his fingers with hers and absorb more of whatever the hell was swirling around her?

"A lot of game playing goes on at Indulgences," he said. "I trust you understand that. What you'll see isn't necessarily the real thing."

"I realize fantasy plays a role in the BDSM scene, if that's what you mean." Okay, if he insisted on keeping things professional, she'd meet him in the middle. Except they were hardly a couple of bean counters divvying up beans.

"In part what I'm saying is, some Indulgence members live the lifestyle twenty-four/seven. Others, the majority, check their real selves at the door and assume new personas."

"What about you?"

"Doesn't matter."

Why not, Mace? What are you hiding from me?

"You don't like hearing that, do you? Get your story, just keep me out of it."

"That's hard to do considering I can't get the story without you body guarding me."

"That's not all I'll be doing."

"You're right. Mace, why didn't we talk about this before?"

There it was, another of his silences. If only she could root around in his brain—and other places.

He tapped the brakes, glanced in his rearview mirror. "We should have."

Until now, she'd successfully kept her hands semi-folded on her lap. Now, thinking about how soon she'd be stepping into a world she'd only fantasized about, she laced her fingers together. The lump that had been in her throat returned, larger than earlier. "I should have brought it up," she admitted. "Granted, I've done my research, but that won't fully prepare me for the real thing, will it?"

Slowing, he flipped on the right turn signal. "Do you trust me?"

"What do you mean?"

They were turning off the boulevard and onto a narrow, ill-lit street. She started sweating.

"This is my turf. If you're willing to follow my lead, you'll get through it; but if you don't trust me, you'll panic."

"Are you sure? You don't know me very well."

"I'll know you a hell of a lot more by the time the night's over."

"Does that work both ways?"

He was traveling less than twenty miles an hour. Because he wanted to finish what they'd started before reaching their destination?

"Maybe." For the first time since picking her up at the *Edge* parking lot, he looked at her. As they passed under a streetlight, she caught a glimpse of his eyes but couldn't see beneath the surface. What she suddenly understood was that he didn't want her getting any deeper into him than she had. Because there was nothing there? Too much?

Her head aching from what she'd just discovered about the powerful man next to her, she stared resolutely at the building looming ahead. A single, subtle light illuminated the word *In-*

dulgences over the door to a single-story, sprawling structure that made her think of a warehouse.

"You know what it means to be a sub, at least the rudiments," he said as he eased into the crowded gravel parking lot. "The regulars will see you for what you are, a newcomer. There's no need for you to pretend to be anything else. However you respond to me will be spontaneous. Here." He tapped the jockey box between them. "Put it on."

Suspicions about what she'd find helped not at all. Her fingers did the jerky dance as she lifted out a dark leather collar with an oversized metal locking device. The lock would take a key to undo. A metal ring was imbedded in the leather.

She could do this. Her growing up had prepared her for facing life head-on. Beating it down if that's what it took.

The leather was softer than she'd suspected and felt almost like velvet around her throat. Still, she started as she clicked it in place. Step one taken. Sub label in place.

"Good," he said as he pulled into a parking slot.

"You had doubts I'd go through with it?"

"Can't blame me." He put the car in Park and killed the engine. "Here's the basics. You speak only when I give you permission. I'll keep things basic and hopefully within your comfort zone. I can read your body language. If I'm about to take you too far, I'll know before you do."

She couldn't stop herself from fingering the ring. Couldn't think how to open her door. "What are you going to do?"

"I'm not going to tell you, slave."

Slave.

"You don't want to blow your cover, right?" He watched her restless fingers.

"No."

"Then this is how it has to go down. Be authentic. Keep telling yourself that, authentic. You ready?"

Not trusting her voice, she nodded. Then he leaned toward

her, and she didn't know whether to take a header through the closed window or bury her head in his lap and squawk out her fear. Instead, she dropped her hand so he could connect a chain to her collar.

"Wait here," he said and reached for his door handle.

5

She sat alone in the silent, dark car. A couple of men were going into Indulgences, not that she gave them more than a glance because Mace was walking around to her side. In miniseconds, he'd order her to get out. She'd plant her weight over her too-high-for-safety heels and do whatever he ordered her to. Go inside that mysterious and exciting building, and be changed by the experience.

A quiet click followed by a rush of summer air jolted her. Saying nothing, he reached for the chain and tugged her out. There was nothing playful about his grip and nothing sympathetic or comforting in his cool appraisal.

Changed? Already happening.

Arms dangling at her sides, she trailed after Mace as he hauled her along like some obedient dog. Walking on gravel forced her to concentrate on her footing.

Mace opened the large door, stepped in, jerked her against his back. If the surroundings weren't sucking her dry of composure, she would have slapped him.

"Hey, Master M, good seeing you," a masked and caped

man with a smoker's voice said. "If you'd have let us know you were coming, we'd have made a few calls. Gotten some of your fans in here."

"Not interested," Mace said. "I have another agenda tonight."

"So I see." A soft hand landed on her shoulder. "Your slave have a name?"

"Not tonight. Anything in particular happening?"

The soft hand remained in place, prompting her to stare up at the man who'd invaded her space. He wasn't particularly tall, with a belly that made him look about five months' pregnant. His mask added to her sense that she was out of her element. She also didn't appreciate being pawed this way.

"Master JJ has reserved the center stage for an auction starting soon. Last I heard, he's selling five of his slaves."

Mace's laugh lacked warmth. "Ever the showman. I wonder how much he paid them to play his little game?"

"None of my business." The masked man massaged her shoulder, drawing her blouse off her collarbone as he did. "You want one of the private rooms, or will you be taking this public?"

"Right now we're just watching. Got it, watching. And no sampling."

The man lifted his hand off her. "Hey, don't get your shorts in a knot. You can't blame me for being interested in a little fresh meat. Where'd you find her?"

To her relief, Mace didn't answer. However, neither did he acknowledge her existence before striding into the large, heavily populated, and dimly lit room. At first the room, which was a step down from the entryway, made her think of a gymnasium, but no gym she'd ever been in had held a population like this.

People stood in groups or milled around. Voices, mostly male, clashed. Their *costumes* took two forms. Either, like Mace, they were draped in black, or they'd stuffed their bodies into too-tight leather. Not enough flesh was covered, and a few had their cocks on display. If she had one word for the way they walked, *strut* won hands down. Whether they were pretending or for real, they gave out auras of control and confidence, arrogance, and the capacity for cruelty.

As for the women—well, there was no lack of skin there either. Or collars, cuffs, ankle restraints, even chastity belts. Some were gagged, a few had been blindfolded. Breasts hung out. Shaved pussies were on display. Heads sagged submissively.

The BDSM Internet sites she'd visited had featured nubile young women with painted lips and false eyelashes. Most had helped plastic surgeons pay their bills. The *talent* knew where to stand to best advantage for the camera, how to shout out their supposedly forced climaxes, how to best *struggle* in their restraints so their assets were displayed.

In contrast, the women at Indulgences came in all sizes and ages. Some had nearly nonexistent breasts, while at least two of the *slaves'* breasts hung nearly to their waists. Granted, there were a few prime specimens, but she'd stack up pretty well next to them, pretty darn well.

Not that it mattered.

"You renting her?" Whoever had just spoken was so close behind her that she felt the speaker's breath on the back of her head. "If you are, I'm interested."

Using his hold on her leash for leverage, Mace hauled her against his side. "Take your cock somewhere else, Paul. Haven't you given up by now?"

The still unseen Paul laughed. "As long as you keep coming up with flesh like her, I'm not likely to. What do you think, slave? Interested in sucking on a real man?"

This was happening. She was no longer dreaming, no longer directing a scene that existed only in her mind, and Mace had slipped his hand into her short hair and pulled so she was off balance, her neck burning.

"Go on, slave," Mace said. "Tell him who your master is."

Mace should have given her the playbook before they came in, should have given her a better hint of what to expect.

"Speak up, slave." Anger, either genuine or affected, was laced through Mace's voice. "Whom do you belong to?"

"You, Master." *Until I kick you in the balls, that is.*

"There's your answer, Paul. Anything else you need to know?"

"Hell, I was just joking. In fact, how about you and your bitch join me and mine at my table. I'll buy you a drink while we wait for the floor show to start."

Mace's shrug resonated through her. She had no choice but to reach out, thinking to wrap her arm around his waist for support, but her fingers barely brushed him when he yanked her upright. Tears sprang to her eyes.

"Did I give you permission to touch me?" Although he released her hair, he reined her in via the chain leash.

"New one?" Paul asked. "Training them's a lot of work, but there are rewards. You thinking of doing some training tonight? If so, I'll sell tickets and we'll clean up."

Cheyenne now stood directly in front of Mace and on her toes because he'd lifted up on the leash, causing the collar to push against the underside of her jaw. Her arms were at her sides and ending in fists that wanted nothing more than to punch Mace.

At the same time, damn it, at the same time something hot and heady radiated out from him, and her hungry body absorbed it. Tonight was the real deal, years of imagining coming true, if she had the guts.

Mace turned Paul down, at least that's what she thought he'd said, not that she paid attention. Her breasts were maybe a half inch from his chest and if she leaned just a bit, she'd connect with his cock.

"How about the drink?" Paul said, sounding disappointed. "At least we can catch up."

"Why not. Your usual table?"

"What else? I'm a creature of habit. Even have the same slave as the last time we saw each other."

To her relief, the pressure around her neck let up, allowing her to settle back onto the balls of her feet. She would have relaxed more if Mace wasn't still holding on to her as if she were some unruly dog. At least she could devote some attention to Paul or, more to the point, the tall, skinny woman standing behind him. Even with the lousy lighting, she noted layers of makeup complete with black lip liner. The woman wore, of all things, a spiked collar and was naked from the waist up. A micro mini clung to her nearly nonexistent hips. Her hands were secured behind her. She didn't speak.

Too much! Sensory overload.

Struggling to put all the pieces together distracted her from what Mace was doing. As a result, she found herself being hauled behind him as his long legs wound through the press of bodies. It was too hot in here, claustrophobic.

And exciting as hell.

Paul was already sitting down when Mace and she caught up to them. Instead of joining him, Paul's *slave* awkwardly inched under the table on her knees. Holy shit, was she going to plant herself between Paul's legs and work on his cock? The sound of a zipper tearing loose answered her question. Just thinking how the skinny woman had accomplished that without use of her hands made her teeth ache.

Pulling out his chair, Mace gracefully settled himself on it. He locked eyes with her. *You have the guts for this?* his expression said.

Yes, she answered.

Nodding, he jerked his head, indicating he wanted her to

kneel at his side. She did so slowly, graceful, back straight and arms still dangling. If he directed her under the table, would she?

Did she have a choice?

Thinking about her lack of options made her mouth water and pussy clench.

"More meat on her than my slave has," Paul observed. "Curves where curves should be. How'd you snag her?"

"That, my friend, is none of your business."

Mace reached out with the chain lightly wrapped around his fingers and stroked her temple. Electricity shot from the point of contact to her already overstimulated sex. "So you like my pet, do you?" he asked Paul. "She's raw but shows promise. Don't you, bitch?"

On the verge of insisting Mace take back the offensive word, she bit her tongue. This was part of the act, right?

"I hope I do, Master."

"Of course you do. Otherwise, you'll be punished."

"How does she respond to the flogger?" Paul's voice sounded strained, giving Cheyenne a clue about what was going on under the table.

"Needs work. She prefers restraints."

"How is she at blow jobs?"

Mace's hand slid from the side of her head to her mouth. Taking her lower lip between his thumb and forefinger, he gently drew it toward him. Her lids sagged, and her breath caught.

"My opinion, she's operating at a C level but eager to become more proficient, aren't you?"

Mindless, she nodded as best she could. Her nipples hardened, pressing against the too-tight fabric. The why and how of her response didn't matter. There was only feeling alive.

Mace released her lip only to continue his assault to her nervous system by flattening his fingers over her mouth. His features blurred. The loud driving music and nonstop conversations that had made her ears ache no longer registered. His fingertips were rougher than she'd expected, the contrast between them and her lips erotic.

"What caught my attention from the beginning," Mace continued, "was her response to tactile stimulation. She's very responsive. It doesn't take much to wind her up and a great deal to wind her down."

"Just the kind of *problem* a man like you thrives on. Looks like you're breaking her in slow."

Changing tactics, Mace worked his fingers between her teeth. She obediently opened her mouth, then tried not to gag when he touched her tongue. The chain he'd been holding slid between her breasts. Between his probing fingers, the chain, her tight as hell nipples, flooding pussy, and the leather circling her neck, she wanted nothing more than to fall back onto the floor and spread her legs. Beg Mace to mount her.

"Timing and pace is key to molding a subject into the perfect slave," Mace said. He slid his fingers over her teeth, occasionally brushing her tongue, keeping her mouth open, controlling her. "It's a slow process, yet relentless."

Paul's breath snagged. His chair squeaked. "Re-lentless. Hell yes. Oh, shit!"

Whether Paul expected Mace to say anything didn't matter. Neither did what Paul's slave was doing to him. Her world consisted of Mace's hand in her mouth and her lips on fire.

Blips of conversation let her know Mace was ordering drinks. Then the conversation ended, and he withdrew his fingers only to capture her lower lip again. "Hands behind your head," he ordered. "Arch your back."

Do it. Don't think. She did so slowly, her progress hampered by her heavy arms and flashing colors in her mind. Finally, feeling proud and yet disconnected, she laced her fingers together and drank in as much air as her lungs could hold.

The drawing sensation on her lip sent jolt after jolt through her. The electrical charges emptied out in her pussy. She smelled sweat, alcohol, perfume, aftershave, sex.

"Tell me what you're feeling?"

Mace's voice first touched the edge of her consciousness, then insisted on her attention. "Everythin'."

"Be specific."

She couldn't speak with him holding her like that, surely he understood. "Pleath."

"Point taken." He released her lip only to take hold of her all but useless blouse and draw it down over one breast, exposing it. She looked down at herself, then took another deep breath. Pride in her dark, hard nipple and pale round breast filled her.

"All right," Mace said with Paul's strident grunts for background, "tell me what happens when I do this."

His thumb pressed against her nipple, the pressure flattening her breast and making the hard knot of flesh throb. Her interlaced fingers started to slip from the back of her head.

"Erect, slave! Chest back. Arms in place. Now, don't move."

His words were like hail on a metal roof, hammer blows that dominated her world. Still, she struggled to obey.

"Pay attention," he continued. "One of the tenets of BDSM is the connection between pleasure and pain. Done right by a master who understands the bond results in a slave who doesn't care which she's receiving. Often she's unable to distinguish between the two. As example—" Gripping her nipple between thumb and forefinger, he drew it toward him much as he'd done with her lip.

More electricity flared. It seemed to originate in her chest wall before spreading in all directions. The pressure on her nipple ratcheted up. *Trapped. I'm trapped.*

"I don't need to point out how sensitive your breasts are when it's easy to demonstrate. Pay attention."

He pulled her breast to the right and then the left, followed by a circular motion that had her turning with him. What was that phrase? Yes, fire in the belly. Flames filled her belly. Some licked up into her chest, while others found the smooth, wide route to her sex.

No part of her was immune, and her mind dove into the assault on her senses. She heard herself whimper.

"I'm giving you pleasure and pain," Mace explained. He must have leaned forward because his breath washed her forehead. "As a point of reference, are you able to distinguish between the two?"

There, shards of discomfort. There, rolling heat.

"Drop your arms, slave. I don't want to wear you out. Good. Now concentrate. This is pleasure."

The pressure on her trapped nipple died and was replaced by hot moisture. Shit, shit, he was tonguing her there! Whimpering, she cupped her breast and offered it up to him, then shuddered when his teeth lightly closed over what his fingers had claimed. She froze, followed by nearly losing her balance when he bathed as much of her breast as his tongue could reach. He repeatedly coated his tongue with saliva and deposited it here, there, and everywhere. Her drenched breast felt both cold and hot. Still holding it up to him, she ran her free hand between her legs and reached for her aching, burning core. Five thumbs-up for no panties.

"No!"

Shocked, she tried to shake her head in protest only to be stopped by Mace's hold on her too-receptive nipple.

"Did I give you permission to touch yourself?"

"What?" she snapped. "You get me all hot and bothered and expect—"

A jerk on the leash cut off her air and silenced her. He released her nipple and stood, holding the leash above her.

"Got some work yet to do on her, don't you?" Paul gloated. " 'Course you don't want to beat all the fire out of her."

"Listen to me, slave." Mace's breath washed her forehead.

"This body is no longer yours. It belongs to me for as long as it pleases me to play with it. Stand up."

Orders had been an everyday part of her childhood, and although she'd prided herself on getting past that, she scrambled to her feet. The breast he'd been mauling was exposed, and the burnished lights glinted off the saliva he'd put there.

Mace widened his stance, and his hand moved down. Then pressure on her neck forced her to lean over so she could no longer see him.

"Hands behind you at your waist, slave."

Desperate to obey, she did as he'd commanded. Thanks to the damnable heels, she was again off balance, which had to be exactly what he'd intended. "Now turn toward the stage."

Although her legs threatened to tangle, she managed to comply. Nothing mattered more than being allowed to lift her head, not even knowing Paul, and probably a lot of other people, were watching the display.

"Fuck it!" Paul exclaimed. "That's enough."

6

_____

The sound of a hand striking flesh said Paul was disciplining his slave. She half expected Mace to do the same. Instead, to her relief, the pressure on the back of her neck let up. Lessons learned, she waited for his orders.

"What do you see?" Mace asked.

Taking the question as permission, she straightened. On the stage a beefy man dressed in leather and carrying a hefty flogger was standing to one side of the spotlight trained on the center of the stage. A naked woman fairly dripping chains slowly walked up the stairs.

"This is the auction, isn't it?" she managed.

"Correct. You're going to stand here without moving while you tell me what's taking place. I want every detail, got it."

"Yes, Master," she said. Reaching the top, the so-called slave headed toward the spotlight. "Do you, ah, do you want me to begin now?"

"First I want you to describe your condition."

As if a switch had been tapped, her focus shifted from what had drawn the audience's attention to the chain now draped around her neck and over her covered breast. "My, ah, my hands are behind me."

"Are you handcuffed?"

"No, but it feels like it."

"And why do you think that is?"

"I don't know. The strain maybe."

"That's part of it. The rest is what's taking place inside you. You want this, don't you?"

Mace's voice had gentled a little, and she caught another question behind the obvious one. He wasn't just asking about tonight. "Yes, I do."

"Now back to your description."

The leather-clad man she took to be the auctioneer had picked up a microphone, but instead of speaking into it, he snapped the flogger. The sharp crack made her jump, yet even as she winced at the thought of how being struck would feel, more of the heat that had invaded her the moment she'd entered Mace's car licked her.

"I'm being looked at, not by many because most are interested in the auction."

"Do you like the attention?"

She waited out another snap of the flogger. "I'm not sure. My breast is exposed. I've never done this in public."

"You didn't expose it, I did. How does that make you feel?"

"Helpless," she allowed, although it went deeper. By doing that one thing, Mace had taken responsibility for and control over her body.

"That'll do, for a start." He repositioned the chain so the end now brushed her exposed nipple. "Last question before the main event gets going. How do you think you'd react if you were being auctioned?"

The slave was dwarfed by the chains gripping her wrists and ankles, and circling her throat and waist. One ran between her legs.

"I don't know," she admitted. "I think it depends on how much I understood of what was happening. If I knew the auction was for play—"

"Do you think that's what's happening?"

"Of course." Because he hadn't given her permission to look at him, she fixed on the slave. If the woman wanted to be perceived as terrified and helpless, she needed to take some acting lessons. "People don't really sell each other in today's world."

"Don't they?"

She might have continued the argument if the auctioneer wasn't announcing that the sale was about to start. He began by listing the rules for bidders while Cheyenne mentally placed herself front and center, naked and hobbled with her wrists fastened to a waist chain.

Despite the occasionally squawking microphone, she managed a running commentary. As she did, Mace's drink was delivered; whiskey straight, she thought. Paul's slave crawled out from under the table but remained on her knees with dried cum on the corners of her mouth.

The first slave went for $9,500, but not until the auctioneer had demonstrated her charms by having her bend over with her ass to the audience while he pulled her cheeks apart. He also hefted her unremarkable breasts, followed by leading her in a circle via his hold on her nipples. Looking as if she was in sub space, the woman managed a few half-hearted groans.

"Enough!" someone finally yelled. "This is embarrassing."

The next slave looked to be twenty at the oldest. She, too, dragged chains, repeatedly turned her head, and glanced at the audience only to shiver and look down. Sweat glistened off her shoulders and large, natural breasts. From where she stood, Cheyenne noted that the girl/woman was trembling.

"I don't know if she's excited or afraid," she said because Mace had asked her opinion. "Maybe a little of both. I think she's new at this. Maybe she's trying to figure herself out."

"Just like you?"

"I guess."

She opened her mouth to start again when Mace growled a command for her to face him. Doing so forced her to look at the stage over her shoulder. She should have guessed what he had in mind, but when he pushed up her nearly nothing skirt so it wrapped around her hips, a squeak escaped her throat.

"What—" she started, then stopped. Without a moment's hesitation, he ran his hand between her legs.

"Spread them."

Damn you! That's taking things too damn far!

"Spread them, bitch."

A role. They were playing roles. For Paul and whoever else might question her authenticity. Reminding herself that this was research for a job assignment might have made more impact if not for the increased pressure on her pussy. Mace had trapped her sex in his palm, the heel of his hand grinding against her mons and lifting her onto her toes.

"Get going again," he commanded while Paul and several other people, women included, laughed. "What's happening onstage?"

You're killing me. "She—she doesn't want to be there and yet she does. Maybe she's afraid of being sold to someone cruel."

"Someone who might turn her into a pony?"

In her current frame of mind she was hard put to remember that pony-play called for a submissive to be treated like a horse complete with harness and strenuous training routines. "Maybe."

"What about you? Would you like that?" He punctuated his question by pushing her labial aside and slipping into her sex.

No man had manhandled her like this! She didn't want it, didn't know how to handle it. Most of all, she couldn't control the sticky fluid leaking from her. Not breathing, she waited for him to complete the invasion, but the seconds ticked by with little more than his first knuckle in her. Not looking at her, he picked up his drink left-handed and took a healthy sip.

"A pony," she finally thought to say. "I don't think so."

"Why not? You have strong legs."

"Would ... would I have to live in a barn?"

When Mace chuckled, she realized that was as close to a laugh as she'd ever heard from him. What had delighted him as a child?

"No, because I don't have one. You wouldn't want to disappoint me by losing any races. I can be a harsh taskmaster."

Given the way he was plundering her, she was hard put to imagine what that kind of existence might be like. Bidding on the young slave on the stage was brisk, but as long as Mace didn't expect her to comment further, she didn't have to think about anything except what was happening to her. An electric heat fairly radiated out from Mace, prompting her to ask herself what he looked like under his form-fitting black outfit. She'd spotted the outline of well-defined muscles, but thanks to the low lighting, she could only draw on her imagination.

An imagination pushed into overdrive by the bold invasion. This wasn't her, wasn't! Despite her interest in a submissive experience, she'd always drawn a firm line. Her dates could maul her a bit; she rather enjoyed rough, commanding hands and a playful slap. But that took place only once she trusted the man. Never on their first *date.*

Yet here she was in a joke of an outfit Mace had supplied, standing in full view of everyone, her legs apart and body angled for his easy access.

"She's zoning," Paul said. "Getting that droopy-eyed look. Sure she isn't on drugs?"

Fingernails scraped the inside of her right thigh in a silent command for her to further widen her stance. The too-short skirt tightened around her hips in an erotic bondage. In contrast, her heel hurt.

Another finger joined the one already in her to farther open her. She knew nothing except the increased invasion and Mace reaching deep into her. If only he'd tied her wrists together! That way the decision of whether to fight or not would be out of her hands. She'd be helpless.

"There's nothing as sweet as being surrounded by a woman's sex," Mace said. "Whoever's responsible for the difference between men and women sure as hell got this part right."

He was talking to Paul, wasn't he? Certainly he didn't expect her to offer her opinion.

"What is it?" Paul said. "I mean, pussies aren't much different. You climb into one, you've climbed into all of them. 'Cept I can't get enough. I plant my cock in a pussy and I lose my mind. Good as that feels, it can be scary."

Paul's words swam around her. She wanted to pay attention because he was saying something revealing about the male sex, maybe even about Mace. But her *master's* fingers were fucking her.

"A question, slave," Mace said. "When you come, is it from clitoral or vaginal stimulation?"

Mace was nearly a stranger. They hadn't so much as shared a cup of coffee and here he was asking an intimate question. Possibilities swarmed through her. She could tell him the truth or to go to hell or something in between.

"Guess you'll have to find out," Paul allowed. "The thing is, I'd think you'd have known by now."

"I told you." Using his unoccupied hand, Mace exposed her other breast and then took another sip of his drink. "I'm just starting with her. One more chance, slave. Either you tell me or I'll figure out on my own."

She saw nothing but blurred colors like a rainbow through a rain-sheeted window, heard male mutters punctuated by occasional female gasps or cries, smelled sex and other heavy, indefinable odors. Mostly she felt Mace's fingers in her.

"Clit or cunt?" His breath was harsh and hot against her ear. "Come clean or two fingers become three."

"Clit!" she whimpered. "Mostly clit. Sometimes..."

"Sounds like she lost her concentration again," Paul observed. "Guess you'll have to make good on your threat."

She wanted Paul gone, dead even. Wanted out of this stifling room with human flesh supposedly being auctioned off. Needed to be alone with Mace.

He gave her no warning. One moment two fingers claimed her. The next increased pressure and strength all but exploded in her. Her fingers lost their hold on each other, and she gripped Mace's biceps for balance. Instead of trying to pull him out of her, she bent a little and helped guide him home.

All three fingers were now deep in her, their bases against her sex lips. Her pussy was splayed, open and vulnerable, fire lancing her breasts, belly, hips, and thighs. She wasn't yet close to climaxing, but she didn't care because sensation was enough, everything.

Turning her body over to this dark and unsmiling man was what she'd been created for. There was no tomorrow, no paycheck to earn, no electric bill to pay. Only him. Everything him.

He could wrap her in ropes and she wouldn't object. If he welded a collar around her neck, she'd stand passively while he worked. Anything for his touch and heat. She'd learn how to give head with her hands lashed behind her, crawl behind him, sleep on the floor next to his bed.

Whatever her master wanted, she'd do it.

"That's enough," she heard. "Don't want your brain shorting out tonight."

Comprehension came a half second at a time. Moving so slow she nearly convinced herself she was only imagining the loss, he drew out of her. His knuckles glided, his nails touched.

No matter how fiercely she gripped his arm, she couldn't stop him. Couldn't speak. Couldn't silence her raw whimpers.

"That's enough." He spoke more firmly. "You've taught me everything I need to know for now."

When he turned her from him, she cared only that his hands were on her arms, one of them coated in her offerings. Then he began wrapping a soft rope around her wrists.

"What..." she started.

"I want you to focus on your reactions and responses," he explained. "This way you won't be distracted. Don't think about me. Mentally place yourself next to that auctioneer and imagine that the bids are for you."

His voice had gone from no-nonsense to hypnotic, and she floated into a space he'd created for her, concentrated on nothing except the experienced hands rendering hers useless and her still-hungry cunt.

"The chains are heavy," he said with his mouth now near her ear and his body behind hers. "Your wrists and ankles are chafed because the links dig into them. Your master, a man who no longer wants you, placed them on you, and you try to tell yourself that as long as they're in place, you still belong to him. Are you crying, slave? Perhaps you're fighting to keep the tears from showing. Which is it?"

When he'd finished weaving rope around her, instead of releasing her, he drew her back toward him. His legs were on either side of her, his knees brushing her thighs, and his cock pressing against her, making her whimper.

"Which is it?" he repeated. "Tears freely given or held back?"

"I don't cry."

"Never?"

"Never."

"Because you've taught yourself control or because nothing truly matters?"

The young slave was walking toward the stairs, proof that she'd been *sold*. What was it like to have no ownership of one's body?

"Lessons learned," she heard herself admit.

"I want to know about those lessons and the reasons for them, but not tonight."

7

Cheyenne was silent, not that Mace expected her to say anything. Thousands of words had poured out of her during her running commentary about the auction, and although they'd been delivered without emotion, he hadn't been fooled. Wise in women's ways, he'd tapped into her body language. For most of the time she'd been unaware of her near nudity, to say nothing of the attention directed her way.

His intention had been to keep his hands on her and her body against his as part of his plan to draw her deeply into the submissive mindset, but she'd done things to him he hadn't expected, and not just physically. Instead of staying at Indulgences until liquor and lowered inhibitions turned play into something dark and intense, as soon as the sham of an auction was over, he'd informed Cheyenne that they were leaving.

She hadn't argued. Neither had she asked him to pull the blouse over her breasts or tug the skirt back down. She also hadn't indicated she wanted back use of her arms or the collar's weight off her neck as they made their way through the crowd. Both Paul and Jonus, who manned the door, had asked what the hell he was doing leaving so soon, but he hadn't bothered with an explanation.

The obvious one was that Cheyenne needed a break from her system's overload. The one he'd never share was that his hard-on was getting to him.

"Remember what I said about security at Indulgence's parking lot?" he asked as they stood near his car's passenger's door.

"Ah, that it's good."

"Which is why I'm not going to remove the ropes until we're out of here." He opened her door.

Despite the balance-compromising heels and skirt wadded around her hips, she managed to settle herself in the bucket seat. Instead of helping, he told himself he was presenting a dominating persona when the truth was, he needed to distance himself from her.

After closing her in, he walked around to the driver's side, his teeth clenched against the grinding in his groin. The interior light illuminated her breasts and well-muscled thighs. What he saw of her pubic hair was so pale it was nearly nonexistent. Gripping the steering wheel was the only way he could keep his fingers off her.

Because he wasn't sure he could hold emotion from his voice, he said nothing as he drove out of the parking lot. She was looking ahead, her body at an unnatural angle, the chain dangling from her neck and settled between her legs.

Shit!

When, a quarter of a mile later, he pulled into the alley behind a used-car lot, she sent a glance his way before staring at the cars as if she'd never seen anything more fascinating. Her breathing picked up.

"First, this." He unsnapped the chain and tossed it in what passed for his backseat. "Lean forward."

Because he hadn't fastened her seat belt in deference to her bound arms, she easily complied, and he stared at the rope circling her crossed-over wrists. Tonight's action was over; it was time to return ownership of her body to her. Why, then, the reluctance?

Cheyenne was different from the other women he'd worked with, he just didn't understand why. Or why sliding his fingers into her hot channel had made him feel as if he were drowning.

An image from another life pushed through his defenses to blur his view of her backside. A child, him, stood before a massive closed door. He clutched a half-full paper bag in a dirty hand, his scabbed knuckles stinging. Any moment the door would open and he'd step into yet another strange house. Helplessness weighed him down and made his eyes burn. If only he had someplace to run to!

He did, damn it! That place was the here and now.

"Your shoulders are going to ache once your wrists are free," he said, working on the knots. "Rolling them forward will help."

As he expected, the moment her arms fell free she gasped, and he gripped the steering wheel to keep his hands off her. She did as he suggested. Then, slowly, as if she couldn't put her mind to what she was doing, she hoisted herself off the seat and tugged the skirt back in place. That done, she lowered the blouse over her breasts. Not bothering with the buttons, she fastened her seat belt.

They didn't speak during the twenty minutes it took to get to her car. The whole time he tried not to note what she'd done with her hands, tried and failed. Knowing they were clamped between her legs sent even more blood to his cock. He needed to get laid, damn it. Of course, there was another way of getting rid of this damnable hard-on, a lonely one.

The instant he placed his vehicle in Park, she unhooked her seat belt and opened the door. After swinging her legs out, she took off the blood-red shoes and tossed them behind her.

"Wait while I change in my car," she said, not looking at him. "That way I won't have to return this outfit to you later."

She'd exchanged her clothes for his in her vehicle before they'd taken off. He considered telling her she didn't have to contort herself in the confined space again, that after what he'd seen of her tonight, what was a little more nudity? But no longer looking at her breasts and pussy had eased the transition from dom to the man he usually presented to the world. They were once again *Edge* employees, nothing else.

"Why did we leave so soon?" she asked through the open passenger's window when she emerged from her car dressed in a sleeveless cream knee-length dress that draped her still-unrestrained breasts.

"You'd had enough for one night."

"What makes you think that? You sure as hell didn't ask."

"I didn't need to. Remember what I said about judging your body language?"

Her nod drew his attention to the fact that she was still wearing his collar. Although he could hand her the key, taking on the chore himself would bring them close again. Dangerously close.

Exciting.

She had to know what he had in mind when he joined her in the *Edge* parking lot, which had its own security cameras. Fortunately, because he was in charge of those cameras, he could erase what took place between them—or keep the sequence for himself.

"How does your neck feel?" he asked when he was done. His fingers lingered on her throat, her veins pulsing against the tips.

She didn't move away. "Strange. Mace?"

Her voice stroked him, tipped him in a direction he both didn't want and needed. "What?"

"I've, ah, never experienced anything like what happened tonight."

"I know."

She swallowed. "The way you touched me, manhandled me—"

"Is that how you see it?"

"I don't know. My research should have prepared me for— the real thing's so different from fantasizing."

"Good or bad?"

Still not looking at him, she shrugged. Instead of letting her know he saw through her attempted indifference, he waited her out. The lighting here wasn't as strong as at Indulgences, and except for a trio of company cars, theirs were the only vehicles in the lot. If not for the steadily scanning cameras at the corners of the building, he'd be tempted to believe they were the only two people in the world.

He wanted them to be.

"I don't know," she belatedly answered. "Hopefully I'll have an answer by morning."

Touching her was a damn poor idea, too much like gripping a live electrical wire. Just the same, he leaned closer and wound his fingers through hers. She didn't try to pull away.

"What's next on your agenda?" he asked.

"Going home."

"What about once you're there? Not sleep, right?"

Shivering, she stared at their intertwined fingers. "I can't lie to you, can I? You'd see right through it."

Hopefully you can't do the same thing. "Pretty much."

"All right, then." She raked her free hand through the short and practical hair he'd love to see long and loose and draped over his chest. "It'll be pull out the toys and battery time."

"How long will it take?"

With a sigh, she locked eyes with him. More of the electricity he'd long ago taught himself not to touch shocked him.

"You really expect me to answer, don't you? There's not going to be any discussing the weather between us, is there?"

"No."

"Damn you." She sighed again and shuffled, drawing his attention to the fact that she was barefoot. And sans underwear. "All right, not long. Wound up as I am, I might have to pull over on the way home." She clawed at her hair some more. "I shouldn't tell you this. Damn it, I know better, but hell . . ."

"Hell what?" *Don't take her other hand!*

"This isn't my body." She studied her feet. "It's like I've taken some aphrodisiac, an upper maybe. I didn't have anything to drink, so I know it isn't that."

"Go on."

A quick, low laugh seared his nerve endings. "If I took that literally, gravel might be already digging into my backside." She laughed again. "My clit. Number one trigger. Anything else you want to know?"

A million things, at least. "Not now. This week you got your feet wet, so to speak. Next week we'll go deeper. Make your experience richer."

Her shiver seeped into his fingers, and his thoughts went back a million years to when fear ruled him.

"Same time, same place, same outfit?" She ran a hand over her breast, and her nipple instantly responded.

"Different outfit." He ground out an unemotional response. "Between now and then I'll give you an idea of what to expect."

"Why?"

Her voice fairly sang to him, each note unique, resonating. He didn't just have a hard-on. Understand it or not, which he didn't, he was in danger of bending before her spell. Thinking to fight her impact in the way that made the most sense, he drew his hand free and stepped back.

"Simple," he answered. "Most women have the same response to what I did to you. Sex organs are pretty much the same when it comes to how they react to stimulation."

Clamping her hands over her stomach, she looked at him, glanced away, looked again. "Sounds damn clinical to me. Takes the fun out of it."

"Does it?" Deciding he wanted nothing to do with verbal sparring, he rammed his hands in his back pockets. "Maybe. Next week's about getting deeper into the BDSM experience by introducing pain."

Instead of flinching, she nodded. He wondered if she realized that her knuckles were turning white. "My pain or watching it happen to someone else?"

"Both."

Nodding almost imperceptivity, she closed her eyes. Was she imagining a flogger, wielded by him, striking her flesh?

He'd restrain her so her arms and legs were outstretched, her body forming a X. She'd wear leather bracelets and anklets, nothing else. Or would he test her boundaries by fastening metal clips to her nipples?

Yeah, gold glinting and her breath ragged, breasts hard and hot. Light lash after light lash would sting her, forcing out moans and groans. She'd look at him, only him, her eyes bright and glittering like the gold. Proof of her arousal would run down the insides of her legs, and she'd twist about, her dance tearing him apart.

If he stopped, she'd beg him to continue. If he demanded an explanation of what she was feeling, words would desert her, but her sex heat would fill his lungs. Watching intently, he'd reach between her legs and fasten his fingers around her sex, trap it.

She'd come, her climax long and rolling, forcing cry after cry from her.

Only Cheyenne didn't cry.

Wondering if she'd ever tell him why, he pulled himself back to the present. Her eyes were still closed, and her body sagged as if she'd lost contact with it. Unable to stop himself, he took hold of her arms. Her eyes opened, widened. His undoing came when, instead of retreating into her own space, she leaned toward him.

"You shouldn't touch me," she whispered. "The things that does to me—"

"Do you hate it?"

"No." The word floated on her exhaled breath. "Shit, I'm so tightly wrapped—" Stepping even closer, she pushed her pelvis at him.

The beast that felt most alive when he had a woman under him clawed at his innards. Cheyenne was innocence and witch. Handing herself to him.

"We're going to fuck," he ground out, "unless you get the hell out of here right now."

"I can't leave. Damn it, you have to know that."

He didn't know anything, least of all why she was so seductive. He knew better than to get personally involved. Walking away from a woman ensured his sanity.

Except for tonight.

8

Not explaining, Mace propelled her backward and lifted her off the ground. She didn't need to look behind her to know he was intent on depositing her on her car's hood. That done, he turned her so they were close enough to kiss.

Kiss? Not going to happen.

As long as he remained between her legs, the squared hood allowed her to sit without danger of slipping off. Her skirt had flipped up, which meant the cool metal was chilling her exposed ass. Not caring enough to do anything about it, she wrapped her arms around his neck. Her breasts flattened against his chest, and his arms went around her back.

The seconds ticked off as they clung to each other, simply clung. She was no less in heat than she'd been before he'd picked her up, no less focused on the throbbing between her legs. The question of why this was happening tapped at her, only to fade into nothing.

There didn't need to be reason or sanity with his hard form ruling hers. This man had wrenched her out of her comfort zone and into a world she'd never had the courage for. No wonder she—

"Last chance for you to say no," he said. "Because otherwise we're going to have sex."

"Here?" She winced at the damn stupid question.

"Yeah, I'm the only one who'll see the tape."

"Oh."

Releasing her, he rocked back on his heels, then came at her again. Muttering something, he ran his hands along her thighs, incinerating them. Determined to catch him on fire, she yanked his turtleneck out of the waistband and slid her fingers over the ladder of his ribs. There was too much muscle there, too much hardness.

"Damn it." His grip on her thighs tightened.

"Do you always swear?"

"Only when I need to." His breath scorched her cheek.

"Times like this?"

No answer, only his hands sliding around her thighs toward her ass. The thought of how he felt about touching her flattened and chilled buttocks pulled her out of the whirlpool she'd fallen into, and she waited for a sign that too much reality had invaded. What she got was his fingers digging into her flesh and something squeezing her heart.

Pressing the heels of her hands against his ribs, she inched closer. His mouth was close, too close. If she wasn't careful, she might be tempted to touch hers to his. Wondering if he might feel the same temptation, she turned her head to the side. Even with the hood against her ass, she remained intensely aware of how close his cock was.

Fucking? Sex.

Sudden pressure at the base of her spine straightened her. Gripping his shirt, she yanked up so the garment bunched under his arms. He again pressed his fist against her spine, the grinding sensation immediately centering in her pussy.

"Not fair," she whimpered, as she pressed the heels of her hands against his collarbone.

"What isn't?"

"Getting to me's so damn easy for you. You got me all wrapped up earlier and now—"

"So leave if you don't want this."

Leave? Not in this lifetime.

She tried to pull his shirt over his head only to give up when he made it clear he had no intention of releasing her. Keeping her in place with one hand, he trailed his nails over her spine.

"Oh, shit. Damn you!" She raked her nails down his chest, not stopping until she reached the waistband she'd give anything to shred. She began retracing her steps only to forget what she'd had in mind when he ran his thumb into her ass crack.

"Oh, shit!" Leaning forward, she tried to bite his shoulder only to wind up with her mouth full of fabric that tasted of him.

His nails laid thin, hot lines on either side of her spine. Angry and excited, she rested the side of her head on his shoulder and returned the favor. When she tried to straighten, she realized she'd slipped into the space between his legs with his cock pressing in the last place she needed to be pressed.

Sinking into something dark that existed only in her mind, she tried to scoot back. "Let me—"

"Too late. It's going to happen."

She needed to say something, anything, maybe simply finish the sentence she'd started. Instead, she drank in more of his smell and the feel of him everywhere on her. Logic and civilization be damned. Considering the consequences of her action, double damned. Mace was different from other men. He'd claimed her sex at Indulgences simply because he'd wanted to.

"Not like this." She demonstrated by working her hand between their bodies and cupping his cock through his pants. "I can't reach the main participant."

"Then do something with the damned zipper."

His command reminded her of the dom/submissive roles they'd played earlier, but what did she care if he thought of her as his slave, his possession? The metal ripping sound closed her throat, and once again she didn't quite believe this was happening. He backed off long enough to tug his pants and briefs down his hips and then sank into her again. His erection ground against her sex. Lifting her head in order to pull in enough oxygen, she again slipped her fingers between them. Lingering over her clit, she separated her sex lips.

Instead of pulling out and letting him claim her, however, she kept her hand in place. Despite her attempt to provide a barrier, if that's what she'd intended, his tip teased her opening, prompting her to rock from side to side. She was wet, her sex weeping the tears she denied herself.

"You're killing me," he hissed. "Don't you get it, there's no wait in me tonight."

"Me either."

"Then what—"

"You're so soft. And hard." Reaching around him, she gripped his ass cheek, but as much as she wanted to reposition herself so he could run himself into her, something held her back.

He pushed at her. The effort squeezed her fingers between their bodies. "What's this?" he asked. "You change your mind?"

"No." She needed more hands, one to tear at her hair, another to grasp her breasts, still another to cup his cock. And air. There wasn't enough of that.

"Cheyenne?"

Say my name again. Make it a song. "What?"

"This is real. Man and woman. No games."

"I know." Trembling from the effort, she withdrew her hand

and wiped her sticky offering on his thigh. Only then did she look down. His taut cock appeared blood red with potent yet fragile veins. It looked like something alien next to her pale thighs and too massive for her body to swallow. A drop of moisture clung to the tip.

"Protection," she blurted.

"Shit, shit!"

Fear that they couldn't go further froze her. Then he hauled his pants higher, digging into a rear pocket as he did, and pulled out the necessary package. Her eyes burning, she watched him roll the condom over his erection. Then, trapped in a place she was certain she'd never been before, she brushed his hand aside and took over. She guided him to her, settled him at her entrance.

"Do it," she ordered the man who'd called her his slave earlier tonight. "Now."

This time he shoved into her, burying his head in her waiting tissues. Then, although she dug at his flanks trying to get him to finish his task, he stopped. Panting, she waited him out. Another half inch filled her. His features blurred, and he claimed the air she needed. Turning her head to the side, she went in search of some he hadn't already used.

As she inhaled, he clamped onto her buttocks, pinning them so she couldn't move.

"We're both going to regret this," he said.

"It's too late for that, damn it." *And I'm too much of an animal.*

Yes, that's what she'd been waiting for! Pressure and being expanded. He took her slow yet hard, his cock relentless and promising. Placing her hands behind her, she leaned back and lifted herself an inch, maybe two. His grip on her buttocks held.

The instant his balls pressed against her, he pulled back, robbing her and making her sex throb. Then he buried himself in her again. Determined not to let him go again this time, she closed her aching inner muscles around him. He growled something she didn't catch.

"What?" she asked.

"Nothing, damn you. Ah, shit!"

The more frenzied his movements, the more she slid back and forth on the hood until she had no choice but to cling to his neck to secure herself. There was something frightening about him, wild and powerful. No matter how much she wanted to prove herself his equal, the more impossible it became to face him. Much easier was staring off to the side while her breasts flailed.

Clit or cunt? Was there a difference between the two? Maybe her entire sex had bled together. Something tore at her chest. Again she felt her heart being squeezed, and now her rib cage couldn't contain her lungs.

A riptide signaling her impending climax hit her. Always before she'd needed extended stimulation to throw her over the top. But this wasn't yesterday, it was now. Him. Night claiming the parking lot and her buttocks burning from the friction.

Forgetting her fear of a moment ago, she turned toward him, and he closed his teeth around her lower lip, forcing her to lean forward awkwardly. His relentless cock still pummeled her, compelling her to attack him in return.

Incapable of speaking, sounds nevertheless burst from her. The helpless cries swirled through her, inflaming her sex.

There! she wanted to tell him. *There! Climax!* The sensation lifted her up and held her suspended. She didn't care what was happening to him, couldn't tell whether he was equally lost. This rolling shudder was all hers.

Everything hers.

9

Not bothering with the light in her bedroom, Cheyenne peeled off her clothes and dropped them on the floor. Grabbing a nightgown, she headed for the bathroom. While waiting for the shower to warm up, she stared at her reflection in the mirror. Her hair looked like hell, partly because she'd driven home with the windows down, the rest the result of the bumping and grinding that had taken place on her car's hood.

Her attention wandered to her neck and the faint mark left by the collar. More marks served as reminders of how Mace had tied her wrists. The growing knot in her groin insisted she replay her responses. She'd loved every minute of his handling of her. Hell, what had dried between her legs left no doubt.

Sighing, she stepped into the shower and let the spray run over her short hair. Did Mace like the style? Maybe he'd prefer it long so he could use it to haul her wherever he wanted, like she'd seen on some BDSM sites.

They'd had sex. She hadn't expected that. More to the point, the act hadn't taken place at Indulgences while they'd been on display, and she at least under scrutiny. Tonight was supposed to be about getting accepted at Indulgences so she could write a knock-it-out-of-the-park article and prove herself at *Edge*.

Edge? Didn't matter tonight.

Her mouth started to sag open. Closing it to avoid drowning made sense, not that she was interested in self-preservation.

What was Mace doing? If his only concern was whether to grab a bite before going to bed, she didn't want to know. In true wham-bam style, he'd said little once they were done, nothing about calling or seeing her again, not a word about what a great lay she was.

Stepping back from the water, she reached for the shampoo, only to stop with her hand outstretched. She could no longer see the rope marks on her wrists, not that it made a difference because the impact remained. No denying it, she'd loved being handled like a sub. That had to be why she'd come so quick and hard.

Thinking about the way she'd stood there dumb and silent and oozing while Mace fingered her at Indulgences made her shiver. She'd expected her first time in bondage to require steel nerves and too much teeth grinding. Fear.

Instead, she'd reacted as if she'd been born to the life.

Shivering again, she turned so her back was under the spray. Water sheeted off her breasts, over her shoulders, and coated her belly and thighs. Some found the channel between her legs. At first she resolutely kept them closed, but as memories of the night piled one upon the other, they slid apart. Giving up, she ran both hands into the space she'd created.

If only she still had on *her* leather collar. If only Mace was here, maybe holding on to the chain, maybe securing it to the shower head so she couldn't leave until it pleased him.

She didn't know the man and had no idea what he was capable of. Yet, dangerous as it was, when she closed her thumb and forefinger around her clit, she too easily imagined that those were his fingers instead of hers.

* * *

"I'm home."

Mace's announcement was unnecessary because Rio was already standing at the front door looking up at him. The pit bull's switch-like tail lashed slowly.

"Don't give me that look, all right. I know I said I might be out all night, but plans changed."

Not giving away what he was thinking, the sixty-pound dog stuck his nose between Mace's legs and snorted.

"Can't keep anything from you, can I? Yeah, I had sex. And don't blame me because your clip job makes that activity impossible for you."

Rio snorted again. His tail continued its slow wag.

"Are you going to let me all the way in? Do I need to remind you who pays the bills around here?"

Pulling back, Rio yawned.

"I've got it. You don't give a damn about bills because you figure your looks are the only key you need to a roof over your head."

Rio planted his rear end on the tile entryway in the first house Mace had ever considered his. Because he hadn't bothered with the light, he saw little more than Rio's outline. Thinking about the scars, he rubbed between Rio's ears and then stroked the ears themselves. The right one was perfect, while most of the left had been torn away, leaving a stump Mace always handled gently. In addition to the destroyed ear, Rio bore scars on his forelegs and muzzle from being used as a sacrificial lamb by trained fighting dogs while Rio was still a puppy. Mace hated thinking what would have happened if animal control hadn't stepped in.

"You're a piece of work. Worthless and ugly as sin," he told Rio, when truth was, he'd never loved a living thing more. "Just because I'm the only human you tolerate doesn't mean I feel responsible for you."

Yawning again, Rio licked Mace's arm. Then they walked together into the kitchen and Mace refilled the dog's water bowl. As his last dog servant chore of the night, he opened the back door and let the pit outside. When he'd bought the house, a cyclone fence had closed in the yard, but then he'd rescued Rio and learned that the dog went nuts every time he saw movement near *his* turf. A six-foot-high wooden fence on either side had eased his neighbors' minds and given Rio a sense of security. Wetlands were behind the property, and Rio all but put out the welcome mat for the endless birds who landed there.

His evening constitution dealt with, Rio came in and headed for the bedroom. By the time Mace joined him, Rio had jumped onto the bed and was circling, mindless to what he was doing to the dark blue spread.

"Anyone tell you how worthless you are?" Because he didn't anticipate a response, especially an honest one, Mace sat on the edge of the bed and removed his shoes. Standing again, he undid the zipper on the shiny, black-as-sin pants he'd never wear anywhere except at Indulgences.

Stripping down to nothing took longer than usual because he kept getting distracted by thoughts of how the evening had played out. The part at Indulgences had been pretty much according to code, all except for his unexpected need to know what she smelled like. He'd also found ways to make her speak simply so the sound of her voice would settle in him. As for fingering her—hell, that had been part of expected procedure, so no need asking himself why there.

She was so soft, her cunt warm and inviting. The strength in her pussy muscles had surprised him, in part because from what he knew about her, she didn't spend a lot of time training that part of her anatomy.

Was it possible she'd risked the equivalent of a torn muscle trying to keep him inside?

"Gotta stop thinking about her," he told Rio, who'd settled into a tight ball and whose eyes were already closing. Instead of crawling under the sheets, he rested his head on Rio's belly and listened to his dog breathe.

"She's just another broad in a long line of broads. Granted, our relationship blurs the usual lines but—maybe that's it. I've become a creature of habit. I want same old, same old from my subs, not whatever the hell she is."

10

"Ten minutes are missing," Robert told Atwood as he stepped into his partner's office and closed the door behind him. "Mace said it's happened before, some kind of short stopping the camera and then letting it start again, but I don't buy it."

Atwood minimized the financial report he'd been working on and waited for Robert to continue.

"You aren't going to ask why this is something we should be interested in, are you?" Robert asked. "Going to make me spell it out, aren't you?"

"You do a good job of it." Atwood indicated the tape in Robert's hand. "Why should I risk distracting you with irrelevant comments?"

Robert's sigh was noncommittal, unlike his coolly glittering eyes. It occurred to Atwood, not for the first time, that their partnership had rough edges. But then, hell, life without edges wasn't worth living.

"Maybe you'll be more interested when I tell you what timeframe is unaccounted for," Robert said.

Although he and Robert had every right to review *Edge*'s security tapes, he couldn't remember the last time he'd felt a need to. Obviously Robert thought differently. Keeping his expression neutral, he watched as his partner settled himself in the handmade leather seat that had taken five damn months to get done.

"Saturday night. From a little before eleven until a good ten minutes later. The interesting thing is, just before the blackout, Mace and Cheyenne's cars were in the parking lot. By the time things start rolling again, they're gone."

"There was something Mace didn't want us seeing," Atwood surmised. "A little hanky-panky perhaps?"

"You think? What gets me is this sudden attack of modesty. The man's a player. Keeping his cock under wraps should be the least of his concerns."

"Maybe his concern is with the *lady's* modesty."

Frowning, Robert looked around. "You want a drink?"

"Little early for that, isn't it?"

Grumbling, Robert got to his feet and walked over to the built-in wine rack. He pulled out an imported burgundy and two glasses. Placing the glasses on Atwood's desk, he began pouring.

"Careful," Atwood warned. "That's mahogany."

"I know it is." Robert handed him full glass. Then he held up his own. "Celebration time."

"Already?"

"I think so." Robert took a sip and sat back down. "Maybe it was just hormones getting the best of them, but I'm thinking he's starting to care about her."

Atwood took a slow sip. Making the drink last would keep the impact at a minimum and allow his head to remain clear. "That's good?"

"It's better than if he didn't give a damn about her. Look, I had the man investigated. Having a sex slave at his feet turns the man's crank. What's better than one he cares about? He's going to want her being part of his new role at the Blind Spot."

"I don't know." Atwood started to shake his head, only to stop. His toupee didn't feel as secure as he wanted it to. "Don't we want him focusing on his duties there, not a particular woman? What if he objects to our plans for her?"

For the first time, Robert looked worried. "Then we make it worth his while not to object. Mace has his price. Everyone does."

"Hmm." Atwood was about to voice his concern that Mace's price might be too steep when a cell phone in his bottom drawer chirped. He pulled it out, aware that Robert was watching. Only he and Robert knew that the phone wasn't affiliated with any of the world's cellular companies.

He read the displayed number, locked eyes with Robert, and punched the Send button. "Atwood here."

"I thought you'd want to know that Fergo's face-the-music date has been set. Wednesday. You and Robert are going to be here, aren't you?"

"I can't speak for my partner, but I intend to be. Does Fergo know?"

The man on the other end chuckled. "Just told him. I thought he'd try to bust out of his cell, but he's curled up in a fetal position."

"Because he can't face the consequences of his crime."

"He isn't the same heartless bastard when the shoe's on the other foot. He stopped demanding an attorney and is crying."

"Damn, but I'd love it if the loved ones of those he killed could see and hear him now."

Robert perked up at that. When he mouthed *Fergo*, Atwood nodded. Robert smiled and gave a thumbs-up. "Robert's in my office," Atwood told the unseen man. "From reading my partner's body language, I'd say, yes, he'll be there. What mode of execution has been decided?"

Another chuckle. "Fergo loved knives because they're silent."

Atwood mouthed *knife*, prompting Robert to hold up his glass in another salute. "We couldn't be more pleased," Atwood said. "Too damn bad *Edge* can't run his obituary."

"Those at the Blind Spot know. It's enough."

"Did you go into the back rooms?" Atwood asked Mace as soon as Mace stepped into the older man's office.

Although Atwood had indicated he could sit in one of the expensive-as-sin leather chairs, Mace perched on the coffee table. According to what he'd been told, Cheyenne was expected to join them, but so far it was just him, Atwood, and Robert at this meeting. He'd seen her when she came to work, but neither of them had spoken, and, of course, he hadn't called her over the weekend.

"She isn't ready for that," he said.

"When is she going to be?" Robert pressed. "She's not going to be able to fulfill her assignment until—"

"This is a hell of a lot more than material for an article, and you know it," he interrupted, then chided himself for his unexpected anger. "You can't turn a non-swimmer into an Olympic finalist the first time she's in the water."

"Interesting analogy. Unfortunately, I fail to see what it has to do with this."

Mace might have pointed out what he considered the obvious if the door hadn't opened just then. Cheyenne was wearing a virgin white blouse and a skirt that was somewhere between red and brown. The blouse was sedate enough, complete with elbow-length sleeves, a collar, buttons. It was the buttons that got to him. Two seconds and he'd have them dispensed with and the blouse down around her waist.

Atwood and Robert seemed inordinately pleased to see her. Nothing would do except she sit between them. It occurred to him that they'd deliberately left that chair vacant, which shouldn't bother him since he couldn't see her joining him on the low table. She gave him maybe a second of her time, then split her attention between Atwood and Robert. Only then did he note the folder she'd brought in.

"Mostly notes." She held up several pieces of computer paper. "I've made no attempt to start structuring my article, so I doubt if you'd get much out of what's here. But of course you're welcome to look."

"It's not necessary, Cheyenne," Robert said, smiling one of his patented thick-lipped smiles. "In fact, we were just talking to Mace about the journey you're on. My partner and I need to remind ourselves that immersing oneself in BDSM takes time. So, what did you think of you first experience?"

If Cheyenne was nervous, she gave no indication. From what he could tell, the notes came complete with numbered points, proof of her reporter training or an attempt to objectify what couldn't be?

"I'd prefer not to say much about my *experience*," she said, sounding as if they were discussing the weather. She crossed one long, slim leg over the other. Did she have a clue how much thigh he could see from here? Or know how close he was to an erection? "It has only been one time. I have no way of making comparisons."

"We respect your privacy," Atwood said. "We also know that you're cognizant of our deadlines and *Edge* readers' voracious appetites for the new and, shall we say, titillating."

"What are you saying?" Mace asked, barely able to keep from demanding the men stop dancing around.

"That the four of us need to come to a meeting of the minds about what will take place this weekend."

When Cheyenne nodded, Mace too easily envisioned his collar around her neck. "I take it you have something in mind," she said.

"That's what we were just starting to talk to Mace about,"

Robert supplied. "Undoubtedly you're aware that there is more than one level to Indulgences, specifically the back rooms."

For the first time Cheyenne gave him a look that lasted. "I can't remember if I heard—"

"She isn't ready for that," Mace interjected. "There's no point in discussing it until she is."

"Wait a minute." Cheyenne held up a hand that had embraced his cock not enough long ago. "How can you say what I am or am not ready for? That's my decision to make."

"Based on not enough information," he pointed out. "What you saw the other night was play. The other is the real deal."

"The real deal?" For a heartbeat her eyes went dark. Then the bland expression she'd presented when she walked in the room returned. "Explain it to me."

"Cheyenne," Atwood interjected. "We have a pretty good idea which Internet sites you visit. Some are hardcore BDSM."

She, reluctantly it seemed to him, turned her attention to Atwood. "How could I have forgotten about your investigation of me? Then I'm to surmise that the back rooms contain cells and cages, maybe a dungeon?"

"No cages."

Making a note of what Robert knew, Mace concentrated on the unspoken messages flying between Robert and Atwood. At the same time, he acknowledged the desire to separate Cheyenne from them with orders for her to never get close to the pair again.

Where was the protective impulse coming from? It wasn't in his makeup.

"I seriously doubt I'm going to see something this weekend that I haven't before," she said. "I'm pretty shock-proof."

"Are you?" he challenged. "The Internet is shy a couple of senses, specifically smell and taste. The cells and dungeons you've visited digitally can't prepare you for the full impact. Also, you've never been handled by a man who sees you as property, have you?"

Something in her fleeting expression said she wanted to re-peat what had happened between them, but if she thought he'd viewed her as property the other night, she was wrong. Strangely wrong.

"I'm sure you'll educate me about the whole property issue," she said, and again faced Atwood. "So I understand the timetable, when do you want to see the article?"

"Articles," Atwood corrected. "And as soon as possible."

11

"You want me to what?" Cheyenne asked moments after Mace stepped into her cubicle.

"Come to my place tonight. I'm ratcheting up your education."

"Your place, alone?" Mentally kicking herself for the uncertainty in her voice, she affected an interest in her keyboard she didn't feel. The meeting with Robert and Atwood had ended less than fifteen minutes ago, hardly enough time for her to put it behind her.

"Are you afraid?"

"Don't play that card! If you were a woman, you'd understand."

"I've dealt with a lot of women."

Her cubicle was too small to contain both of them. All right, so it had enough space for her desk, several filing cabinets, a bookshelf, and the plastic/metal chair he was bracing his arms against, but he—why did he have to wear a short-sleeved pullover shirt that showed off his biceps and buff chest?

"I'm sure you have," she said noncommittally. "What does that have to do with me?"

"Look, you probably think I shoved you into the deep end the other night, but truth is, I took it easy on you."

"I'm glad you told me." Never a fan of verbal sparring, she contemplated ways of getting to the point. Obviously the direct approach made the most sense. "I thought you were an advocate of jumping into the deep end. So you pulled your punches?"

"To some extent, yes. The decision's yours. However, I believe you need to experience at least a little of what you'll see this weekend in advance."

The man was making too much sense. "I want someone to know I'll be at your place. I'm sorry if that offends you, but I insist."

"Fine. Who's it going to be? A boyfriend?"

"No," she said, when the truth was, she hadn't made time for a man in her life in more than a year.

"Girlfriend? Parents."

"Not my parents," she said sharper than she'd intended. "Ah, they live two thousand miles away. Besides, who I choose is none of your business."

"Hmm. What's your stand on anal?"

Whew! The man sure knew how to change topics. "In regards to what?"

"Isn't that obvious?"

He was still bracing his body via his locked arms while staring steely-eyed at her, and she felt his gaze all the way to her toes. She wanted him gone. Wanted him looming over her as she lay sprawled on her desk.

"I've seen, never participated," she admitted.

"Any legal, moral, or political objections?"

Grateful for the lighthearted question, she shrugged. "None

of those. Mace, you're asking me to make a decision about something I have no frame of reference for. Watching some porn star take an ass hook up her hole is hardly the same as experiencing it myself, if that's what you're talking about."

His nod made him look wise and a little predatory. "Point taken. I'll give you directions to my place. How about a little after seven? That'll give you time to go home and change."

"Change?" She worked at completing a swallow. "Into what?"

"As little as possible. I'll take care of the rest." That said, he straightened, turned graceful as a big cat, and walked out.

Nerves buzzing, she looked down at her desk where her folder with the notes on Indulgences lay. Shit. Holy shit.

Instead of the sleek, high-rise apartment or condo Cheyenne pictured Mace living in, the address he'd given her took her beyond the city limits. She couldn't even call the area a suburb. At the moment she was about to turn off a country road that included everything from single-family homes to small farms or ranches, all with rural mailboxes she'd had to slow down to read. As her headlights caught his, she noted that it was flanked by other ranch homes, each with considerable land around it. The gravel circular driveway led to a large, covered porch decorated with bushes and flowers in clay pots. Only one chair, a large, white, wooden rocker, had been positioned so whoever was in it could easily see the road. Brickwork was on either side of the white front door, and several solar lights illuminated the three stairs leading to the porch. Otherwise, it was dark where she parked her car.

Because she had no desire to be pulled over by a cop while dressed in a bikini, she'd opted for a muumuu-style dress she'd picked up the only time she'd been to Hawaii. She hadn't bothered with underwear, thinking that might be easier than having to strip for him.

After wiping her sweating hands on the cotton dress, she rang the doorbell. A dog started barking, the sound deep and strong.

Telling herself it made sense for him to have a guard dog considering how far he lived from the nearest police station got her through the waiting. Then the door opened, and she knew absolutely that she hadn't prepared herself for this moment. Her toes curled in her sandals.

He wasn't wearing a shirt, damn him! No shoes either. And the faded and frayed jeans hung too damn low on his hips for any woman's sanity.

A dog stood at his side, large and solid with a mouth full of white, potent teeth.

"What's this?" Working at keeping the gulp she felt out of her voice, she indicated the staring dog.

"Rio."

"He's a pit bull, isn't he?"

"Yes."

"And you trust him?"

"As much as he trusts me."

Mace's response so captured her attention that she was in the living room before she noted her surroundings. The most prominent feature was a brick fireplace with a wood-burning insert. The walls were painted a calming cream. Framed photographs of outdoor scenes were on every wall. Where were the artful nudes she'd expected, the stark skyscrapers against a dark sky?

Large windows were on either side of the front door, and half of the wall to her left was nearly all window. There weren't any curtains. The furniture was leather and wood, old and well-used. She envisioned him haunting used furniture stores and then repairing what had appealed to him. A stack of hiking magazines rested on the solid-wood coffee table.

The way he was watching her, she expected him to ask what

she thought, but maybe he didn't care about her reaction and was deciding whether he really wanted her in his space.

Rio seemed to be having the same thoughts, but at least the dog wasn't growling.

She swallowed, fighting the impulse to wipe her palms dry again. "What's in the other rooms? Am I going to see a cage?"

"I don't dom here."

"Oh. Then the doming, if that's what it's called, always takes place at Indulgences?"

"There are other BDSM clubs. I've been to all of them, but these days..."

Despite her curiosity, she forced herself not to ask him to finish. He had to know she was nervous, but so far he'd done nothing to put her at ease. The way Rio regarded her wasn't helping. She swore the dog was appraising her with an eye to determining whether she was worthy of his master.

Not caring what Mace thought, she walked over to the wall opposite the one with the picture window so she could study the half dozen or so photographs on it. From where she now stood, she could see into the kitchen. Several dishes and pans were in the sink, making it clear that cleaning up for guests wasn't a priority. Maybe he seldom had people in here.

The photographs ranged from seascapes to a spectacular one taken in the middle of a redwood forest looking up and sunlight streaming down. One was of spring wildflowers growing around a mossy rock, another a lake with hundreds of ducks on it and mist seeming to cradle them.

"This is incredible," she said with her back to him. "You took them?"

"Yes."

Unable to think of anything else to say, she imagined him standing beside the lake waiting for the perfect moment. Judging by how quickly they'd had sex, she'd assumed he was an impatient man. This other side to him, maybe the real man, had her pressing her temple. Bottom line, she didn't know him at all.

She couldn't see him right now, but that didn't prevent her from sensing his presence. Something alive surrounded her, pressing close, demanding and compelling all rolled into one. Sex was a major component of what she felt, but it went deeper than that.

Still pressing the side of her head, she slowly faced him. His being barefoot did nothing to lessen his impact. And his chest, that strong and healthy expanse of flesh, muscle, and bone, was nearly more than she could handle. She knew better than to drop her gaze to his belly.

"Something I want to say right now," he said, his hands in his back pockets and the stance doing too much to her nerves. "If you felt pressured by Robert and Atwood, let me know. I told them not to rush things with you, but I don't believe they listened."

"They are pushing it, aren't they?" Was he feeling the differences between them, feeling her heat as much as she did his?

"More than necessary. Whether your articles start coming out this month or next doesn't make that much difference."

Although her awareness of Mace remained on level ten alert, she mulled over what he'd just said. "I think they want to make sure they made the right decision when they hired me."

"Why *did* they hire you?"

Believing he cared, it took all she had not to touch him in gratitude, but if she did, she wasn't sure she was ready for what might come next. "My understanding is they were impressed by some pieces I'd written, particularly a lengthy one about children for a psychology magazine that won a national award."

"Sounds like you were proud of it."

"It's more than that. It was personal to me."

"What was it about?"

Getting close here. "I thought we were here for, ah, educational purposes."

"You don't want to talk about it?"

If I say too much, you might learn more about me than I'm ready for. "It's not that," she lied. "I was observing high-school students for something else and got to talking to their teachers about why some teens were laid-back about their studies while others seemed uptight. When I said I guessed that was because they were hardwired one way or the other, the teachers said it wasn't that simple. Bottom line, parental influence has a profound impact on personalities."

He frowned, then nodded. "In what ways?"

"I'm simplifying things, but those who roll with the punches have parents who face life the same way. The parents of teens who put pressure on themselves tend to be hard driving. They expect a lot from their children."

Worn out by the lengthy explanation, she waited for Mace to change the subject to the reason she'd come here.

Instead: "Which are you?"

She waved dismissively, then didn't know what to do with the hand that ached to brush his chest. "It doesn't matter."

"Yeah, it does. You aren't laid-back. You wouldn't have gotten to where you are without a fire under you." Pulling his hands out of his pockets, he folded his arms over his chest. "Who lit that fire, you or your folks?"

They started it. "A bit of both I guess. What about you? Do you think your parents contributed significantly to the man you became?"

Something she wasn't sure she'd ever seen in human eyes flashed in his. "They had nothing to do with it."

Rio must have caught Mace's clipped tone because he started whining. When Mace laid his hand on the dog's head, she saw that one of the pit's ears had all but been torn off. Hairless patches dotted his face and forelegs. "Was he a fighter?" she asked. "Shit, you didn't—"

"No!" Mace's nostrils flared. "He went through that hell before I came into his life."

"I thought that once a dog started fighting, he couldn't be trusted."

"If he'd been older, he wouldn't have been salvageable." Mace lightly scratched behind Rio's good ear. "He was only a pup, but the bastards put him in a ring for the older ones to work on."

Horrified, she dropped to her knees before Rio. Only then did she question whether Rio could truly be trusted. He might be faithful to Mace, but what about other people?

Rio regarded her as if she was marginally interesting, unlike most dogs who lost their pea minds whenever someone gave them some attention. How had Mace learned about Rio, and why had he concluded that he was the right person for the physically and emotionally damaged animal? Wondering if she'd ever ask, she looked up. The man dominated her world.

"He isn't demonstrative," Mace said.

"I noticed. Do you think he was born that way?"

"I hope not. Like the kids you wrote about, his upbringing imprinted him."

Her knees were starting to ache from the hardwood flooring, but instead of standing, she held out her hand, palm down. After a few seconds, Rio gave it a lick. Her throat tightened.

"I've never seen him do that."

Drawn to Mace's tone, she again focused on him. They'd been like this before, him standing while she, his sub, knelt before him. She felt the restraints on her neck and wrists. When they were in Indulgences, he'd been dressed in near-vampire garb. Now his naked chest defied her to ignore it.

"I've always loved animals," she came up with. "Maybe he knows it."

"You had a lot of pets?"

"No." Hoping to avoid the logical question of why not, she stood. Her legs felt unsteady, but she'd be damned if she'd hold on to Mace. "I'm glad he's with you. Ah, let's get started."

"You're ready?"

"That's why I came here," she said when what she wanted was for him to tell her about his journey into pit-bull ownership—that and all the other things she needed to know about him.

His expression seemed to be asking if job responsibility was the only reason she'd driven out here. If he voiced his question, what would she say?

"My bedroom."

Startled, she nodded, then glanced at the hall. Because it wasn't lit, she could only guess how long the cave-like space was. She wanted to say something smart ass so he wouldn't guess she was suddenly both scared and excited, but her mind felt empty. In contrast, her body was so full she half expected to explode. This was prom night and college finals all rolled into one.

12

He led the way, his feet silent. In contrast, her sandals put her in mind of pounding hoof beats. Rio remained behind. Perhaps he knew what was going to happen, but Mace had told her BDSM never took place in his house, hadn't he?

What about girlfriends?

A single lamp on the nightstand provided the only illumination, yet she noted that there were more framed photographs in here. The bed was queen size, the spread pulled back to reveal blue sheets. Everything looked ordinary, too ordinary.

Lacing her clammy hands together, she concentrated on learning all she could about her surroundings. More magazines were on the dresser, and a chair was half buried under clothing. Male clothing.

He tapped the dresser. "It's all in there. Do you want to see?"

Oh, shit. What am I doing here?

The answer came, not in a reminder of how badly she wanted to succeed at her career, but the motionless form a few feet away. Mace was Tarzan and Batman rolled into one—courage, strength, and dark thoughts in a single body. She could be at home watching her favorite detective show. Instead, she stood in a man's room waiting for him to imprison her.

His stare beat on. After too long she remembered he'd asked a question. Knowing she couldn't hide her nervousness from him, she walked over to the dresser and opened the top drawer. At first she couldn't concentrate, then had no choice but to acknowledge the coiled flogger, red velvet blindfold, handcuffs, and ball gag. There were other things, but they'd have to wait until she'd processed this much.

"You're shaking," he said.

"Does that surprise you?" No matter how exposed it made her feel, she ran her hands down her hips. "This is like—I keep thinking how I felt walking into my college chemistry class for the final."

"How did you do?"

"I passed, barely."

"It'll be different here tonight. No tests, no passing or failing. Unless you can't handle it, this is what's going to happen. I'll take you down into yourself so you can explore the basics, your body telling your mind things it never has before."

Not sure she was following him, she picked up the handcuffs. They were heavier than she'd expected. "Not the same as the ropes you used the other night."

"No, they're not." He'd moved so he was beside her, not quite touching but imprinting her with his presence. "In some respects, the cuffs are the same as the collar in that you can't remove them."

Wondering where her courage came from, she draped one of the cuffs over her wrist but didn't fasten it. "Part of the collar was soft. These are hard."

"Can you handle that?"

Because she'd been raised to meet challenges head-on, she

snapped the cuff. A rush of something she didn't have a name for filled her.

"There's been a lot of discussion about who wields the ultimate power in a BDSM relationship." Taking the loose half from her, he drew her captured arm behind her. "Conventional *wisdom* says it's with the sub who must approve everything that happens. My take, power constantly shifts."

Something clicked inside Cheyenne, a door locking perhaps? "How is that? I don't have any power."

"Yeah, you do."

"Right." She tried to jerk her arm free. "Do we have to bring up which of us is the stronger?"

"BDSM doesn't operate on strength alone. Because I've done this more times than I'm going to admit, I can explain certain things to you, things you won't need notes to remember."

Thinking to face him, she tried to turn, only to have him stop her by looping an arm around her chest and holding her in place. That done, he tugged on the cuff until her arm was up between her shoulder blades. Her body jolted, then seemed to melt. She had no desire to fight.

"This is what I'm talking about." He spoke with his mouth near her ear. "I'm not a beast. If you started struggling, I'd immediately let you go. What it boils down to is that I do what pleases me, but only when the sub wants the same thing."

His explanation was too complex, and how could he expect her to concentrate when his aroused cock pushed against her backside?

"Do you understand what I'm saying?" he asked.

Fighting the impact of his hot breath on her ear slowed her response. "I'm trying."

"I'm sure you are." He shifted his hold, brought her even closer to him. Then his hand snaked down, capturing her breast. Even with her garment between them, another jolt ran through her. "You came here of your own will, which says you're interested in becoming a player, but if I don't play according to your terms, you'll scream."

"What good would that do? No one will hear."

"Rio will."

Wondering if the dog would attack his master, she closed her eyes. Granted, this wasn't the first time Mace had restrained her, but the closeness got to her. It might always impact her this way. A million miles from questioning her behavior, she pushed back so the contact between his cock and her spine intensified.

"I'm not screaming."

"Which is what I needed to know. I brought up anal play. Have you thought about experiencing it?"

You need to ask? "I'm not sure how to answer. It's not as if I have any frame of reference."

When he chuckled, his chest rumbled, and her body welcomed the sensation. "Then first order of business is for me to supply the frame of reference. One step at a time, right?"

Eyes still shut to hold out everything except the two of them, she zeroed in on her captured wrist, his arm holding her in place and his hand cupping her breast, his breath dampening her ear, most of all his cock saying this was personal with him.

"Yes," she managed.

"Good. I could turn off the light, but I think you need to always know where you are."

Agreeing with him, she opened her eyes, but before her vision cleared, he closed his teeth over her ear. Molten energy filled her, and she fought the impulse to try to jerk free. Until now, she'd been so focused on other things that she'd taken only scant notice of her pussy. Hot and hungry, it pulsed.

After too long, he released her ear and breast. His arm slid lower, skating past her ribs and over her waist. Then he pushed her away only to capture her wrist and draw it behind her. She stopped breathing. A moment later, he fastened the handcuff around that wrist as well.

Trapped said it all.

Taking hold of her shoulders, he spun her around to face him. "Feel everything," he commanded. "Steel on flesh. Me close to you."

"Yes."

"Make your restraint your gift to yourself, Cheyenne. This isn't something I've done to you; it's what you need."

"Need?"

Closing his hand over her chin, he lifted her head. "You make your living with words. Don't pretend you don't know what I'm talking about."

You're asking so much of me. "Are we going to have sex?"

Once more his expression defied her comprehension. "We'll know it's right when and if the time comes. Listen to me. I'm done forewarning you. From now on, I'm going to assume you want what I'm offering. If you don't, you need to say your safe word."

Stop shaking. "I don't have one."

"Choose it, now."

"Rio, all right, Rio."

"All right. And in case you're curious, his hearing is incredible. That's why I closed the door."

He had? How could she have not noticed?

When she shifted her feet, it registered that she was still wearing the muumuu. Reminded that she wasn't totally vulnerable, she squared her shoulders. "You said something about me wanting what you're offering. This has nothing to do with Indulgences, does it?"

"You'll have to decide that." He leaned closer, and his breath again caressed her. "I can't crawl into your mind and find the empty places. All I can do is rely on my expertise."

Empty places? Despite the question, his nearness was robbing her of any interest in psychoanalyzing either of them. At the same time she didn't know how to tell him to get started, not that he hadn't already done so as witnessed by the handcuffs.

"What's your favorite fantasy?" Not giving her time to gather her thoughts, he pulled her around so her back was to him and lifted her dress an agonizing inch at a time. "When you need to get off, where does your imagination take you?"

Intertwining her fingers as best she could, she stared at a photograph taken from a mountaintop that went on forever with distant peaks spearing through the clouds. Had Mace been alone when he'd taken that one, and how had he felt surrounded by wilderness and solitude?

"To a remote area," she answered. "There are lots of trees and a creek running through a valley, acres and acres surrounded by a high cyclone fence I can't climb."

He pressed his fingers against the back of her thighs with the fabric resting on the back of his hands. His touch was firm but sensual, possessive. Biting her lip, she shivered.

"You're inside the fence," he prompted. "Are you trying to get out?"

"Yes, because I'm being hunted."

"By men who want to enslave you?"

Any other time she would have been too embarrassed to continue, but the hands of the man who'd cuffed her were closing in on her pussy, and she could barely think.

"They're, ah, powerful; no law enforcement would try to close them down."

"And some cops are members of the hunting party."

"Yes." He knew! Was it possible Mace understood her cravings better than she did? "I'm not the only woman there," she continued. "We're all naked and barefoot, terrified. If we're caught, we'll become sex slaves; but if we make it through the night, the gate will open and we'll be set free."

"Do you really want freedom?"

Oh, shit, one more inch and the fingers between her legs would reach her sex! Exhaling a long breath, she tried to imagine standing beside Mace on that unknown mountaintop while he took picture after picture.

"Free? I don't know," she admitted. "I've never been in a situation remotely like this one. But the challenge excites me."

"Why do you think that is?"

Enough with the hard questions. "I think because I'm in touch with myself, aware of my nudity and vulnerability. Does this make sense?"

"Go on."

"I need to hide, and yet I want to be thrown to the ground and be manhandled."

Gathering the skirt in one hand, he lifted it over her hips and tightened it around her waist. Only one hand remained between her legs, but it was enough. Everything. A fingertip promising the world simply by lightly stroking her labia. Shuddering, she jerked away only to sag back against him.

"Do you see the other women being hunted?" he asked.

"No." *Oh, shit, shit!* "But I hear them screaming. Then their screams end, and they start moaning."

"Why?"

His fingertip continued its assault on her pussy and sanity. "I . . . don't know."

"Is it that or because this"—thumb and forefinger encompassed a labial lip and drew it down—"is distracting you?"

"Oh, God, I can't . . ."

"Yes, you can. Concentrate on your fantasy. Don't think about what I'm doing to you."

Nearly laughing at the impossible-to-obey command, she noted that her legs had slid apart. "You really like jerking me around, don't you, playing with me."

"What I like is taking both myself and a sub into a new

space. Continue. I want to hear all about what happens when you're inside that fence."

"I've never told—it's my fantasy, my secret."

The drag on her sex relaxed a little. "Tonight it belongs to both of us, Cheyenne."

"All right. Oh, God . . . It doesn't hurt to run, and I love the way the wind feels on my body. My hair is long, nearly down to my waist. I don't have makeup on, no manicure. It's just me, primitive. Me against whoever is pursuing me."

"You're about to be captured," he said seductively, still intimately holding on to her. "You hear the footsteps behind you. Whoever is after you is faster, stronger, laughing because it turns him on to drive you to the ground."

Yes, yes! "I won't make it easy for him!" The fingers working her trapped sex lip released it. Guessing what he intended to do next helped not at all. The instant a wet finger entered her, she gasped and rose onto her toes.

"Go on. Leave nothing out."

"I can't—God damn you, you know I—"

"Yes, you can!" His finger, now bent, raked the front of her channel. Her G-spot! "You've been milking this fantasy for years. You know it as well as you know which side of the bed you get out on." A second touch punctuated his words.

"Stop! Please, stop!"

"If that's what you really want, say your safe word."

Hell no!

"All right, damn you." The invading finger stilled, allowing her a measure of thought. "I hear a sound, something whistling. Suddenly a lasso settles around me. It tightens, trapping my arms against my sides. I'm being pulled back. Off my feet. Landing on the ground."

"You're stunned," he muttered. "Maybe you black out. By the time you can think again, a man is standing over you, laughing and planting his foot on your back to keep you down. You know it's over. You've lost, he's won."

Even as her pussy leaked and her nipples knotted, she realized he'd pulled out of her. Robbed of the impending release she craved, she again dove into her imagination for the trigger that might throw her over the top.

"No, it's not over. My becoming his captive is just beginning."

"But first he needs to secure you. How does he do it?"

She could answer. After all, she'd spent countless nighttime hours spinning the details.

"I try to turn over, but I can't because his foot keeps me on the ground. He keeps the rope tight so I can't use my arms. When I stop struggling, he slaps my ass. Furious, I redouble my efforts. He waits until I'm exhausted. Then he kneels beside me and ties off the rope. Using the loose end, he secures my wrists."

"Like I did the other night."

"Yes," she admitted, no longer able to focus on the mountaintop photograph. Her muumuu was so tight around her waist that in her mind it became rope. She'd never needed a cock in her more, Mace's cock. "That's when he turns me over."

"What does he look like?"

"I don't know." She laughed. "That's the one part of this whole thing I can't control. Maybe I don't care." *Maybe I was waiting for you.*

Unnerved by the thought, she tried to escape Mace's grasp only to have him haul her tight against him. "Safe word time?" he asked.

"No! Damn it, you're going to be disappointed if you think you'll get logic from me tonight." Forcing herself to relax, she again noted the pulled-back bed covering. In anticipation of a night of sex?

"That's good to know, not that I expected different. So, your captor has placed your weight on your bound arms. It would take a lot of effort on your part to get to your feet now. Does he want you to?"

"Not yet." So undone she wasn't sure how much longer she could stand, she welcomed Mace's sex-drenched hand on her hip.

"Why not?"

Think, damn it. "He wants to make sure I can't get free. There's . . . he has another rope. Kneeling, he places it around my neck and knots it. It won't tighten any more, but I can't slip free. When he's done, he manhandles my breasts. It hurts and yet . . ."

"And yet you're turned on."

Nodding, she went in search of what she might say next, but trying to separate imagination from reality was beyond her.

"You're giving up control to this man." He spoke for her. "Bit by bit, self-determination is being taken away."

"Yes."

"But even as you masturbate to climax while spinning things out in your mind, something's lacking, isn't it?"

Although she tried to concentrate, his heat and the insistent pressure of his cock splintered her mind.

"What is it?" A slick hand glided over her hip bone. "I'm getting closer to the truth than you want to admit?"

"I don't know."

"I don't believe you."

"Go to hell."

"Undoubtedly. Okay, time to shake things up a bit."

13

Releasing the woman who was too close to crawling under his skin, Mace pondered if he'd made a fatal mistake with what he'd just told her. Then she faced him, and although her dress slid back over her hips, he fought the urge to throw himself at her and knock her to the ground as her fantasy captor had done.

It would be so damn easy, so satisfying! To hell with rules and regulations. Piss on the self-control he always held tight to. Cheyenne needed a fierce and dominating master. He could be that man. Needed to be.

Rio trusted her.

"Tonight's about you," he told her when that was the last thing he wanted to say. "Pushing your limits."

"I know." She struggled to meet his gaze.

"How can you? You don't know what I have in mind."

"Why are you doing this?" she snapped, straining to free her wrists. "Is that how you operate, by playing word games?"

"You're the one who makes her living manipulating words, not me." He forced a smile. Suspecting he'd regret it, he unfastened his jeans but left the zipper in place. "My expertise lies in another direction."

Judging by the way she shifted from one leg to another, energy was building inside her. The same energy coursed through him, causing his cock to fight its prison and compel him to cradle it. Her attention locked him.

"Wish you were the one doing this?" he asked.

She licked her lips. "Would you let me?"

"Not now." *Because I know what would happen.*

"But maybe later?"

The way she lifted her chin said she was tapping into him, something he refused to let a woman do. Narrowing his gaze and concentrating on not blinking, he waited until she lowered her head.

"Kick off your sandals," he ordered. She did so without looking at him.

Spurred by what she'd said about imagining she had long hair, he stepped into her space and took hold of the short strands. She tried to pull away, then stopped. After a moment, he pulled down, forcing her to bend over. The ridiculously loose dress billowed out. Seeing no reason not to, he ran his free hand up under the fabric until he reached her dangling breasts. Capturing the one closest to him, he hauled her, stumbling, over to the chair that held his discarded clothing.

Sitting down while maintaining his hold on her hair and breast was far from the most graceful movement he'd ever executed, not that he figured she was paying much attention. Her breathing sounded strangled.

"We're going to go back into your mind, your imagination," he told her. "But first . . ."

Positioning her so she was on her knees and bent over his thighs called for letting go of her breast, which he hadn't wanted to do. Both breasts now pressed against the outside of his leg, and he didn't know what would be better, the safety of his jeans between them or the sweet pressure of her breasts on his naked thighs.

The dresser was close enough that he was able to retrieve what he wanted without having to dislodge her. From the way she tried to twist her upper body, he knew she wanted to see what he'd chosen, but she'd find out soon enough. For now he placed the toy next to him on the chair.

Grasping the links between her wrists, he lifted her arms so her upper body no longer rested on him. Her head hung down and she panted, distracting him. Mindful of the strain on her shoulders, he hauled up on the stupid dress until he'd wadded it under her armpits. After making sure her breasts were exposed, he let her down.

"What are you going to do?"

She sounded lost, not afraid, just off balance. Exactly how he wanted her. "Have you forgotten? Tonight's about taking you to the next level."

"Which is what, Mace? Please—"

He slapped her naked and inviting ass, the sharp sound echoing through the room. "No questions, got it? The only thing you need to do is experience." Punctuating his comment with another slap, this one on her opposite ass cheek, he pushed on the back of her head and forced it down.

Although he knew what he intended to do and was eager to experience her response, he studied her. The line of her spinal column captured his attention, and he trailed a finger over the bones. She whimpered but didn't try to wiggle free.

"We were talking about what turns you on," he said, relaxing the pressure on the back of her head. "Speaking is difficult for you now, and pretty soon it's going to be impossible." Releasing her head, he lightly massaged the faint red splotches he'd left on her buttocks.

"Oh, God, oh, God."

"There's no deity in here." *And if there is one, he doesn't know I exist.* "No one coming to your rescue—just like when you were hunted down and roped."

When she caught her breath, he took that as proof that she was sinking back into her make-believe world. Fine. He'd help her bring it to life.

"You're still on your back, your arms helpless like they are now." He lifted them for emphasis, then went back to memorizing her spine. "With a rope knotted around your throat. Your captor is just about ready to take you to his camp, only one thing left to do."

Wise in the art of anticipation, he fell silent and started slapping her ass cheeks again, one followed by the other, falling into the rhythm. At first she lay still and submissive over him, but as he put more and more effort behind the *punishment,* she started squirming.

Her buttocks were changing color, blood coming to the surface. Continuing the pace that vibrated through her and came out centered around his cock, he ground his fist into the small of her back.

"A gag," he said, because if he didn't distract himself, he'd throw her on the bed and spread her. "Made from rags and stuffed in your mouth, more rags knotted to keep everything in place. Now you're silenced, isolated."

"Yes," she moaned, writhing against his thighs.

"Being locked inside yourself turns you on." Cupping his hand, he slapped her again, making her flesh shake.

"Damn you!"

"No question about that."

Seeing his fingertips imprinted on her ass sent flames through him. It took everything he had not to change from dom to bastard. Somewhere deep inside a remnant of his upbringing lived. The helpless boy he'd been raged, on the brink of leaping into hell and taking whoever was with him down with him.

Fighting the boy he loved as much as he feared, he stroked Cheyenne's abused flesh.

"Tell me, when I spanked you, what did it feel like?"

"It hurt, damn it!"

Grunting, he ran his hand between her legs. As he expected, her pussy was drenched. In fact, moisture was seeping through his jeans. "Do you always get turned on when you're being punished? How did you explain that to your parents?"

"What? They never spanked me."

"Never?"

"No need when a lecture cut me in half."

Sensing she'd just scratched the surface of something important, he swiped his sticky finger over her asshole. Another man might ask her to explain further, to unburden herself, but hell if he'd go there tonight. Or any night.

"Your captor has been staying at a hunting camp surrounded by evergreens." He picked up the toy and ran it down her spine. "He wants to get you there by dark and is looking forward to when it's just the two of you and no one will ever know what he's doing."

"Am . . . I afraid of him?"

"Yes, but that's coupled with excitement. You don't know what to expect as he hauls you to your feet. Just as you resign yourself to being dragged behind him, you learn he has one more trick up his sleeve."

With that, he rested the blood-red butt plug on the small of her back and lubricated her puckered opening with the juices rolling out of her. Her breath became more ragged, and she ground herself against his leg. His cock was on fire, a hurting, demanding force.

When he pushed past the tight ring of flesh, she arched, her nearly useless fingers reaching for the plug. "No! It's too big. I can't—"

"Yes, you can. All you need to do is relax."

"Relax? Are you out of your mind?"

"That's possible. You know what's expected of you, slave, the pleasure that'll accompany your obedience." He slapped her buttocks. "Did I give you permission to talk? Focus on what I'm doing to you, nothing else."

Turning her head from side to side, she started shaking. Having her head hang down had to make her dizzy, but then he didn't want her clearheaded. "You have no choice but to stand watching as your captor secures the lead rope around a tree. You're stuck there. Things are going to happen you have no control over; nothing else is important."

Certain his words had gotten to her, he placed the bulb end of the butt plug against her opening.

"He has another rope, one you didn't notice before. He holds it in front of you, laughing as he does. You take an involuntary step back. The rope around your neck tightens, stopping you."

She was relaxing a little, responding to his hypnotic tone. Although maybe he should have taken her further into her personal zone before doing what he'd intended from the moment he'd invited her here, eagerness spurred him on.

"Your captor kneels before you and starts wrapping a rope around your ankle." Holding his breath, he pushed on the plug. It met resistance. Her trembling intensified. "You try to shake off the rope, but he threatens to whip you, so you stop and let him hobble your legs."

Taking hold of an ass cheek, he pulled it aside. Her rear hole opened a little, and when he pushed again, the toy's head slipped in.

"Oh, shit!" Lifting her head, she tried to look back at him. Her toes curled, and her calf muscles knotted.

"Perhaps not the best choice of words," he pointed out.

Hopefully she knew the plug's flared end ensured it wouldn't slide all the way in her.

When she kept straining to see what he was doing, he released her cheek and took hold of her cuffs. Lifting up, he again raised her arms and forced her head down.

"Not much to see like this, is there?" he observed. "Nothing to do except experience." He made his point by pushing the plug as far as it would go. "And listen. Now, where was I? Oh, yes, your legs are now tied so you're forced to shuffle along. Your captor leads you to a trail you've never seen before. Much as you want to, you don't dare look around because you might fall. He wants you to walk faster than you can. You start sweating. The insides of your thighs are getting chafed because you can't separate your legs. The bottoms of your feet are bruising, and the ropes rub. No matter how hard you try, you can't get him to understand that you're in pain, but maybe the truth is, he doesn't care.

"Does your imagination ever take you there?" he asked. "Your master is a cruel man. To him, you're nothing but a piece of meat, maybe something to sell for as much as he can get."

Mace's words swirled around Cheyenne. She was drowning in them, sinking deep into a place she'd never been. Blood pressing on her temple contributed to her confusion, but there was another kind of pressure taking place, an invasion of her body she'd only contemplated before.

No modesty left, no control over the most intimate of parts. Her bung hole was full, invaded. Fighting the loss of self-control, she again tried to straighten, only to have him force her back down. In truth, she didn't care. This way everything was his responsibility. She could only experience. Listen.

"Your captor intends to sell you," Mace said. The pressure in her rectum was both relentless and fascinating. "But first he plans to train you. A subservient sex slave is valuable, and he knows how to turn you into one. He could simply let you imagine what he has in mind, but the bastard wants to see you sweat and hear you beg. What about the two of us, Cheyenne? Are you going to beg me to stop?"

The plug started twisting inside her, confusing her. Then splintered parts of her mind reconnected, and she realized he'd thoroughly lubricated her back there so the plug would move freely. Her pussy clenched, demanded more.

"Losing focus, are you?" He slapped her ass. "I asked a question. Do you want me to stop?"

"No."

"That's what I thought. Maybe it's the same between you and this captor you conjured up. Because you're the one who ultimately controls how things play out in your sex fantasies, you decide how much and what kind of things are done to you. As an example, instead of wasting time on the long, hard walk to his camp, you've jumped things ahead. Now that you're there, what do you see?"

"You want—"

"An intimate look into your mind, yes. What is it, Cheyenne? Your imagination needs a jump start? This should help."

He tapped the end of the plug. Jolt after jolt rocked her, forced her forward. Her breasts scraped his jeans. Hating the gag, she tried to gnaw on it. When that failed, she pressed her side against his cock.

"No, you don't!" Dragging her closer to his knees, he planted a hand on her spine and held her in place. "You might be able to pull your captor's strings, but that doesn't work with me."

"Fuck you!"

"Hold that thought."

As the pressure on the plug continued, he reached under her, stroked her clit.

"Oh, shit! Oh, my—shit!"

"Unnerving? Now pay attention, because I'm not going to

repeat my performance. And for your information, my thumb is all that's keeping this not so little toy in you."

She was ready. Anticipating. In control. At least that's what she told herself. Then the plug drummed inside her, and his all-knowing fingers captured her nub. Screaming, she wrenched to the side and would have rolled off his knees if he hadn't hauled her back into place.

"Not gonna get away that easy, my pet."

More jolting deep inside sent her heart to hammering. The pressure caused by the plug wasn't as intense as earlier, not that it mattered. He rolled her clit about.

"Oh, my God! I'm going to come!"

"It is what you want?"

"I don't know."

"Why not?"

I'm afraid. It's all too much. "Stop asking your damn stupid questions!" Her throat felt raw, and even with need crawling over her skin, she knew she'd given away too much. Dreaming up submissive scenarios was one thing, reality quite another.

"All right." The plug stilled. Although he didn't release her hardened nub, at least he was no longer putting it through hell. "Sounds like it's time to change a few things. Do you want up?"

"I . . . don't know."

"Then I'll make the decision unless you want me to make you come first."

He could do that, force release? Of course he could. Unnerved, she shook her head. "You'd like that, wouldn't you! Playing with me. Getting off on control."

"In case you haven't noticed, I'm nowhere near getting off."

Point taken. "What do you mean by changing things?"

"This, in part."

The strange drawing sensation left no doubt that he was withdrawing the plug. He also left her clit, leaving her confused, relieved, and disappointed. He held the glistening toy in front of her. It was smaller than she'd thought, the deep red overkill.

"Not so intimidating this way, is it?" he observed. "It's glass, in case you're interested. Another time we might try a battery-operated one."

"I, ah, take it you have that among your arsenal."

"A staple for the well-supplied dom."

"Something you've had a lot of need for?"

"Don't."

He was right. Not only wasn't his past her business, digging into it wasn't what tonight was supposed to be about. Just the same, the realization of how little she knew about him tamped her arousal down a little.

When he pushed her up and off him, still on her knees, she studied his features. His dark eyes belonged on a man accustomed to keeping certain doors closed. And if he kept countless secrets, she'd do the same. At least she'd try.

"What's with the jeans?" she asked to have something to say. "They can't be comfortable given the state of your cock. Why don't you get out of them?"

"Because this is about you. Now—"

"Is it ever going to be about you?"

His jaw clenched, he turned his attention to the plug. If she said or did the wrong thing, she'd lose him. If she was ever going to get anything out of him, she'd have to choose her words carefully, not easy for someone on her knees with her hands cuffed behind her, and her dress now hung up on her hips.

"We're going back inside your mind." Dropping the plug on the floor, he reached for the dresser drawer and pulled out a strip of black fabric. "Locking you into what turns you on."

She flinched both at the sight of the blindfold and what he'd said, then forced herself to settle back so her ass rested on her heels. Her buttocks still felt abraded from the spanking, a glorious and erotic sensation. If she played according to his rules tonight, if she earned his respect, would he eventually open up to her?

And what would she do with the knowledge?

Then he slid the velvet over her eyes and everything went away. Steady pressure left her with no doubt that he'd tied the blindfold in place. Robbed of a vital sense, she cocked her head, hoping to hear him. For a while there was nothing beyond her heartbeat and less than steady breathing, and sounds that led her to conclude that he was rummaging in his drawer of tricks. When he slid his finger under her neckline, she clenched her teeth. Sweat slickened her armpits.

A new sound set her to trembling. Only when warm air slid over her breasts did she fully comprehend that he was taking scissors to her muumuu.

"Who said you could do that?" she demanded. "Do you have any idea how much that cost?"

"You're my possession. I can do anything I want to you and your belongings." A ripping sound accompanied by air cooling her belly punctuated his words. "There. Better. Now, slave, take me back into your fantasy. Your captor has taken you to his camp. He intends to turn you into a well-trained and valuable sex slave, so how is he going to make that happen?"

14

If she told Mace that picking up the threads of her fantasy was the last thing on her mind, he'd only press her, either that or spin out his own images. In this one thing, maybe, she'd be in charge.

"He, ah, he begins by informing me that I must be broken down so he can rebuild me as he sees fit."

"Do you know his name?"

"I'm to call him Master. Nothing else matters."

"How does he break you down?"

Concentrate! You know how this goes. "By flogging me."

"Flogging." Mace rested his hands on her breasts, pushing them down. "What does he use?"

She couldn't think after all, didn't give a damn what happened to the woman in her dreams.

"Don't you know?"

"You're . . . touching me."

"As is my right and responsibility." The pressure increased a little. "You have beautiful breasts, Cheyenne. The areolas are dark, the nipples even more like a deep tan. The men in your life must love sucking them. Is that something you'd like me to do?"

The question swam through what remained of her mind. The truth was, she couldn't think of anything she wanted more, but would she survive? "I don't know."

"I don't believe you."

"It's the truth, damn it."

"If it is, I don't think you'd want to admit it."

Running his hands under her breasts, he gently lifted them. "You're not going to tell me this isn't pleasurable, are you?"

Her sagged to the side. "Why ask? You know the answer."

"I can surmise and read your body language, but I want you to tell me the truth. Back to your captor, although we really should call him your master now. Does he show you what he's going to whip you with? Maybe he blindfolds you first?"

Was Mace going to take a flogger to her, maybe a switch? She couldn't force the question past her dry throat.

"Need help tapping into your imagination? All right, here's how things start. He ties you to a tree with your arms over your head so you're on your toes. In addition to the rags he stuffed in your mouth, he's knotted a blindfold in place. Next comes a rope that secures your hobbles to a nearby bush. You can't move more than a few inches in any direction. It doesn't matter that you can't see it, you know what your naked body looks like. What about your breasts, Cheyenne? Are they swollen and sensitive?"

Working a little moisture into her mouth, she muttered, "Yes."

"Of course they are, because this is what you've been wanting for. Only now you aren't sure which is stronger, anticipation or fear. What about now? Between you and me? Are you looking forward to what I might do?"

Half of her remained tied to the tree Mace had told her about, while the rest was on her knees with his hands claiming her breasts and her pussy soft and ready.

"I don't want to be flogged," she whispered.

"Hmm." Increasing his hold on her breasts, he massaged them. "Maybe you aren't as much of a submissive as you wish you were. You don't see anything erotic about pain?"

"This doesn't hurt, not really."

"What about when I spanked you?"

Laughing, she shook her head.

"Felt good, then?"

"Yes."

"As I intended. Back to the pleasure–pain thing. How much have you explored?"

"Not much."

"Do you want to?"

Knowing this was what he'd been leading up to didn't help. Even as her breasts throbbed and tingled, her throat again dried. "I don't know."

"I do."

His words like hammer blows, she flinched.

"But I don't expect you to take my word for it. Example time." He fingered her nipples, dry skin grating against dry. "For the true submissive, pain brings pleasure. Perhaps their nerve endings don't process the difference. As a result, the message reaching the brain is a confused one. Some people can climax from pain alone. Do you think you might be one of them?"

"What . . . are you going to do?"

"This." Vice-like pressure closed around her nipples only to end almost before she realized he'd pinched them. "What did you feel?"

"Surprise." Her knees were starting to ache and her world had closed in on her, blackness embracing her.

"Was it a turn-on?"

"It happened so fast I can't answer."

"Besides, you're used to me handling your breasts."

"If you say so."

He chuckled. "Got it. However, that doesn't get us any closer to learning what we both need to. A reminder, there's a return visit to Indulgences on our schedules and toward that end . . ."

As the silence dragged on, she realized he had no intention of finishing. Her overactive nervous system told her he'd pulled back. Alone, she tried to visualize what he was doing. Then he pushed her ruined gown off her shoulders and down her arms until the cuffs stopped him.

"I'm not going to flog you tonight," he said. "Maybe another time, but not now."

"What—"

"Silence! Put yourself back in that captive's place. Surround yourself with trees and bushes. There's a hawk flying overhead. A coyote watches from behind a boulder as your master reaches for this."

Something hard clamped onto her left nipple. Shuddering, she tried to pull free only to have the grip tighten. Tears stung and her toes curled. "What—"

"Silence." He slapped her free breast. "And hold still. Experience."

Mesmerized and afraid, she froze. At first the only thing she could think was that Rio was biting her, but that couldn't be.

"That's better," Mace said. "You're shaking, but you aren't trying to get loose. That's the kind of thing a master requires, obedience in spite of fear."

And pain. What about that?

"Ready?"

Before she could ask what for, another set of *teeth* closed around her right nipple. Careful not to test her strength against whatever had ahold of her, she breathed through flared nostrils. Something hot ground into her sex.

Whatever had hold of her nipples appeared to be made of steel with blunt-edged *teeth* ensuring she couldn't dislodge them on her own. Although the stinging sensation held her attention, she no longer felt as if the top of her head might explode. Calming herself with an effort, she acknowledged that Mace had fastened nipple clamps on her.

"I tried them," he explained, "so I have some idea what you're feeling. But a woman's breasts have much more to grip. These are called Japanese clover clamps complete with a chain. Ever put them on yourself or have anyone else do it?"

She shook her head.

"But you've seen them. They're at all the BDSM sites."

"I've . . . seen. They hurt."

"Do they?"

Suddenly her right nipple vibrated. She'd seen both silver and gold clover clamps and knew how big they were, how they adorned a woman's breasts like hardware, how easy to manipulate.

"Pay attention." He sent the other clamp to vibrating. "What beyond discomfort?"

Her breasts were on fire. How did he expect her to concentrate on anything else? Desperate to escape, she sucked in her breath only to exhale it as something drew her breasts down.

"I let go of the chain," he explained. "You're feeling its weight. My preference is silver. I love the contrast between pale flesh and something man-made. When a woman can't use her hands, they become part of her until her master decides otherwise. Of course, you could beg me to remove them. Is that what you want?"

"Beg?" The word had a bitter taste. "No."

"Ah, pride. Concentrate. What am I doing now?"

Something was drawing her nipples away from her body. Holding her breath and trying to lean forward did nothing to lessen the sensation.

"Mace, please!"

He slapped her cheek. "Call me Master."

"Master, all right, Master." Hating her pleading tone, she struggled to accept the inescapable. Maybe her nipples were becoming numb because she no longer defined the sensation as discomfort.

"That's better. I repeat, tell me what you believe I'm doing."

Think, damn it. Don't make him angry. Even as the warning wrapped itself around her, she realized she wanted him to possess her. Forcing herself to think of nothing except him, she went in search of the answer.

"You have hold of the chain. Every time I move, the chain tightens."

"You're getting there." Keeping the tension on her breasts constant, he patted her cheek. "Think about this. You're naked and helpless. You can't see what I'm doing. My attention is on your breasts. I love the way I've altered them. There's nothing natural about the shape and certainly nothing natural about what's hanging from them. And yet the clamps are works of art, a combination of the practical and erotic."

Her mind hung up on the last thing he'd said. He must have released the chain because she felt it sliding over her flesh. Moving carefully, she leaned back. The sliding increased.

"Next to clamping a woman's clit, there's no more failsafe way of controlling her. Everything her breasts feel is echoed in her sex."

He was right. It was as if her breasts and pussy were connected. "What do you want me to say?" Holding her head up was becoming harder and what did it matter? She couldn't see.

"Whatever you need to." The weighted sensation faded,

leaving her to guess he'd again palmed the chain. "Right now my intention is to demonstrate the union between pain and pleasure."

Lowering her head, she pressed her legs together. Flashes of sexual energy attacked her pussy.

"I still don't want to be whipped. Maybe the day will come when—no, I don't care. I want this." She hunched her shoulders. "Not daring to move. No choice but to wait for you. Feeling things that—"

Something pressed against her knees, jolting her thighs, belly, and then breasts. It had to be his knees but what—

Oh shit! His hand between her legs, sliding over her thighs and testing her resolve. Shivering, she willed herself to remain still. Masculine fingers marched upward, inward, slow and steady. Whimpering, she strained to see.

"You don't want to fight me, slave. You know not to try, and yet your body needs to protect itself."

Closer to her sex, the anticipation lasting forever.

"Don't move, understand." He slapped the top of one breast and then the other, making her whimper.

"This lesson is about self-control, slave. If you don't demonstrate restraint, I'll sell you."

"I'm sorry, sorry."

"Apologies mean nothing to me." Two more light slaps to her breasts punctuated his comment. "And if you think I'll regret what I'm putting you through, you're mistaken."

Something in his tone cut through the morass of her mind. "Do you ever wish you hadn't done something?"

He'd gripped her chin before, but that time she'd been able to study his expression. Now darkness awaited her, that and the lengthening silence between them. "Life's a never-ending succession of decisions, slave. Not all are right."

"Then—"

"But I have no doubts about what I'm doing now." His breath

washed her cheeks. Anticipating while not knowing what she was waiting for wrenched her focus from her waiting sex. Then his lips settled over hers and became everything. Mace was kissing her, pressing his mouth against hers anyway. She tried to open her mouth only to have him lightly bite down on her lower lip. Seconds later, he let her go but continued to hold her chin.

"What's going on behind that blindfold?" he asked. "Are your eyes pleading for me to stop? Perhaps, but I don't think so." With his thumb and little finger pressing against her thighs, she inched her legs apart.

"What are . . . please tell me what you're going to do."

"Quiet. Patience. Trust."

"Trust?" The blindfold had locked her in a small, darkened cave. She could listen and speak, nothing more.

"Trusting me is what brought you here, Cheyenne. Now that you are, you're learning whether that trust was warranted or misguided. You could fight, you know. Throw yourself at me, aim your head at my chin. Maybe you'll knock me out, but then what?"

Why was he trying to frighten her? But was he?

"Pain and pleasure. The marriage between the extremes. Are you ready?"

"Yes," she heard herself say. "Yes!"

"Good." The all-knowing hand went on the move again, pushing against her inner thighs. Her chin was free, her head lowering, again trying to see.

15

Maybe she should have anticipated, but when he grasped the chain and pushed two fingers inside her, she cried out. Although she wanted what he was offering, she tried to scoot away.

"Not going anywhere, slave. I'm not done with you."

"Not—fair!"

"Of course it isn't. But then you really aren't complaining, are you?"

Waiting for his fingers to trigger an explosion, she paid scant attention to her breasts. Then, suddenly, her right nipple was free! Blood rushed back into it, making her whimper. She was trying to get on top of the sensation when he began rubbing where the clamp had dug in. Pain slid off into a place that didn't concern her as she focused on the current weaving through her.

"One down, one more to go. I'll go slower this time so what you feel will be different. Hold your breath."

Whether focusing on breathing had anything to do with the slow return to life in her left breast, she couldn't say. He took what seemed like forever with her nipples, running his nails over them.

"No lack of sensitivity there," he said unnecessarily. "I feel sorry for women who don't experience what you just did."

Other fingers were inside her, waiting and ready. No escaping. No wanting to. "You don't feel sorry for anyone," she snapped. "Otherwise, you wouldn't do that."

"Maybe. One last lesson, Cheyenne. Then, if that's what you want, you can go home."

He'd called her by her name instead of slave. Did she dare do the same in return, ask him about that last lesson?

"If you could see and weren't wearing cuffs, would you let me do this?" Drawing out of her sex, he circled her clit. She fought to keep from drowning.

"What about it? If you were free, would this be happening?"

Another circle brought her high on her knees. Could she get to her feet and if so, would she run?

"You're going to climax soon," he said. "I, however, am going through hell."

"Not my doing. I didn't—" Her body stopped, froze. The seconds ticked down. Two, she thought, two. Maybe.

Without warning, he pushed on her chest, forcing her onto her back. Her legs were no longer under her, but straight and splayed. Saying nothing, he ran his hands under her buttocks and lifted her so only her shoulders and feet were on the floor. Something wet and warm lapped at her sex.

"No! Oh, my—God!"

Her body shuddered, and her hands dug into her own back. The attack on her pussy increased as Mace drew her into his mouth. Holding her tight, he controlled her climax.

Her head thrashing from side to side, she screamed. Screamed again.

* * *

Cheyenne was back on her knees, but her arms were no longer fastened behind her, and he'd removed the blindfold. Looking down at the top of her head, Mace told himself he was still in charge, but any man who said that while a woman cradled his cock in her mouth was a fool.

Her hands gripped his thighs, steadying herself as she turned her head this way and that, sucking much as he'd done to her. Because he didn't trust himself to touch her, he'd fisted his hands. His back was slightly arched, his toes trying to grip the carpet. His eyes burned, his jaw ached from clenching his teeth, and his jeans were down around his ankles.

Cheyenne wasn't a pro at sucking cock, yet. But she was making up for it in enthusiasm, although maybe determination to prove herself drove her. Whether she drew him in as deep as she could or adjusted her hold so his tip pressed against the inside of her cheek made little difference to him.

It was all good! All unnerving.

"Keep it up," he ordered, because that was what a dom did. "Don't stop. Put your tongue into it."

Her understanding nod brought him onto his toes. A groan pressed against his teeth, but damned if he'd cry out like she had. He might come; hell, there was no might to it! But even then he'd hold it together.

Somehow.

"Hands on your thighs," he commanded. "I didn't give you permission to touch more than my cock, did I?"

A shake of her head sent fire running down his legs. If she was doing this on purpose—

"You remember what Paul's sub did at Indulgences, don't you?" Not giving her time to nod, he continued. "She crawled under the table and did him because she's his obedient pet. She hasn't earned the right to climb in bed with him. Maybe she never will."

Cheyenne's lips slowed. Done with trying to act as if he wasn't on the edge, he ran his fingers into her hair and pulled her against him until her nose was against his groin. Mindful of not forcing her to go too long without breathing, he held her in place.

"Keep at it," he ordered. "Put everything you have into pleasing your master."

Although he heard her try to suck in air, she obediently ran her tongue along his cock's underside. Her mouth was open wide, the corners looking strained; even when she met his gaze, he wasn't sure how much she was seeing.

Letting up a little, he allowed her to fill her lungs. He'd given her damn little time to recover from climaxing. Granted, he'd let her down once her juices coated his mouth, but then he'd flipped her onto her belly so he could straddle her hips. Lowering his weight onto them had felt good, but nothing like what was happening now.

"Faster. Put more effort into it, slave!"

Her nodding, bobbing response robbed him of air. Hell, he could barely think. What he remembered was rubbing against her buttocks followed by unlocking the cuffs. Then, not particularly wanting to, he'd gotten off her and told her she could sit up.

The blindfold had remained in place as, in response to his command, she'd pulled down his jeans. Then, wanting her to see what she was about to do, he'd yanked the cloth over her head. Static electricity had left her hair standing on end.

"What . . . what do you now think of the marriage of pleasure and pain? Change your mind? Think you could fall in love with a flogger after all?"

She stopped moving, eyes wide and knuckles turning white.

"Doesn't damn matter," he ground out. "Not now. Get back to work."

Releasing her hair, he slapped her shoulder. His hand didn't leave a mark, but then drawing her into a sub's life was hardly his priority. Damn it! For a man whose world revolved around independence, having his cock in her mouth was wrecking him.

Wrecking him good.

Shit! The point of no return coming. Plowing over him like a tidal wave. Gripping her hair again, he dove into the explosion. Shards of sensation first circled around and then into him.

He wouldn't look into her eyes anymore! Damn it, wouldn't let her see the truth of him! Instead, he'd force her to hold his cum and struggle to breathe. Keep the balance tipped in his direction.

Mostly.

Coming! "Ah, shit, shit!"

Her strength tightened down around him, pulling him into a deep, dark pit.

"God damn!"

Lights in the pit. A rainbow of color.

"Damn you!" *Damn me.*

Cheyenne had painted her condo's living room walls cream with a hint of green. The female employee at the paint store had tried to talk her into trying yellow, saying that yellow was mood-lifting, but Cheyenne believed that color worked on flowers and the occasional butterfly or bird. Same with pink. Who had died and declared that all women preferred to surround themselves with pink?

Of course, she acknowledged as she let herself in after driving back from Mace's place, it was more than a little likely that her parents had influenced her opinion of pink. Her adoptive parents. No sissy, girly-girl nonsense for their project. Instead, they pounded home their insistence on primary colors, the stronger the better.

The message light on her phone was blinking. Hoping it was Mace making sure she got home all right, she punched Play. Instead of the deep voice with the ability to run chills down her spine, she heard her *mother's* voice.

"Your father and I want to make sure you read this month's *Finance Today*, the magazine we gave you a subscription to. There's an important article in it about the economy's impact on IRAs. You are feeding yours, aren't you? The maximum allowed by law. If you'd focused on computer technology as we advised you to, you'd be making much more than you are and retirement funding would be less problematic. However, your career is what it is. Our hope remains that you're intelligently leveraging yourself for the future. The article begins on page twenty-two."

"I love you, too, Mom," Cheyenne muttered, erasing the message. "And I wonder what you'd think if you knew what I did tonight. Probably cut me out of your wills, not that that hasn't been the subject of more than one conversation."

The pit of her stomach hollowed out, but because it wasn't the first time, she knew how to deal with it. Surround herself with emotionless walls. The successful couple who'd opened their lives to her when in their early forties was set in their ways. They had cast-in-stone standards she'd never lived up to, but they had provided her with a roof over her head and pounded a strong work ethic into her.

"The standoff continues," she muttered as she headed for the bedroom. "I just wish I could find a way to get you two to listen when I say I'm going to do what turns my crank, not yours."

Speaking of cranks, hers had been turned and then some tonight.

After kicking off her sandals, she stripped out of the shirt Mace had given her to wear home and dropped it on the floor. Naked, she stepped into the bathroom and turned on the light. Maybe because she was avoiding her reflection in the mirror, she first noted the dark blue highlight wall to the right of the sink. Not into over-the-top decor, she'd painted the other walls white. Because hers was the only name on the mortgage, for the first time in her life she hadn't had to ask permission.

Mace's pale walls had retreated into the background with the result that his photographs stood out. Where she'd brought her modern and impersonal condo to life with mismatched pieces of furniture and a paintbrush, he'd relied on photography.

Spectacularly.

Thinking to ward off replaying what had happened at his place, she focused on her image. Her hair was a disaster. Nothing short of a shampoo and lots of conditioner would remedy things. Her shadow and mascara was smeared, making her ponder whether there was such a thing as blindfold-proof make-up. Probably not, and even if there was, did she have the courage to ask?

Red splotches began at her cheekbones and ran clear to her chin. Her lipstick was history, undoubtedly because what she'd started the evening with was on Mace's cock.

Groaning, she rested her chin in her hands. Her eyes had that deer in the headlights look. Clearly she'd seen and experienced things she never had before. Deliberately turning her next groan into a sigh, she got around to the real reason she'd come in here.

She couldn't be sure, but her breasts seemed a little larger than usual, a lingering by-product of being stimulated. Most remarkable, if that was the right word, were her nipples. They were darker than the rest of her breasts all right, no surprise there. Still hard and erect. And with faint marks on either side.

Giving a crooked smile, she lightly touched the marks. Not pain, not really. But far from same old, same old. No way would she want to have to shove them into a bra right now.

Planting her hands on the counter, she leaned closer. She'd seen the clover clamps as she was getting ready to leave, so knew there'd been nothing claw-like about them after all. Instead, spring-loaded flat disks had connected with the sides of each nipple. No wonder she hadn't been able to shake them off.

If she'd agreed to being flogged, would that have satisfied Mace?

Gnawing on her lower lip did nothing to supply the answer. The idea of pain for pain's sake made her slightly sick to her stomach. No way would she stand still for that kind of treatment. But what if Mace wielded the flogger?

16

"I understand," Mace said. "It's not as if I need telling how to do my job."

A few minutes ago, Atwood had summoned Mace into his office, and although the executive hadn't said what he wanted to talk about, Mace had a damn good idea. Being able to concentrate on Atwood instead of splitting his attention between him and Robert made it easier to focus, something that hadn't come easily since Cheyenne had been to his place.

"I didn't say that," Atwood countered, "but Cheyenne was noncommittal when I asked if the two of you had finalized plans for Saturday night. When I brought up her submissive tendencies, she shrugged me off. I understand her reluctance to discuss it with me, but Robert and I have a right to assurance that—"

"I know what you're getting at. You want to make sure I get her into the back rooms."

From his expression, Atwood hadn't expected the conversation to jump right to the point. Instead of agreeing, he pointed at his liquor cabinet. "Interested?"

"Not on duty." *And never when I'm doming.*

"Suit yourself." Atwood held up a glass. "As you can tell, I'm welcoming Thursday evening a little early. So, is she ready? So far I'm seeing no indication she's embracing the lifestyle."

"What do you mean by indication?"

Atwood's smile made Mace think of a kid caught with his hand in the cookie jar. "Proof. Physical proof."

"Such as?"

"Hell, you know what I'm talking about. She can't phone in the BDSM lifestyle."

When did a magazine article become this important? Making no attempt to shrug off his question, he watched Atwood sip.

"Seeing her in chains is important to you?" he asked. "Why? Do you intend to be there?"

Atwood's denial took a moment longer than it needed to. "Although I must confess that the thought of seeing her restrained is, ah, intriguing, that scene's not my style. Too edgy. And the costumes some of the regulars wear—"

"You've seen them?" *And don't give me this shit about the back rooms not being your style.*

If Atwood was caught off guard, he gave no indication. "Research, Mace, research. I needed a guarantee that she'd be writing about the real deal, albeit an extreme real deal."

Hardly for the first time, Mace wanted nothing more than to end a word game. "Granted, my responsibilities don't call for me getting involved in the magazine itself," he said, "but Cheyenne's articles can't be the most important *Edge* has ever published."

"That's where you're wrong."

On alert, Mace worked at keeping his own poker face in place. "So educate me."

Atwood's smile was slow to develop and left his eyes untouched. "Economics. *Edge* exists because of its advertising.

Subscriptions don't come close to covering the magazine's operating costs."

"I'm aware of that."

"I'm glad to hear that. Simply put, in order for *Edge* to attract top-tier advertisers, we have to offer a solid subscriber list. That has been achieved because we offer what other magazines are afraid to. Reality. Life in the raw."

"Content that occasionally gets you in trouble with the morality police."

Atwood grinned. "Which is why we keep a legal firm on retainer. Mace, we recently signed contracts with two national companies with generous advertising budgets. One produces the most popular brand of TVs on the market today. The other—not naming names—is a highly successful drug company."

Atwood finished his drink in a single swallow. "A key factor in their signing those contracts was because we told them what Cheyenne's working on."

"In other words, sex sells."

"In other words, so-called deviant sex attracts big money." He chuckled. "How's this for an idea? The photo accompanying her byline shows her wearing a collar."

"You're joking."

"No, I'm not." He paused. "I trust you know what I'm talking about."

"You bastard."

"What do you care what does or doesn't adorn her? It's not like she matters to you, does she?"

Atwood waited several minutes after Mace left, then took out his cell phone and accessed a number in his address book.

"He's making me uncomfortable," he said after the obligatory small talk. "I can't tell if he's buying what we're feeding him."

"So cut him out. We don't need trouble."

Chuckling, Atwood stared at his empty glass. "The Blind Spot knows how to deal with reluctant *members*. I'm simply telling you not to expect him to immediately fall into line. I just issued him a challenge. It'll be interesting to see how he responds."

"You're putting a lot of effort into this particular recruit."

"Because we need the kind of service he's capable of providing. The man called me a bastard, but the word fits him."

Rio was standing at the back door when Mace opened it, looking as he usually did, a little disappointed.

"I'm sorry," Mace apologized as he let the pit bull in. "I know you don't like being cooped up in the backyard, but I can't take the chance on someone freaking out."

Rio didn't appear inclined to forgive him, at least he didn't until Mace held up what he'd gotten at the grocery's meat market. "A beef knuckle bone," he explained. "It won't splinter and wind up in your gut. You promise to keep it in the kitchen?"

Rio snagged the bone, dropped it, and settled over it.

"Thanks for nothing. The maid's going to kill us. Oops, no maid."

Leaving Rio to his treat, Mace headed for his bedroom. Thanks to a distraught woman's insistence on seeing whoever had interviewed her mother for a Hunted piece, he was more than an hour late getting home. The woman had been furious, declaring that the journalist writing the piece should have been sensitive to her mother's emotional state.

"My mother's sister was killed by a monster," the woman had pointed out around her tears. "There isn't a day she doesn't relive that terrible time. To be asked to describe how it felt to learn the killer was Aunt Viola's ex was unconscionable. You tell that damned reporter that thanks to her, my mother's not sleeping again."

In the end, he'd gotten the woman to agree that the chance

of someone recognizing her dead aunt's ex would increase when incensed readers saw his picture and read about the hell the family was still going through.

Cheyenne was writing the piece.

Despite his growling stomach, Mace couldn't put his mind to throwing something together. Instead, he pondered what it had been like for Cheyenne to hear a woman sob about her murdered sister. No wonder Cheyenne fantasized about giving up control and responsibility when off the job. Given similar circumstances, he might feel the same way.

No, he wouldn't, he admitted as he stood with his hand on the drawer holding his dom equipment. He knew what it was to be helpless, to live a nightmare. Coming out intact on the other side had required shutting down his emotions and embracing control.

Enough with the journey into his childhood! What he had to concern himself with tonight was how to deal with Atwood.

Opening the drawer, he took note of what it contained, not that he didn't know what he was after. Telling himself he was simply doing what had to be done, he selected a collar made of silver links resembling a dog chain. Sitting on the side of the bed he'd come close to putting Cheyenne in, he pulled out his cell phone.

"There's going to be something in your desk when you get to work tomorrow," he told Cheyenne as soon as she said hello. "You'll know what to do with it."

"Mace, what is this about?"

"Maybe my helping you transition into what you think you want to be. Maybe job security."

"That doesn't make any—"

"Just do it."

Mace wasn't at his usual early-morning spot by the front door when Cheyenne arrived the next morning, thank goodness. Instead of taking the crowded elevator, she opted for the stairs. Once she started climbing, she realized that while she didn't have to engage in gossip and chitchat here, the claustrophobic space brought back memories of what had happened between her and Mace.

Not like thoughts of him didn't blindside her no matter where she was or what she was doing.

You'll know what to do with it, he'd said. As a result, she'd spent the night half convinced she'd find a battery-operated dildo in her desk. Realizing he'd tapped into her ragged physical state was unnerving. He had to be crazy to think she'd slip into the bathroom at work and pull down her panties so—

A catch in her side distracted her, and she managed to reach her floor with just a tad of juice on her panties' crotch. Her cubicle consisted of three portable walls and an open space next to a short hall. Fortunately, no one was in the hall, and she didn't share her cubicle. Sitting down, she, not for the first time, wondered when and if she'd be promoted to an honest-to-goodness office. *Edge* might be a slick publication, but the powers that be believed in Spartan surroundings for most of its employees. All flash on the outside and no substance beyond the public area.

Resigning herself to what was, she started opening drawers. It wasn't until she got to the bottom one on the left that she spotted something that hadn't been there yesterday. The brown paper bag was anonymous in the extreme. Resting her hand on it, she looked up to reassure herself that she was still alone. Then she opened the bag and took out its contents.

A slave collar. Made of links of chain. Silver. Choker length. Not slender enough to pass as ordinary jewelry. A not so unobtrusive ring welded into it.

Oh, shit.

As she reached for the interoffice phone, disbelief slid into embarrassment followed by a tingling hopefully no one would know about.

"You can't be serious," she said when Mace came on the line.

"Deadly serious."

His tone told her this was no joking matter. "If I wear it, people are going to know what it represents. They'll point and talk behind my back."

"Let them."

"Why?" she demanded. "I thought you believed in separating your personal life from the professional one. You can't want me telling folks it came from you."

"What you say's up to you. My only stipulation is that you put it on, now."

Feeling weak and other things she needed to keep to herself, she fingered the collar. She had no doubt that like the one she'd worn at Indulgences, this would remain locked around her neck for as long as Mace wanted.

"You aren't going to tell me what this is about, are you?"

"I'm trying to decide. For now the only thing you need to know is that your master is making this request of you."

"Request? That doesn't sound like you."

"Okay, command. Is that what you wanted to hear?"

I don't know. "I have to do it today?"

"Now. Cheyenne, just do it."

"I'll talk to you later," she said and hung up. Thinking he might call back, she tucked the collar in her purse and headed for the bathroom. Two women from the art department were in there, their expressions somber.

"You can't keep avoiding the calls," one was saying. "Those collection agencies are relentless."

"I call back, but all I get is recordings. How am I supposed to—"

Leaving the women to their conversation, she headed for the stall farthest from them. She sat on the toilet and clutched her purse to her, her lips numb. If she could, she'd wait until she was alone, but who knows how long the women would be in here. They might ask if she was okay.

Well, she wasn't. Or maybe the truth was, she was more than okay. Turned on.

Staring at the closed door, she retrieved the collar. She'd worn a button-down blouse and slacks, which meant her throat and even a hint of cleavage was in sight. She supposed she could button the blouse all the way, but the garment hadn't been designed with maximum modesty in mind. Besides, she'd be failing Mace if she hid the collar—his collar.

Her fingers tingled so much she almost dropped the piece of *jewelry* but managed to drape it around the back of her neck. Now came the hard part. Putting off the inevitable, she noted weight and substance. The collar wasn't ornamental. There was nothing fashionable about it.

Just get it over with!

Teeth grinding, she pushed the ends together. The instant she did, energy raced through her veins. She sucked in air that smelled of too much freshener.

A distant door opened and closed. The room went silent.

Standing, she shuffled out of the stall and over to the bank of sinks with a long mirror behind them.

There she was, collared. Her pale skin looked vulnerable and trapped, the links dragging and the ring resting against the base of her throat.

"Oh, shit."

Someone looking on might surmise she was horrified, but in truth, she loved knowing she was bound to Mace in inescapable ways—even if he didn't feel the same way. Closing her eyes, she fingered the solid links.

17

"We intend to keep this short, ladies and gentlemen," Robert announced as he and Atwood entered the conference room. "All of you have deadlines. Never let it be said that management got in the way of meeting those deadlines."

From her place at the opposite end of the table from where Robert and Atwood always sat, Cheyenne noted that Atwood's cheeks were somewhat flushed. Gossip was he was having trouble regulating his blood pressure, but more gossip centered around the opinion that the man imbibed, a lot. Whichever it was, she was glad Robert was running the meeting.

"It occurred to us"—Robert nodded at Atwood, who was staring at some papers in front of him—"that although there's a lot of talk about *Edge* employees being family, reality is that each of you is so focused on your own responsibilities that you might not be aware of what your fellow journalists are doing. In an attempt to remedy that, I'm asking each of you to spend a few minutes talking about your current project."

Sighing, Cheyenne shifted in her seat. If anyone had noticed her collar, they hadn't said anything, although if the tables were turned, she would probably keep her mouth shut. She'd been wearing it for no more than an hour and already she felt changed. Mace didn't have to be anywhere near for her to sense his presence. Most distracting, certain parts of her anatomy insisted on reminding her of the activities that had taken place between them.

As Mace's slave, she'd obey his every command. Hell, he could walk in the room and order her to strip and splay herself on the table and she wouldn't take time to breathe before complying. A pat on the head for a *job* well done and pride would engulf her. His cock sliding into her pussy and—

"Cheyenne, I'd like to begin with you," Robert said. "You've only done one other Hunted piece and that was about a serial bank robber, which financially inconvenienced the banks but wasn't particularly compelling for our readers. This one—what's the killer's name?"

"Carl Schulz," she supplied. Giving herself a mental shake, she pushed Mace and the incredible things he was capable of to the back of her mind.

"Oh, yes, Schulz. You'll be turning in the finished product before the end of the day, right?"

"Yes."

"Why don't you fill us in on the police investigation, your interviews with family members, everything you've done." The corner of Robert's mouth twitched. "And if you don't mind, I'd like you to stand up. How tall are you, an even five feet?"

"Five feet one."

Both wishing she could crawl into a hole and feeling a bit like an exhibitionist, she stood. All eyes turned to her. A few expressions didn't change, but most fixed on her collar. Eyes widened. Robert nudged Atwood, who muttered something and then leaned forward.

No one asked about her new decoration, but she sensed the unspoken questions as she described Carl Schulz's violent attack on his wife followed by more than a year in hiding on his part. Viola Schulz had filed for divorce and taken out a restraining order on her estranged husband, not that pieces of paper had stopped him from coming through Viola's sister's back door where Viola had been staying while trying to pull her life back together.

"Her family has been traumatized," she said. Thinking of the haunted look in Viola's sister's eyes killed the energy humming through her. "I'm not holding back in the telling. Readers need to know how important it is to get him off the streets."

"In other words," Robert said, still staring at her throat, "you're writing an impassioned article."

"You're damn right I am. He didn't have to kill her. She wasn't asking for much, just her half of the house when it sells. They have two children, fortunately grown, who'll spend the rest of their lives dealing with what happened to their parents."

"Give him hell," someone muttered.

"Where do I sign up for the lynch party?" someone else asked.

"String the bastard up by his balls."

Robert clapped his hand on the table. "Do you see the potential there, Cheyenne? If you write as well as you just spoke, which we know you can, you're going to have people all through the country turning over rocks looking for Schulz."

Nodding, Cheyenne started to sit down.

"Just a minute," Robert said. "Our young lady here might be vertically challenged, but her journalistic skills make up for that. I have no intention of leaking information. All I'm going to say is, she's now working on something that'll knock more than people's socks off. As your one and only hint, take a close look at her *necklace.*"

* * *

"If looks could kill," Atwood told Robert when just the two of them remained in the conference room, "I'd be picking out your casket. She didn't appreciate you saying that."

"I knew she wouldn't."

"Then why—"

"I wanted to leave no doubt in her mind that I understand the meaning and purpose behind the collar. She did squirm a bit."

"I loved seeing that."

"What I don't understand"—Robert pinched the bridge of his nose—"is what prompted her to put it on. If she wanted to remain under the BDSM radar scope, she went about it the wrong way."

"It wasn't her idea. Wasn't Mace's either."

"What are you talking about?"

Even with his alcohol-produced haze getting in the way, Atwood loved the look on his partner's face. "I had a talk with Mace," he explained. "Gave him the impression that we're questioning his expertise in a certain area."

"What the hell are you talking about? If you've got something to say, spit it out."

"I don't have to do any such thing. However, since it pleases me to do so, I'll explain. Our nominating Mace for a position at the Blind Spot puts our necks on the line. Before we take that step, we need to be absolutely sure we're offering him what he wants and needs."

Lips thin, Robert shook his head.

"Elementary my dear, elementary. In essence, I asked Mace if he had the balls to make Cheyenne jump through his hoops. Her sporting his slave collar answers that question."

"Shit."

"Shit as in good?"

A smile as broad as Robert ever offered transformed his features. He slapped Atwood on the shoulder. "Damn good. You know, I'm becoming more and more convinced that Mace is as much of a bastard as we are."

"He'd see that as a compliment."

"What about her? Think she'd agree?"

Atwood belched, the taste of booze coating his tongue. "Doesn't matter."

"What are you doing? Damn it, Mace, I don't—"

"Shut up. Getting what you want no longer matters. Now it's my turn."

Less than a minute ago, Cheyenne had opened her door to let Mace in. But instead of handing her what he'd decided was appropriate attire for tonight as he'd said he'd do, he'd grabbed the front of her dressing gown and torn it open, popping several buttons as he did.

She could have screamed. Her neighbors would have heard. Instead, caught up in her sudden nudity and Mace propelling her backward out of the living room and into her bedroom, she'd remained silent. Despite her struggles, he'd thrown her onto her bed and flipped her onto her stomach. Now he was wrapping rope around her elbows, forcing them so close they nearly touched. Mixed in with confusion and fear was a heady dose of expectation. Losing use of her arms this way was, hell, sexy. Her breasts ground into the coverlet, sending shards of energy through her.

Don't let him know.

"What is this?" she asked, turning her head so her face wasn't in her pillow. "What about Indulgences?"

"We're going there." Done with knotting the rope in place, he patted her ass. A sigh pressed against her teeth. "Just not the way you thought."

"No!" she exclaimed as more rope went around her wrists. "Don't I get any say in this? What if I don't want—"

"Want? You're a sub. You do what your master tells you to."

Oh, yes. "Wait." Although she tried to pull free, her tethered elbows made that impossible. "You're not going to take me there naked. Mace, I don't want—"

A rag being shoved into her mouth stopped her in mid-sentence. As if that wasn't enough, he wound electrical tape around her head to seal the rag in place. That done, he went back to binding her wrists. *Helpless. And turned on.*

The final ropes went around her ankles, forcing her legs so close together she knew she couldn't stand. Not that she wanted to.

Helpless. Needing him.

He rolled her onto her back.

"Here's how things are going to go down," he told her. "At least in part. There's more to the back rooms than you know, maybe more than you want to know. But you're determined to write those damn pieces, and I've committed to making your experience authentic."

Watching her with his head cocked to the side and his entire body yelling *masculine,* he closed a hand around her left breast. At first it was all good, everything she'd ever wanted her make-believe dom to do to her. But Mace kept squeezing, pressing tighter and tighter until the good was replaced by pain and a wave of fear. She struggled to escape.

"I love your breasts." Still holding on to the first, he cupped her other breast. "They're natural. Sensitive and responsive."

Still not comprehending the reason for Mace's rough treatment, she forced herself to lie still. Fortunately, her breasts had recovered from his earlier treatment, but it wouldn't take much for that to happen again. Was this playacting on his part, a role he'd become an expert at?

But what if he'd stepped across the unspoken line?

"Something for you to chew on," he continued. "I have no doubt you've been looking forward to tonight. The chance to dive into a sub role—well, here's the rub. There's no games being played tonight. This is the real thing."

Eyes wide, she stared up at him.

"Didn't expect that, did you? Not after everything you've heard about BDSM being about equal rewards and the sub holding the real power."

Releasing her breasts, he stood and walked out of the room. Before she could gather her wits, let alone try to formulate a plan, he was back carrying his jacket. He reached into a pocket and pulled out what might be the same leash he'd used on her earlier. After clipping it to her collar, he dug into another pocket. Out came a Magic Wand. Watching her, he plugged the heavy-duty vibrator into the nearest socket.

Oh, shit, shit!

"Do you have one of these?"

Her first inclination was to shake her head. Then, deciding one of them needed to be honest, she nodded.

"Hmm. Works pretty quick, does it?" He brought it near her crotch.

Another nod briefly distracted her from anticipation and a little trepidation.

"That's the response of most women I've used it on. A lot more punch in this than battery-run toys." With no warning, he placed the Magic Wand's head against her clit. Trying to bend her knees, she shook her head. Damn it, didn't he know anything about warming a woman up? Giving her a sample of the main event ahead of time?

"Hold on." He pushed her legs flat against the bed. "I'm looking forward to seeing your reaction."

A loud buzzing reached her ears a half second before her pussy recorded the touch. A swarm of vibrations enveloped not just her clit but her entire sex. Nerves jolted to life. Her over-wrought system let go, and she flooded her spread.

Overwhelmed, scared, and reaching climax, she threw herself to the side only to have him haul her back into place again. Holding on to her ankle restraints with one hand, he reintroduced the wand.

"What's it like in there? Brain not functioning like you want it to, right? No matter how much you want to keep on top of what's happening, it's a lost cause. This isn't your body anymore. Instead, it belongs to me."

Was she climaxing? Maybe being dominated had thrown her so off balance she no longer knew her body, that and the toy's relentless energy.

Stop, oh, God, stop! she screamed behind the gag. If he understood, he gave no indication.

"Okay, enough of that. For now."

The assault ended. Although her nerves remained tangled, the sense that she was trapped in violent river current decreased. Scared he wasn't done with her, she fixed her attention on his arm.

"A question for you," he said, leaning so close their noses nearly touched. "I just gave you a taste of what you're likely to experience tonight. Still sure you want to go through with it?"

Her first impulse was to shake her head as hard and fast as possible. The last thing she'd expected when she opened the door was to be treated this way. How worse would things be in a place devoted to master and slave, control and helplessness?

But she hadn't hated the forced sexual stimulation, far from it.

"I don't have all night." He ran the silent wand from under her chin all the way to her ankles. "What's it going to be? You going to bail, or do you have the guts to go through with it?"

Damn it, the pair who'd raised her had believed that throwing challenges at her was the only way to give her a backbone.

Well, it had worked. Furious and still on sexual high alert, she glared at him.

"Still thinking about it?"

She shook her head.

"In other words, you have an answer?"

She nodded.

"Okay." He positioned the damnable tool between her legs, then extended his finger, reaching inside her, making her jump. Withdrawing, he placed his drenched fingers under her nose. "Ready for me to untie you and walk out the door?"

Tense because he might bring the wand back to life, she nevertheless shook her head.

"Let's make this clear. You're not going to go to the cops after I haul you to Indulgences?"

Despite the image conjured up by the word *haul*, she responded with an unblinking stare and a shake of her head.

"All right." Maybe she was imagining it, but his expression seemed to say that wasn't what he'd expected. Or what he wanted. "But don't say I didn't warn you."

Mindful of how close Cheyenne's neighbors were, Mace had turned off the outside lights in preparation for leaving. Then he returned to where he'd left her. If looks could kill, he might be six feet under, but along with anger he caught hints of other emotions, not that her sopping sex hadn't spelled things out. As he'd expected, he'd confused and frightened her with the way he'd manhandled her, but now wasn't the time for an explanation, if ever.

Instead of immediately going about the business at hand, he took a moment to gain an impression of her bedroom. There wasn't anything frilly about it. The bland walls, hodgepodge of furniture, and large plant on top of her dresser said not enough about the woman who lived here, or maybe the truth was, she hadn't found a way to express herself in here.

Why not?

And why no family pictures?

Pushing the questions to the back of his mind, he approached her, careful not to look into her eyes. Tonight was going to change her; she just didn't know it. Maybe change him too.

After pulling her toward him so her legs hung off the side of the bed, he sat her up. Grunting dramatically, he slung her naked body over his shoulder and turned toward the door. One arm held her in place while the other headed for her buttocks. He slapped her repeatedly, albeit lightly, so she wouldn't be inclined to struggle.

Out of the corner of his eye he acknowledged the small surveillance camera tucked in among the plant's leaves.

18

The back rooms weren't at all what Cheyenne expected. Based on her online forays into bondage sites, she'd envisioned an elaborate dungeon or fanciful prison cells, maybe *stalls* filled with chained subs. Instead, when Mace stood her up, she found herself looking at an elegant, albeit dimly lit, banquet room. Perhaps a dozen men sat around an oblong table laden with what looked like fine china and crystal wineglasses. Dinner hadn't been served, but wine bottles were being passed around.

Unable to stand with her feet bound, she was forced to lean against Mace, although truth was, she took comfort from his warmth. She might have relaxed enough to thoroughly study her surroundings if she sensed he cared about her. Instead, except for the hand around her, he didn't acknowledge her existence.

"Mace, good to see you. How long's it been?" a middle-aged man in the process of filling his wineglass asked. "And who's this? Damn but you can pick them."

"She doesn't have a name, yet. I took away the one she had, just haven't bothered coming up with something."

"Slave always works, doesn't it? Why don't you park her and join us?"

"I was just about to. Where's the handler?"

"Here," someone said from the shadows. "You got preferences."

By way of answer, if that's what Mace had intended, he grabbed her hair and yanked her head back. Even more off balance, she prayed he wouldn't step away.

"There's nothing like a crotch rope to keep a slave on her toes," Mace said. "But really, I don't give a damn." With that, Mace shoved her away from him. Her chest collided with a solid male form, and unfamiliar arms engulfed her.

"What about the gag?"

"Leave it."

"Suit yourself. But if she's a moaner, you'll be missing part of the show."

"I'm not interested in anything she has to say. At least not until I've eaten."

This wasn't happening! The arms lifting and dragging her into the shadows had to be part of a too-vivid dream. Then the shadows gave way a little, and she was looking at a number of white floor-to-ceiling pillars. Women had been tethered to some of them. Two had their arms tied over their heads, their backs to the pillars, legs spread and ankles restrained. Like her, they were gagged. Ropes had been erotically woven around their breasts.

Shocked, she strained to locate Mace, but the body of the man holding her made that impossible.

"Don't make the mistake of trying to move," her handler said as he propped her against an unoccupied pillar. She was still trying to get her balance when he dropped to his knees and began doing something to her ankles. A moment later, although the rope remained in place, he'd loosened it so she could stand.

He took his time standing, running his hands over her body

as he did. To her shock, the touch turned her on. Was she really that addicted to being manhandled? Or was fear of the unknown responsible? "Nice fresh meat," he said. She wasn't sure whether he was talking to her. "Don't know what's going to happen tonight, do you? Not what you expected."

Although she didn't want to, she forced herself to focus on him. If anything, he was taller than Mace with a weightlifter's arms and days' worth of stubble adding to his sinister look. To top things off, he was dressed all in black.

"I'm going to take the strain off your elbows. It's a bitch having to put up with that for long. And I'm going to untie your wrists, but don't try to boogie out of here. You don't want to miss being part of the show."

The moment her elbows were free, blood flooded her veins. She moaned behind her gag. The idea of boogying anywhere with her ankles still tied would have been laughable if she hadn't just noticed yet another naked woman. This one, mostly in shadow, had on a collar so wide it forced her to stare straight ahead. Her arms were behind her, her elbows so deeply bent that Cheyenne guessed some kind of restraint ran from the collar in back to her wrists. A chain fastened to a ring imbedded in the pillar over her head ended at her collar. As if that wasn't enough, she also had on iron ankle restraints.

Cheyenne's arms still tingled when her handler positioned them in front, one wrist over the other and wound rope around them. Another rope soon circled her waist. Seconds later, her handler had secured her wrists to the latest rope, preventing her from moving her arms.

"Now comes the fun part."

Because he was working behind her, all she knew was that he was attaching yet another rope to the one around her waist. *Crotch rope*, Mace had said.

If asked, she couldn't describe what she was experiencing. When Mace first brought her here, she'd been intent on comprehending her surroundings. Then he'd roughly turned her over to another man. The sight of other helpless women and the change in her ties pulled her into herself. Yes, Mace remained part of her world, just not as important as what she was experiencing.

Her handler's hands slipped between her legs and pressed against her pussy, bringing her onto her toes. Just like that, she felt both less than human and more feminine than ever before.

"Not bad. All puffy and soft, just like I like it," he informed her. What did it matter that this was her body? His strength and bonds gave him every right to do what he wanted to her.

"Damp, but not drenched," her handler announced. "Mace, you sure she wants this?"

"Guess we'll find out."

What about my reaction to the Magic Wand, she wanted to demand as her handler continued his wanted/unwanted exploration. *I nearly came then; you nearly made me come.*

"Medium tight," her handler observed as he slipped a finger into her. "At least she hasn't been ridden by every stud in town."

"If I'd known she was into the scene," a new male voice said, "I would have put a saddle on her. She loosening up? Welcoming you in?"

Being talked about as if she were a piece of property had her so off balance Cheyenne was hard put to remember how she'd gotten here. Then there was the manhandling, the clinical exploration.

"Not making much progress," her handler said, still probing. "Guess it's time to kick things up a notch."

When he slipped out of her, she acknowledged a mix of relief and disappointment. Having a stranger maul her had never been at the top of her list of things she wanted to experience, but her body operated independently from her mind, all instinct and anticipation.

His hand returned, only this time he brought the rope with

him. Even though she twisted to the side, he easily threaded it between her legs. For the first time in her life, twisted cotton trapped her sex. Thank goodness it did little more than rest against her labia. If there'd been pressure . . .

"Just about done, or should I say, my role in this is damn near finished." He spoke with his mouth near her ear. "However, things are just getting started for you."

Threading the rope's loose end under her *belt*, he tugged. The rope rubbed her belly, but that was nothing compared to the increased pressure on her pussy. *Trapped?* What came after that? More than helpless? When he reached over his head, she looked up. A metal ring was imbedded in the top of her pillar.

Moaning, she watched as he looped the rope through the ring and tied it. When he stepped back, she stared at him, willing him to promise he wouldn't leave her like this. Although he returned her gaze, there was no humanity or compassion in his eyes, only the look of a man who took pride in a job well done. Then he was gone, swallowed by the darkness.

By experimenting, she determined she could stand comfortably on the balls of her feet, but that did little to quiet the sensations circling through her. Pleasure and helplessness bled together until she could no longer separate them.

A thin red light suddenly streamed over the body of one of the women with her arms over her head. Then another band of red highlighted the second similarly tethered woman. Next came concentrated light on the woman in chains. Then it was her turn followed by more until by the time all the shafts of light had been turned on, she'd taken note of a dozen *slaves*. Only a few were gagged, but except for moans and sighs, they were silent.

Even trapped in her own body's responses, she concentrated on what she was hearing. She caught hints of discomfort, but that only touched the surface. The others, like her, were deep inside their bodies, experiencing things that made them feel rawly alive.

The sounds sank into her and became part of her experience. With the blood-colored beam trained on her, she could no longer see the dining table and could only guess where Mace was, whether he was watching her.

She wanted him to note her silenced mouth and prayerful arms, the pale brown lengths wedded to her waist. Most of all she hoped he'd noted the way the rope hugged her belly and disappeared into the valley between her ass cheeks. If he could see her pussy . . .

Despite the others, she sank into a space where only she lived. She had no command of her body, and yet it was doing what she'd long wanted it to. If the handler returned, he'd find her sopping and the rope soaked. He might ridicule her lack of self-control, but even as his words exposed what had always been her secret, she'd slide even further into herself. Maybe climax.

19

_____

"**S**he's getting off on it," the man to Mace's left observed. "This her first time?"

"First time she's been this far," Mace replied because something was expected of him. "Hell, if I'd known she'd have so much fun, I'd have left her behind."

"Tied up and waiting for you, I trust."

"Got a cage. No need for anything else."

"You're not shittin' me? You really keep her in a cage?"

Heinz—wasn't that the man's name—spoke with enough of a slur that Mace suspected he wouldn't remember the conversation. But even if that was the case, he had a reputation to uphold. Long-time Indulgences members knew him as a coldhearted bastard. As long as the label stuck, Cheyenne was safe because other doms, unless they were stupid drunk or stoned, knew to leave his property alone. And if they were, there was always the pistol against the small of his back. He'd never come into this place without it.

"She's not a full-timer if that's what you're getting at," he told Heinz. "Not yet."

Heinz nudged him in the side, causing Mace to clench his fists. "But you're working on her, getting her there. Ain't that a kick! Making some bitch think BDSM's her idea when you're brainwashing her."

"Every slave's different." Although he wanted to keep an eye on Cheyenne and not Heinz, he shifted position. With his side safe from another jab, he noted that others were listening. What he had to remember was that this was about Cheyenne. Her experience. Memories that would find their way into her damnable articles.

Mostly he didn't dare lose focus by wondering what the hell the security camera in her bedroom was about. That had to wait until later.

"She's still wrapping her mind around what she's feeling," he continued. "She begged me to take her slow tonight. Not sure she's going to get her request."

"Hell, Mace, holding back has never been your style. You love taking a broad to the edge. Sometimes past the edge, which is why you go through so many. They can't take it."

Mace looked across the table and to his right to where the voice was coming from. "Yoel. Long time no see, man."

"I've been here. Where have you been?"

To Mace's way of thinking, Yoel was as far from the stereotypical dom as a man could get. Late fifties, no more than five and a half feet tall with a runner's lean body, he didn't look as if he could get any woman to see him as macho man. But he had a couple of slaves, good-looking women in their twenties, who followed him like puppies. For all Mace knew, they were part of tonight's pillars scene.

"I've been busy," Mace replied. *Trying to wrap my mind around how I'm going to handle the rest of my life.*

"How long since you've been in here?"

Mace shrugged. "A while."

"Don't tell me it's because you've been playing privately

with the one you brought in tonight. What's the world coming to when dom 'em and leave 'em Mace lets some broad get her hooks in him?"

"No hooks. Not interested in that." *Ever.* "I just wanted a break. No matter how interesting it is at first, too much of the same thing gets old."

Yoel's expression couldn't have been more incredulous if Mace had just told him there was no Santa Claus. "No way. You've been in prison or witness protection or something." He stuck out his hand. "Good to have you back. I learned a lot from you."

"Did you?"

Yoel nodded, drawing Mace's attention to the man's receding hairline. "About not getting emotionally involved."

"Are you saying you don't care about those two *children* you've been hooked up with forever?" Mace challenged.

Yoel's expression didn't change as he shook his head. "I said I learned a great deal from you. I didn't say I incorporated those lessons. In fact, the more I thought about it, the more I realized I needed exactly the opposite."

"What are you talking about?"

"Simple man, simple. What's the point of getting physically close to a woman without letting the heart in?"

The older man had asked similar questions before. As he'd done in the past, Mace chose not to answer. Back then his response would have been that his heart's only task was to keep the blood pumping in his veins. Now he wasn't so sure.

Putting down his barely touched wine, he stood and walked over to Cheyenne. He cared not at all that they were being watched.

"Getting the point of this?" he asked.

His intention had been to tug the crotch rope, but her skin against his knuckles distracted him. Feeling contemplative, he ran his fingers over her belly. She was so damnably soft in the places a woman should be, dangerous and unsettling places.

Noting that her eyes were nearly closed told him that, as usual, the handler had done his job. Restrained and silenced with her senses in overdrive, Cheyenne cared only about what was happening to her. Probably any man or even a woman could touch her and she wouldn't care.

"Enjoying yourself, are you," he observed as he reluctantly withdrew his hand. "In that zone you can't find words for, a place where the world revolves around you."

Other than blinking, she gave no indication she'd heard. Several men had left the table and were positioning themselves near their slaves. Always before, a part of him remained removed from what he was doing in case intervention was needed. This time, however, someone else would have to step forward if a dom went too far.

"I want to keep you in that zone," he continued. "I also want you to tell me what it feels like." Studying her, he ran his knuckles over the hip closest to him. She started, but instead of trying to draw away, she leaned into him, eyes still at half mast.

"You don't care what I'm saying. The only thing you give a damn about is being the center of my attention. You'd hate it if I left you. What if I traded or sold you? Seeing me dom with someone else would piss you off, not that you could do anything about it."

Her eyes were now open, suspicion sneaking into her expression. Maybe she wasn't as far gone as he'd thought.

Tired of asking himself questions only she could answer, he continued to stroke her hip. A woman to Cheyenne's left whimpered. There was no mistaking the sound preceding it. Someone had slapped her. She whimpered again.

"Shut the fuck up," a man ordered. "You should have cried uncle when you had the chance."

Reminded of the primary reason he'd stopped frequenting Indulgences, Mace reached into his jeans for his pocketknife. Holding Cheyenne's hair to steady her, he cut through the tape keeping the rag in her mouth. As soon as he pulled out the rag, she licked her lips.

"I can gag you again just as easily as I got rid of it," he said as much for the benefit of their audience as her. "Which I will if you do anything except what I want you to do, you got it?"

Because he still had a hold of her hair, her nod was barely perceptible. Still, it told him she was listening.

"Good." Reaching up, he unhooked the rope over her head. That accomplished, he draped the loose end over his shoulder and took off for another section of the room with Cheyenne behind him. Mindful of her tethered ankles, he walked slow, and much as he wanted to study her expression and note how the pussy rope separated her labial lips, his primary concern was keeping his pulse under control.

He'd nearly reached the flogging stand before she stopped. Anticipating her reaction, he turned, keeping the tension on the lead going.

"Take your time," he said. "And take a good look at where you're going to be until I decide different."

The flogging stand consisted of two long four-by-fours in an upright X shape. Metal rings had been imbedded into all four ends so someone could be secured with their arms and legs apart.

"When you and I started," he continued, "you went off on how you weren't into pain, but how can you say that? You spoke out of ignorance, a condition I'm about to change." He jerked his head at a table near the stand on which a half-dozen floggers had been laid out.

"You're not—you can't—"

"Quiet!" His jerk on the rope between her legs had her

stumbling toward him. "What'd I tell you about not speaking unless I've given you the right?"

Her eyes big, she nodded. Then her attention dropped to the tether sealing them together.

"I'm going to untie your hands and feet," he explained. "But because this"—another jerk—"is staying in place for a while, I strongly suggest you don't try to resist."

In almost perfect timing, an unseen woman moaned. If he hadn't been so focused on Cheyenne, he'd know whether the woman was playacting.

Leaving Cheyenne to digest what she needed to, he squatted and freed her ankles. Despite the strain in his calves and thighs, he took his time standing, running his fingers over her legs as he did. Goose bumps broke out on her. Her hunched position took him back to the first time he'd seen Rio. Despite his clean kennel, because he had no reason to trust humans, Rio desperately wanted to be free. Rio was the first dog he'd owned, but he'd instinctively known the pit needed time and love. In the end, Rio had become his best friend and confidant. As for Cheyenne, he'd do what was necessary to bring her to a place she didn't know existed.

She trembled as he reached for her wrists and was still shaking by the time he'd finished freeing them, reminding him of his first days with Rio. Taking hold of the loose end of the crotch rope, he lifted it, forcing her to acknowledge his continued control.

Something he'd never tried to give a name rolled through him. Energy explained it as well as anything, energy born of dominance after a helpless and too-often fearful childhood. Once he'd been on the other end of restraints, but what he'd endured back then had had no sexual component. There'd only been surviving.

Acknowledging how much had changed and that he now

held the pace and beat of everything he did made him strong. Powerful.

Sliding a hand under her breast, he lifted it. She made fists but kept them at her sides.

"There's nothing more erotic than a captured breast," he muttered. "From what I've observed, it's the same for both men and women, taker and receiver." With that, he slid his fingers to her nipple. "We've been through this before, but it's my opinion that the experience hasn't been exhausted. What is it like knowing you could stop me from doing this"—he drew her breast upward—"but not being sure you want to? The only thing holding you here is what's around your waist and between your legs. Why don't you make a break for it?"

The world came to Cheyenne in fits and starts, bits and pieces without meaning. She had a rudimentary knowledge of where she was and, if pressed, could explain how she'd gotten here, but those things were unimportant. Having back use of her arms and legs felt strange, almost as if she was in water and moving in slow motion. She could throw a punch, but it would have no impact. Her constricted pussy took a great deal of her attention, wonderfully so. Between that and what Mace was doing to her breast—

"You gonna use it? Because if you don't, I want to."

The unexpected male voice distracted her. Both grateful and resenting the intrusion, she looked around. Unfortunately, or maybe fortunately, the ever-shifting mix of shadow and ruby lighting hindered her. What she did know was she was looking at two people, one male and the other female. The man was dressed, the woman naked.

"Mark your own turf," Mace said. "I've staked my claim here."

"Then do something. This bitch needs a good old-fashioned tanning."

Fortunately, the man laughed, calming her fear that the

woman in question really was in trouble. There seemed to be a lot of posturing among the men. They were like dogs or wolves trying to figure out who was alpha. So far Mace seemed to fit that role.

Mace who was effortlessly dominating her.

The man moved on with his sub or slave scurrying after him. Releasing her breast, Mace flattened his hand against the base of her throat. "Your pulse is racing and you're sweating. Why do you think that is?"

"The way he was treating her . . . I have a video that shows—"

"A video you watch a lot?"

Despite the hand still on her throat, she nodded. "It, ah, always turns me on."

"Because you wish it was you?"

"No." She tried again. "Only if I trusted the man."

"Sometimes trust is ill-advised. And sometimes the error is discovered too late."

Confused, she tried to read his expression, but he didn't give her time. Grabbing her arms, he pulled her over to the X. She knew its function and had imagined herself fastened to it. The moment he kicked her legs apart, her sex creamed. Behind him were a number of lounge chairs with men heading toward them. Some were alone, others were accompanied by nude and restrained women, all on hands and knees.

It was happening! Her longtime fantasy come to life. The only difference was, Mace and not she would dictate everything that happened.

Kneeling, Mace placed something around one of her ankles. As it closed, she realized it was made of metal. Her hands fluttered, free and yet useless.

"Spread. More."

She widened her stance, then stood numb, dumb, and off balance as he secured her other ankle. When he straightened and stepped aside, she found herself looking out at a sea of faces.

Unable to determine how many people were watching her, she caressed her throat where Mace's hand had been a short while ago. Those who knew Mace had drawn their own conclusions, thus the air of anticipation.

"Think that's what she wants?" someone asked.

"Who cares. Make her whimper."

"What about it, Mace? This consensual or forced?"

Her arms were heavy, too leaden for anything except letting them dangle at her sides. She concentrated on keeping her balance.

"Depends on how she responds," Mace said.

Deciding he wasn't talking to her, she stopped trying to make sense of what he was saying. How strange it was not to care that she was naked and center stage. Granted, there were other nude women in the room, but they didn't matter. Only what lay ahead for her did.

20

Mace reentered her field of vision, filled her world if she was being honest. He positioned himself to her side, then grasped her hair as he'd done other times. When he pulled her head back, she reached out thinking to anchor herself on him.

"Don't touch me," he warned. "You haven't earned the right."

Any other time she'd call him out on that. However, submitting to his command, she pressed her hands against her thighs. They remained there even as his free hand went to her pussy. Pushing the crotch rope aside, he touched her lightly, perhaps lovingly.

Shocked by the possibility, however remote, that he loved her, she held her breath while he invaded her. His finger remained in her channel, moving about, speaking of right and command. Triggering primitive responses.

"She's wet," he announced.

"Just wet?" someone asked.

"Hell no," Mace replied. "The proverbial flood."

"From a half-assed hand fuck job?"

"Come clean, Mace, what you been doing to prime her pump?"

"You know the answer to that as well as I do." Mace remained at her side, his forefinger joining the middle and pushing her inner tissues aside. Tearing into her mind. "Draw your own conclusion."

"That's a no-brainer. She's a rope slut."

"In part," Mace said. "Truth is, just about everything I've tried on her turns this one on."

Something about Mace's tone brought her mind back to life. He was speaking as if she were an object, not a human being, certainly not someone he cared about. What a fool she'd been to think—

"Hands over your head."

She'd done as he'd commanded before the words fully registered. She even extended her hands toward the upper ends of the X, only then comprehending that Mace's fingers were no longer inside her. The rope back against her crotch tightened.

Tears sprang to her eyes, compelling her to focus on blinking weakness out of existence while he released her hair and secured her wrists as he'd done her ankles. Something soft had been fitted to the insides of the cuffs.

"That looks damn fine," a man who'd spoken earlier said. "There's something about fresh meat that makes all our effort worthwhile."

Exhausted, she looked down at herself. Although her breasts prevented her from seeing the crotch rope, that part of her body sent clear messages. Having her arms and legs restrained fed her libido, but a lingering sensation where Mace's fingers had been reached every part of her. Her body hadn't belonged to her since Mace touched her for the first time tonight, maybe even before. No denying it, he knew her better than she did herself.

Pressing his body against hers, he took hold of her chin. "It's just going to be you and me, Cheyenne. But mostly it'll be you looking inside your body and soul, going places you've never been, learning new things about yourself. I'm going to cause you a kind of pain I believe you're hungry for. You have your safe word, which I don't believe you'll feel compelled to say. You remember it, don't you?"

"Rio."

"Yes, Rio." His tone softened. "I'll be mixing in pleasure. What we need to determine is the right balance. I'll do the work, you the experiencing."

You promise?

"You won't be able to articulate where you are in terms of that experience, and that gives me the burden of reading you. Do you trust me to be able to do that?"

"I, ah, want to."

"Yes, you do." Releasing her chin, he stroked it. "And I want to earn your trust. Never doubt that."

Tears again dimmed her vision. Even when he turned his attention to untying the rope that had all but become part of her, she replayed what he'd said. His goal was to earn her trust.

Why?

As he pulled the rope from between her legs, drawing out the sensation and making her long to close her sex around it, she again tried to look down at herself. With the cotton strands no longer pressing against her clit and labial lips, she felt exposed. Everything she'd experienced and was about to came from him, this man who'd taken her freedom.

This stranger.

"I don't have a preference when it comes to floggers." He seemed to be speaking to their audience. "Each woman I've worked with has been different. It takes them a while to lock into themselves. I'm starting with deerskin because I've heard it described as feeling alive."

"You ever try it on yourself, Mace? Maybe you got some dike to tee off on you."

Whatever Mace's reaction to the comments, she couldn't tell, or rather the truth was watching him walk over to the table and pick up one of the floggers was all she could concentrate on. The dark handle fit his hand, and the slender strands looked soft. She'd watched enough sex tapes to believe she knew how a flogger responded in the hands of a pro, but only once had touched one. Furtively caressing a flogger in a sex toy shop was hardly the same as the real thing.

"It's you and me again, Cheyenne," Mace whispered. "The others don't matter. You can focus, can't you?"

Not trusting her voice, she nodded. If she cried out, would he gag her again? But maybe he got off on hearing her scream.

Scream? Please, not that.

Positioning himself in front of her, he rolled his wrist so the strands moved in a series of circles. Nothing touched her, yet she sensed her future in the way air moved against her side. Sweat bloomed in her armpits, and a wave of liquid heat dampened her inner thighs.

Closer and closer the flogger came, the air now pushing against her. She couldn't say what suddenly compelled her to stare at her master.

Master. Owner of her body. Giver of pain and pleasure.

"Starting easy," he muttered, reinforcing that what was about to happen was between the two of them. Something flicked her hip bone, the touch so light it barely registered. "Giving you a base of sensation." Another touch, this one less imagination and more reality had her tightening her belly.

He repeatedly *struck* her belly, each so-called blow easy. Calling it painful didn't occur to her. Yet the potential was there. Maybe a half-dozen times he stroked the same place. Then he pulled his arm farther back, and she readied herself.

"Ah," she whimpered as a stinging sensation settled over her thigh. Again and again, the deerskin strands landed on one thigh and then the other. Despite the rhythm, she couldn't fall into it.

The flogger danced from the joint between hip and thigh to the top of her knees, never twice in the same place. Each strike seemed stronger, but maybe that was because her skin was becoming more sensitive. She wanted these moments to end, needed it to be over so her nerves could recover. But if she begged Mace to stop, would he listen? Maybe only using her safe word would work, and she wasn't there.

Needed to prove herself.

Her thighs burned, her muscles kept contracting. Her breathing rasped, and her temples throbbed.

Slap, slap, slap.

"Stimulation," he said. "There's a fine line between experiencing not enough and too much. You're on the edge."

Needing to connect with something other than her body, she went looking for him. How had he moved to her side without her knowing? His *assault* on the thigh closest to him continued. Sighing with each breath, she struggled to concentrate on her other thigh, to find sanity in what wasn't being attacked, but the pace was picking up, sting upon sting upon sting, now moving around toward her ass cheek. Mewling, she tried to turn away.

"Not going to happen." Grabbing a nipple, he hauled her back into place. "No getting away from this. You're climbing a mountain, one we both need."

He'd released her nipple, yet the tugging sensation slipped along her rib cage to touch her other breast. Amazed, she looked down. Both nipples stood out. Aroused!

He was directly behind her now, expertly guiding the flogger around the X so the tips reached her buttocks. How ignorant she'd been to think the wood would protect her. There was nothing gentle about the strikes now, no more of the earlier sweet buzzing. Yet was this pain?

"Hmm, hmm."

"Overwhelming, right?" He struck the back of her right thigh and then the left. "Feel like you're flying and drowning at the same time?"

"Yes, oh, yes. Can't . . . can't."

"Doesn't matter." Snap, snap. "Because you're going to."

Rio! God damn it, Rio!

Men were speaking, their words tumbling over each other, someone laughing. A woman cried out. Another sighed. Somewhere a man grunted repeatedly.

One moment she felt boneless; the next every muscle locked. Her head fell back, only to sag to one side and then the other. The flogger came at her everywhere, kissing her mons, the back of her shoulders, calves. Jerking this way and that, she let sounds flow. They made no sense, had no beginning or end. Her pussy was on fire, threatening to explode. And her knotted nipples ached.

Then, with no warning, everything stopped. The fire in her pussy continued to blaze, and if anyone touched her breasts, she'd scream. Fragmented memories of what she'd just lived through rolled over her. Not trying to fight the waves, she blinked the world back into focus. Mace stood to her right, the flogger dangling from his fingers, his stare stripping her down to her core.

"Starting to get the idea?" he asked.

Even though she wasn't sure what he was referring to, she nodded. Behind him, a man laughed.

"Changing tactics a bit," Mace informed her as he dropped the deerskin flogger. "Introducing you to other sensations."

"What kind—"

"No! No speaking."

"But I need to understand," she insisted. "There's so much . . . so many sensations . . ."

"I know." Closing in on her, he reached between her legs and glided his finger over her clit.

"Oh, God, oh, God!"

"Sensitive?"

The second time he touched her, she struggled to wrench loose. Not granting her relief, he moved his finger back and forth. Had she ever been so sensitive? Incapable of differentiating between pleasure and pain?

"Don't! Oh, please, don't."

Chuckling, he kept after her, brought her onto her toes and trying to lean away. Overwrought, she settled herself around the experience.

"I can't—God damn, I can't . . ."

"You don't want to climax?"

"I do. But not like this." *Because if I let go now, I'll fall apart.*

"That isn't your call, Cheyenne."

His tone had gentled. She was still trying to absorb the change when he patted her cheek with a hand coated in her juices. As she leaned into the caress, he ran his fingers over her lips. Opening her mouth, she tasted herself.

"Starting to get it, aren't you?" he said so softly that maybe no one else heard. "A few moments ago your body was trying to tell your mind that it was being hurt. But another part of you, something primitive and primal, recorded those sensations as sexual stimulation."

"I don't understand."

"Not surprising. My observation is that the human system isn't designed to comprehend the conduit between pleasure and pain. However"—he pushed his fingers between her teeth—"trying can be endlessly fascinating. Let's see if that's true for you."

Licking his fingers, she pushed his comment aside. Too soon he drew free and walked over to the flogger-covered table. Her body softened and became so loose she wondered if she might melt.

"Suede this time," he announced. "Ridiculously expensive, but then most everything associated with the sex industry is." His expression neutral, he again stood before her and studied her.

"What?" she finally blurted. Her arms ached, and the strain caused by her widely spread legs was getting to her. "You want me to say or do something?"

Instead of reminding her that she had no right speaking, he shook his head. She couldn't comprehend his expression.

"Get on with it, Mace. Finish the demo."

"Give her some welts to remember you by."

Welts? Shouldn't she be cut and bleeding? Instead, her flesh felt intact, alive, ready. If she ever had the chance, she'd praise his skill with an instrument of torture that wasn't in his hands.

"You might not be aware of it," he told her, "but your skin has been, shall we call it, scraped. It's sensitive everywhere. I deliberately didn't touch you in certain places. Do you know what they are?"

Answers, he wanted answers from her. "My, ah, my face."

"Yes." He reached out as if to touch her cheek only to drop his arm. "Only a sadist would do that. Think, if you're able."

She took inventory of her body, naming off the untouched parts as she did. Not a single strand had reached her neck, forearms, or hands. Her ass felt as if she'd been spanked, yet her spine was untouched, as were her feet and ankles, knees.

"Do you know why?" he asked when she ran down.

Aware of little except his breath on the top of her head, she shook it.

"Because most of the places you mentioned have no padding between skin and bones. The veins are close to the surface."

He had her so off balance she didn't risk responding. She needed to believe she was more than yet another sub to him, that her safety meant a great deal to him, that paramount to him was giving her an unforgettable experience.

But Mace had been a dom long before she'd met him. And probably would be long after . . .

"I'm shaking," she admitted. "I don't know if I want you to continue."

21

A cool smile lifted the corners of Mace's mouth. "Oh, I'll continue all right. The only thing you have to concern yourself with is when it'll begin. Wait, there's something else. You don't know if this session will feel the same as before or be different."

The first time she'd gotten behind the wheel of a car, her hands had been so slick from nervousness she could hardly hold on. Fear of how her judgmental *parents* would react if she made a mistake had turned those early lessons into disasters. In frustration, they'd hired a professional driving instructor to take over the, to them, distasteful chore. Out from under their criticism, she'd quickly caught on and enjoyed driving.

Because of a pro like Mace.

By the time she'd pulled herself out of the past, he was behind her. Anticipating the first blow, she tightened her buttocks.

"Relax." Something brushed her ass cheek. "It'll hurt if you don't."

If he thought her capable of relaxing, he didn't know her. But he did in ways she'd never thought a man could.

Willing her muscles to let go, she focused on the audience. The easy chairs around where she'd been placed were full. Only men sat. The women knelt before their masters; some between the men's legs, others with their heads touching the floor. She'd seen some of this behavior the first time she'd come to Indulgences. But in the back room, instead of the earlier playfulness, fear and despair had a smell and weight of its own.

Was that what she'll write about?

"Give it to her! Show her who owns her."

"Yeah, enough with the playing around."

Other commands echoed around her, not that she cared from the moment Mace started flogging her again. The blows began stronger, came faster. She found herself in a place defined by sensation, felt as if she were being thrown about by a powerful current. However, she struck no rocks. No sharks circled her. There were massive waves, endless water, no definition between sea and sky.

And she was alone. How she'd come to be here was beyond her comprehension. As for when it might end ...

Her buttocks were on fire with flames running down the backs of her thighs. More flames licked between her legs. No matter how much she strained to close them, they remained open and vulnerable.

"Ah, ah, oh, shit, ah!"

"Sing for me. Let it all out."

Faster and faster. Not stinging, but an endless series of deep, thin caresses. Although her bonds held her nearly immobile, she pushed her buttocks back and into the flogger.

"Yes, yes!"

"Feeding off it, are you? Let's see what happens to your appetite when I do this?"

How had he gotten in front of her? The question became unimportant the instant he pushed her away so she was pressed against the X. That done, he rotated the hand holding the flogger so the strands whirled in smooth circles. Time after time the suede flicked over her breast.

"Hmm, hmm."

"Drunk on it, are you?" He punctuated his question by shifting his hold so the flogger now landed on her other breast. "Drink deep, slave."

"Hmm."

"Go deep. Keep going. Find the pain lover in you and became a slave to it."

His tone was rougher than before. Things kept changing, one area after another being subjected to his expertise. One moment, an electrical current ran over her ignited skin. The next, the current penetrated her surface to circle ever deeper. She was being scraped everywhere, shaken, dancing to the wild tune. Magical drums beat in time with her heart, and the air in her lungs was so hot it threatened to scorch them.

"Can't . . . I can't!"

"Not hearing you."

Stroke followed by stroke followed by yet another in rapid succession turned her world into a kaleidoscope of reds and black. Her head throbbed and her core pulsed.

"Too much. Oh, God, Mace, too much!"

"Call me Master."

The flogger found her thigh. "Master! Oh, shit, Master."

"That's what I want. You getting close, the crevasse just ahead. Do you see the dark hole waiting to pull you in? It wants you, already owns you."

Now her other hip was on fire. She both loved and feared the out-of-control sensation. Burgundy hues surrounded Mace.

"Help me!"

"Too late for that. The pit's just ahead, waiting for you, its victim."

"No! Don't make me—"

"The hell I won't. I live for this."

Just like that, the inner drumbeats moved from her heart to her sex as lash after lash surrounded her clit. There was nothing painful about them, nothing she wanted to escape. Then Mace, her owner and master, slapped her pussy with a cupped hand. Every inch of her body jolted.

"Oh, God! God!"

"He isn't here, slave. Just me showing you the way and getting off on doing it."

Mace was a masterful drummer and her sex his instrument. His song had only one note, the rhythm fast and strong.

Suddenly her cunt became her world. The rest of her body evaporated, died maybe. Her stretched arms and legs could have belonged to another woman for all it mattered. Mace, her dom, had led her to the edge of that bottomless cliff, and she teetered at the brink. In her mind, she held on to and fought him at the same time. She feared, not him, but her own body.

"Help me!"

"I am," he whispered against her ear. Then louder: "I'm not here to help you. Surely you know that."

"I need . . . please, Master!"

"Don't beg!" He slapped her mons repeatedly. "Listen the hell to me. I'm ordering you to hold back." The slaps intensified, became almost cruel. "Don't come. Got it, you climax and I'll hurt you."

Climax? Oh, God, yes, she was there.

"I can't stop . . . I have to—"

"The hell you do." His hand quieted and pressed against her pussy, shielding and covering it at the same time. "You do what I tell you, when I tell, got it!"

"Master, please." The eruption gathered deep inside, grew ever stronger.

He swiped a finger from the back of her pussy to the front, ending at her clit, staying there. Challenging.

"Oh, please, stop! I can't—"

"Can't what, slave?" The pressure and movement on her clit increased.

"Stop!" Even before the word was out, she knew it was too late.

She'd never climaxed like this. Always before she'd sensed its approach and relished that last heady rush, known that if she needed to, she could pull back. This time there was no warning, no pause at the end, no thought of freedom.

Her pussy spasmed, the muscle contractions so strong they frightened her. She dimly comprehended that Mace's hand rode the waves with her. No, not just rode, he kept the waves going.

"Ah! Oh, shit, ah!"

"Watch her," he said as she bucked in her bonds. "Listen to her cry."

No tears! Never that. But no control either, nothing but earthquake after earthquake assaulting her helpless body.

"Who owns you, slave?"

Although she didn't immediately answer, Mace had to give Cheyenne credit for lifting her head and meeting his gaze. Her eyes had that post-climax glazed look. Sweat made her entire body glisten.

"Say it!" he commanded, mindful of their audience. "Who owns you?"

"You, Master."

"And you'll do everything I tell you to, won't you?"

Her head bobbed, causing her ruined hair to bounce. He'd freed her as she was coming back to earth, but although others undoubtedly expected him to command her to unzip him and wrap her mouth around his hard-on, he'd simply watched, fighting his own body, as she sank to the floor. She'd lain there in the proverbial heap, lungs heaving, prompting him to fold his arms over his chest and glare down at her as if she were some deer he'd just bagged. The truth was, although he'd wanted to back when he controlled nothing, he'd never shot anything.

"We're getting out of here," he said in his stage voice. "You know where the door is, don't you?"

When she gave him a confused look, he jabbed an impatient finger. "Get going." He punctuated his command by swatting her ass. "Crawl."

More confusion clouded her eyes, but to her credit, she did as he ordered. Although tradition said he should lead the way, he followed behind, occasionally slapping her, other times nudging her ass with his shoe.

"Where you going?" someone asked. "Party's just getting started."

"Yours, not mine. I'm taking this private."

"Ah, don't. We're all more than interested in seeing what you have in mind for her. Come on, Mace, there's some new-bies in here who could learn a lot from you."

"Not tonight." He shoved Cheyenne with enough force that she fell forward. "What the hell's your problem, slave? You're going to get punished for moving so slow."

Rising off the floor, she continued crawling without looking back at him. He pondered whether she was crying, then squashed the thought; the last thing he wanted right now was for his expression to hint at compassion.

When she reached the door, she stopped and straightened, waiting as a dog would to be let out. Stepping around her, he reached for the door only to have the Handler stop him.

"That's not the way the game's played, and you know it," the beefy man said. "The *entertainment* doesn't leave until the night's over."

"She's no one's entertainment," he countered. "She's my property." He poked Cheyenne in the side. "Like I said, I'm taking this private."

The Handler made no move to get out of the way. "Management won't like it."

"Then they can take their gripe up with me later. Right now

the only thing I care about is getting her to sing some more, for me. By the time I'm done with her, she'll have forgotten she had a name. Pleasing me will be the only thing she cares about."

"Then why aren't you taking the floggers?"

They'd attracted a small crowd he had no doubt would grow if he didn't immediately get out of here. "Those belong to Indulgences. I have my own collection. Damn it, the night's young. I intend to make the most of it."

Although the Handler's nostrils flared, he backed away. "Bring her back next weekend," he ordered. "Let us see how well her education's going."

"You know me, I take pride in my work. I just hope security comes to the same conclusion."

"What are you talking about?"

Mace leaned close so he was nearly nose to nose with the Handler. "The camera that's been following us since we got here. First time I've seen one inside."

"You just haven't paid attention."

"The hell I haven't."

Shoving what he couldn't do anything about now out of his mind, he risked a glance at Cheyenne's back. He'd gotten too close to her tonight. Damn it, he'd spent years perfecting his solitary existence. No way was he going to let down his defenses now.

But she might be in danger. Him, too, but he'd never put that much stake in his own life.

22

Camera? Cheyenne couldn't make sense of the brief conversation between Mace and the man who'd initially tied her up. Neither was she ready to face the fact that she'd submissively crawled through both the back and public rooms. At least, she tried to comfort herself, he'd let her stand and walk once they reached the parking lot.

When Mace ordered her into the trunk, she gaped at him but said nothing because his glare warned her not to. Feeling less than human, she did as he ordered. The lid slammed into place, locking her in a small, silent, albeit not too uncomfortable world. Although her pussy was still hot and sensitive, she didn't touch it, because if she did, she wouldn't be able to concentrate on anything else.

Curled into a ball and trying to find something to rest her hip on, she first fought the memories and images, and then gave in. It hadn't been her in there! The competent professional she'd worked so hard to become would never let herself be restrained and flogged for the amusement of a bunch of arrogant men. Admitting she'd been naked with her legs spread and her sex on display while those men gaped at her made her moan with embarrassment.

She didn't blame Mace. He'd simply done what she'd asked him to, or rather what Robert and Atwood had talked both of them into doing. Doming her had come naturally from Mace's personality, which put the responsibility squarely on her shoulders. She'd been the one who'd—

"Enough!" She couldn't smell exhaust fumes, and although the air wasn't the freshest, she wasn't having trouble breathing. How long did Mace intend to keep her in here, and where were they going? Did he expect her to remain naked for the foreseeable future?

And what about everything she owed Mace?

Tires humming over the road quieted her thoughts. She might not want to risk touching her so-sensitive sex, but other parts of her anatomy were pleading for attention, most notably her breasts. Fortunately, or perhaps not, her hands were curled against her middle, which made lightly touching her nipples a simple matter. Had they ever been this receptive to stimulation?

Mace was such a pro. Maybe he'd been born with a sixth sense about the female anatomy and how each part of that anatomy responded to various stimulations. He should be a teacher.

What was she thinking? His brand of expertise didn't belong in a classroom.

Wrapping herself in memories of the ways he'd restrained, touched, and flogged her a little while ago, she gave up trying to make sense of her surroundings. Yes, she was still wrapped in post-climax lethargy, but she trusted him. Mace hadn't hurt her tonight. He never would.

As the car slowed, she told herself he might only be responding to the traffic, but then she heard crunching under the tires followed by the vehicle rocking to a stop. Breathing as slow as possible, she listened to his shoes on what she thought was gravel. A quiet click and the trunk swung up.

They were somewhere without streetlights or traffic, a place illuminated by stars and the nearly full moon. Mace appeared as the faintest of shadows standing above her. Studying his motionless form, she wondered if she might be falling in love with him. No, it couldn't be that! She hadn't known him long enough to grasp what there might be to love about him. Truth was, she knew nothing about his background, family, childhood, none of the things that comprised a complete human being.

Yet, something about him caressed her senses. That something went beyond sex in the forms they'd experienced.

He held out his hand. Taking it, she sat up, then stepped out of the trunk. As soon as she was on her feet, he gathered her in his arms and headed for the passenger's side. Not giving herself time to think about what she was doing, she wrapped her arms around his neck but resisted the impulse to snuggle against him.

"I don't want to run the risk of you stepping on glass," he explained. "As for putting you in the trunk, it was part of the show."

"What show? Everyone was inside."

"Were they?"

Letting go with one hand, she opened the door. He deposited her on the seat and stepped back, leaving her full of questions. Now he was back in the shadows that treated him so well, a silent and powerful force.

"I don't know if you noticed it," he went on, "but there are video cameras stationed throughout the parking lot. And inside. The ones inside are what concern me."

Bending her knees, she wrapped her arms around her legs but made no move to face ahead. "Who would be looking at them?"

"Good question. A syndicate owns and manages Indulgences. Club members like myself don't know who belongs to it."

"You make it sound like the mafia, maybe a drug cartel."

"You might not be too far off. Scoot around. We need to get going."

Earlier tonight she'd complied with his every command, but this was now, and her future and safety were back in her hands. Her emotions where he was concerned might be complicated, but her *parents* hadn't raised a fool.

"Where are we going? You owe me at least that much."

"My place."

"What about mine?" Was he taking note of her breasts flattened against her knees or what he could see of her crotch? Like it mattered.

"Not yet. We need to talk."

"Why can't we do that at my house? That's where my clothes are, where I feel safe."

"Are you? Look, we can do this easy or hard. Either way, we're going to wind up where I say."

"What's this? You aren't done playing the role you assumed at Indulgences, at least I guess it was a role."

He leaned closer. "Are you sure it's a role?"

Unnerved, she faced front. She started a little when he closed the door, then hugged the passenger's door as he slid behind the wheel.

"Seat belt," he said.

Her hands shook, so he wound up reaching over and snapping the belt into place. Thinking he might demand to know what was on her mind tied her stomach in knots, but when he turned the radio to an easy-listening station, she relaxed a little. If only she knew where Mace's dominating side ended and the compassionate pit bull owner began.

Mace hadn't said anything the whole time they were heading

for his place. The car doors automatically unlocked when he turned off the engine. After a moment, she reached for the handle because she had no choice. Noting her bare arm reminded her anew of her nudity.

Much as she wanted to cover what she could, she refused to let Mace know what she was thinking, so she let her arms hang at her sides as they went inside. Rio was waiting for them, his tail slapping the wall. Seeing him, her heart softened.

Dropping to his knees, Mace embraced the solidly built dog.

Watching them, she was reminded of the weekend she'd spent with a friend when she was in the fifth or sixth grade. Her friend lived on a sheep ranch, and she'd fallen absolutely and completely in love with the family's two trained sheep dogs. When not on duty, they were gentle, loving couch potatoes, but at a command, they changed.

At first she'd been intimidated by their single-minded energy and determination. Then the smaller female had crawled onto her bed and she'd held on to it all night. When she went home, she'd begged her *parents* to let her have a dog, only to force the dream to die when she saw the denial in their eyes.

Rio licked his cheek as Mace looked up at her. "We need to talk."

"What about?"

"For starters, there are some things I need to know about you."

"Me?" Even on his knees, he looked masterful. And she'd be a fool not to remember that Rio had been bred as a fighting dog. "What about you? I know nothing about you." *Except that you have more self-control than any man should have.*

After giving Rio a final hug, he stood, seeming taller than he'd been a moment ago. Her collar felt as if it had become a living thing, an extension of him placed on her for reasons she might never fully understand. "I'm going to let him out. If you want, get something from my closet."

If I want. Feeling dismissed, she studied his back as he left the room, a now calm Rio walking beside him. Although she wanted to look at his photographs for assurance that she was safe with him, she headed for his bedroom. Once there, she hurried past his bed and into a small closet. His clothes were basic, nothing trendy. They'd been hung up with little consideration for order or wrinkles. She grabbed a plain blue T-shirt because it looked as if it was the longest. Even before she pulled it over her head, Mace's scent enveloped her, and although she shouldn't, she held it to her nose. Her cunt stirred, and her throat felt flush.

"Why can't we have this conversation at my place?" she asked when he came into the living room where she was sitting in a dark brown leather chair. "If we have to have it at all, I'd prefer it happens where I feel comfortable."

He seemed to be considering her comment, but when he sat opposite her some three feet away, she knew she'd lost the argument. And that she wasn't going to get an explanation.

"Tell me about your friends," he said. "I know about the ones at work, but there have to be others."

He'd concerned himself with whom she hung out with on the job? If that was so, then he was aware that those relationships were casual and not always comfortable. He probably didn't need her to explain that as the new kid on the block, yet being handed some plum assignments, the more established journalists weren't inclined to embrace her.

"What's this about?" she asked, although she sensed this question, too, would go unanswered.

"I can investigate if necessary, but it's to your benefit if I don't have to spend valuable time doing so."

"My benefit? What do you mean?"

He'd been sitting back looking so comfortable she envied him. Now he leaned forward and his expression changed,

warned. This wasn't the same man who'd turned her body inside out a little while ago. Gone was the BDSM expert, in its
place, what?

"I debated telling you this, but I don't see any way around
it. Your house is bugged."

"Bugged?" she repeated, feeling stupid.

"There's a camera in the plant in your bedroom. My guess, it
isn't the only one."

Going from hot to cold, she struggled to keep her mouth
closed.

"Who knows how long it's been there or what they're looking for?"

"They?" She had to stop repeating him somehow.

"That's what I intend to find out."

"By . . . by asking for the names of everyone I've ever had
anything to do with?"

"I doubt if that'll be necessary. Let's start by making a list of
everyone who's been in your place and when. Better yet, tell me
about your security system, if you have one. There's a dead
bolt. What else?"

She kept her eyes open because otherwise she risked being
emotionally sucked into her home that had always felt safe but
now felt alien and dangerous. Mace had to be mistaken. No one
meant her any harm. She had no enemies—except maybe the
man she'd done a Hunted article on, but not only hadn't it come
out yet, she couldn't possibly be at the top of Carl Schulz's hate
list.

"Who installed your security system?"

"I don't have one."

Mace's expression was natural for a man whose job revolved
around keeping the people entrusted to him safe. How could
she make him understand that a lifetime of physical security
had impacted her? In fact, feeling physically safe as a child had
made up, a little, for the lack of emotional warmth.

"Just the locks then," he muttered. "At least tell me you secure your windows when you're gone."

Feeling as if she'd been found guilty of a crime, she shook her head, then hurried to explain that she loved fresh air. "The screens are fine. I've never seen any sign that—"

He stopped her with a shake of his head, the movement and dark eyes touching something in her that needed to remain quiet tonight. The man who'd taught her the meaning of submissive pleasures should have nothing to do with what was being discussed. If only denying that man's existence wasn't so hard.

"Cheyenne, anyone capable of installing a camera so the homeowner isn't aware of it can get in and out without leaving any sign."

"You saw it," she said, then regretted it because security was his job. "My bedroom. That really makes me sick. Wait a minute!"

Not sure she could handle her thoughts, she stood and walked over to the oversized window. It was dark out there, no streetlights and trees growing close, the stars and moon barely made an impact. Turning, she focused on Mace. She hadn't turned on a light when she came into the living room, thinking that was Mace's right and responsibility, but only the adjacent kitchen illuminated the room. Too damn many shadows led to her unease.

"Damn you, Mace. I thought that what happened in my bedroom was about you and me." For a moment she thought she was going to be sick. "But you were playing to the camera. Hell, for all I know, you planted it."

He didn't move, and from here she could only guess at his expression. Upset as she was, she wanted to feel her skin against his. "Is that what you believe?" he asked.

"I don't know." She pressed a hand to her throbbing forehead.

"Think about it."

She nearly snapped that that's exactly what she was doing. Instead, she wound up heeding the messages from her body. Bottom line, it trusted Mace.

Despite another voice insisting she was a fool if she let her body be in charge, she retraced her steps and sat down. She even managed to lean back and *casually* cross her legs, careful to keep his shirt tucked around her thighs. "If it's someone at work, it won't be long before everyone knows you and I were, ah, together."

"If that's the case, we'll deal with it. At least that way, we'll have our answer. Cheyenne, do you have any enemies?"

The unexpected question had her gripping the chair arms. "No, I've never done anything to—"

"What about jealousy from your coworkers?"

"I haven't taken anyone's job from them."

"Look, I understand your reluctance to entertain the possibility that another reporter could resent you enough to want to destroy you. What about someone from your past? Anyone you locked horns with?"

"Besides my parents, you mean?" she blurted.

Cocking his head to the side, Mace nodded. "You're joking, right?"

"About the possibility that they'd want to ruin my reputation, yes." She took a deep breath, then let it out. "But I didn't turn out the way they tried to mold me. I'm adopted. There was a lot of locking horns. There still is, although I keep that at a minimum by having as little as possible to do with them."

Her admission had nothing to do with a camera secretly recording her movements. She expected Mace to dismiss what now sounded like a disgruntled child. Instead, he leaned forward. "That's where the idea for the article that got you the job at *Edge* came from. You needed to try to understand their impact on the person you turned out to be."

"I'm not sure how well I succeeded. Maybe I should have seen a shrink, but I didn't."

"Did they say you didn't measure up?"

"Not in so many words." Now she was grateful for the dim lighting because hopefully he couldn't see how deep the pain ran. "But a child needs simple acceptance and love. When it isn't there, he or she knows it."

"Yeah, he does."

She wasn't the only one in pain; his tone left no doubt. She also knew he wouldn't say more than he had, and if she pushed, he'd throw up countless barriers.

"They set the bar high starting with a prestigious preschool where I was taught how to read almost while still in diapers. Being in diapers by my second birthday was seen as a sign of immaturity and defiance, so there were consequences."

"You remember that?"

"I'm not sure. Something about my early years overwhelms when I try to look back. I knew I couldn't ask them, so I turned to my aunt, my adoptive father's sister. She and her brother were estranged, but she decided I needed to know, as she put it, how they'd screwed me up."

"You aren't screwed up."

"Aren't I?" *No tears, damn it!* "I get off on being flogged."

"Submissive tendencies are natural, Cheyenne. Don't ever think there's something wrong about them."

"I want to believe you." At least she no longer felt as unsure as she had when, at four, her *mother* declared she was too old for training wheels.

"Then do. Cheyenne? Why did they name you that?"

Mace was a voice in the dark, a compelling presence, the vital link to the present. Compassion and caring when she needed that. "They didn't. I was named Udele, which means prosperous."

"The hell."

"Yes." She laughed. "The hell. When I went away to college, I legally changed my name to something that symbolized freedom to me. They were furious."

"Are they still?"

"On occasion. Chasing the almighty dollar rules them. They don't understand why I don't feel the same way. They're concerned I'll give away my inheritance. In fact, my *mother* said she was going to draw up a new will appointing their financial advisor as executor so I can't. He'll handle the distribution based on their orders."

"How do you feel about that?"

"It's their money, their only real love. They can do what they want."

Mace's silence enveloped her. Maybe it was nothing more than fallout from what she'd dumped on him, but she sensed a compassion she hadn't expected. Their relationship was complex, unlike any she'd ever experienced. And in the aftermath of the most explosive climax of her life, she'd be a fool to trust her mind.

"What are you thinking?" she asked when the silence became too much.

"About something I heard about tigers eating their young. Too bad it doesn't work the other way around."

"What? That's horrible."

"Maybe. Maybe not. Ready to change topics?" he asked.

"Yes, I never thought I'd . . . obviously my parents haven't bugged my place, so why were we talking about them?"

He could have pointed out that she'd been responsible for that. Instead, he asked if she was warm enough.

"Yes."

"Let me know if that changes. Now, back to who's been in your place."

Answering didn't take long. A self-diagnosed hermit when

not on the job, she loved owning her own place. That probably had its roots in her childhood when her every move and activity had been scrutinized. Before Mace could ask, she admitted that since buying the condo, she hadn't brought a date home. In fact, she hadn't dated any man more than three times in years.

As for women friends, there were two from where she'd worked before and several college friendships that had endured. Her closest friend was her roommate from her last two years of college.

"Does she know about your interest in BDSM?" Mace asked.

"She's the only one who does. I sometimes accuse her of corrupting me because she supported herself as an exotic dancer all through school."

"What about you? Dancing makes good money."

"I'm not that kind of an exhibitionist."

"I know what kind you are."

Mace's comment stung. Earlier tonight she'd been too involved in what she was experiencing to think about her audience. Not trusting what might come out of her mouth, she studied her legs. Mace's shirt covered about half of her thighs, much more than she'd worn at Indulgences, but she still felt exposed.

"What is it?" he asked. "I said the wrong thing."

"Yes."

"Look, I'm sorry."

"That's all right. After all those years of not measuring up, I have a thick skin."

The last thing she expected was for him to stand and walk over to her. Then he knelt and placed his hands on her knees, and her heart slammed against her chest.

"You were an innocent child. It took a long time for you to realize that the way you were being raised was wrong, and even once you did, there wasn't anything you could do about it."

They'd started this conversation trying to determine who had invaded her privacy, but she'd allowed it to go in another direction. As a result, he was now in her personal space, both physically and emotionally. This felt different from when her body had been under his control.

"Are you speaking from experience?" she asked.

His fingers clenched, pressing on her knees.

She shook her head. "You aren't going to answer, are you?"

23

No, Mace acknowledged, he wasn't. Cheyenne might be willing to hold her past up to the light, but he'd be damned if he'd open himself up that way. She was a subject, a duty.

Then why the hell had he brought her back to his place, and why was Rio dozing near her chair?

"I'm sorry," she went on. "I had no right." She ran her fingertips over his knuckles, started to withdraw, then squeezed his hand. "Can you do anything with the information I gave you? I don't see how it can be useful."

"I have my own suspicions. I just wanted to eliminate—"

"What suspicions?"

Noting the alarm in her voice, he tried to come up with a way to tell her she wasn't in danger, but they both knew better than that.

"I prefer not to say until I've done my investigation. In the meantime, I want to go through your house and remove every camera. Once I have, I'll try to determine where they came from."

"You'd do that?"

Her hands still gripped him, and he felt the pressure and warmth throughout him. "Of course."

"Because it's your job?"

Tell her yes. Don't get any closer than you are. "Because what's happening pisses me off. You're entitled to privacy, everyone is."

"I keep trying to come up with a reason. Blackmail maybe. God, the idea of revealing pictures of me all over the Internet makes me sick. Mace, what if the room was dark? Could the camera still pick up something?"

"Like what?"

"Me masturbating. When I did, I wasn't always under the covers." Her nails dug into his knuckles, compelling him to release her knees and close his fingers around hers.

"What are you thinking?" he demanded.

"Did you—"

"No."

"No what?"

"I had nothing to do with it. That's what you were going to ask, isn't it?"

Nodding, she straightened, still not trying to get free. "I had to," she whispered. "The things we did, or rather what you did to me in my bedroom . . . if that was made public, it would ruin my career."

"Yours wouldn't be the only face out there."

Her sigh coming from deep inside, she collapsed against the back of the chair. He reluctantly let go of her, but instead of returning to his chair, he stood and looked down at her. Hopefully the dim lighting prevented her from noting his growing erection.

"It's been a hell of a night," she said.

"For both of us."

The ensuing silence gave him too much time to ask why the hell he'd admitted what he had. Hadn't rule number one always been to keep his emotions locked away?

Tell that to his cock.

"Yes," she whispered. "It has been." Dropping her gaze, she spread her legs and rested a hand on her mons. "What's that saying, something about being rode hard and put away wet. That's me."

Chuckling came easily. "Not interested in a repeat performance?"

"I don't know," she muttered. "Sex right now would be interesting to say the least. I'm not sure how I'd respond."

"Because I flogged you?"

"That felt fantastic, sort of as if I've been out in the sun, all warm and excited, content. Alive. Does that make any sense?"

They'd have to get back to the issue of security and safety, but not now. "It's the reaction I hoped you'd have."

"You've perfected your technique. I feel as if I should send you flowers."

Roses. I love the smell. "Not necessary. It's part of the job description."

"Is it, Mace? That's how you see it?"

For someone who'd spent years distancing himself from other people's emotions, he had no trouble reading hers. She didn't buy what he'd just said. "It makes doming easier if I concentrate on the sub's physical cues. My primary responsibility is ensuring she has a safe and satisfying experience."

"So you get nothing out of playing the dom?"

"That isn't what BDSM is about."

"Then what—never mind. I'll write my article later." She glanced at his crotch. "So where do we go from here?"

Horizontal. "Not home for you tonight," he said. "I need to check it out first."

"I'd feel better if you did. Mace, I hope you'll give me an honest answer about something."

Honesty might backfire on him, but the way he felt right now, he couldn't deny her anything.

"Studying me tonight, touching me, helping me climax, did that reach you sexually?"

"Here's the answer to that." He cupped his cock, then released it before the hair trigger went off.

"Occupational hazard?"

Grateful for the lighthearted turn in the conversation, he looked behind him to measure the distance between her and his chair. Too damn far, more than he wanted to endure despite the danger. "Maybe I can get workmen's comp."

"Too much paperwork. I have a suggestion."

Was she still joking? Not if her body language was any indication.

"Mace, please." She rubbed the chair arms. "Don't make me do all the talking. I'm offering, hell, I'm offering my pussy to your cock. That obvious enough for you?"

He didn't want crude from her. The thing was, he couldn't say what he needed to hear, if anything. Animals had it easier. If the female was in heat or the male in rut, they got it on. Otherwise, life revolved around filling their bellies.

"I'm sorry," she whispered, still rubbing. "My folks would have sewn my mouth shut if they'd heard me say that. Do ... you have a spare room? I could sleep on the couch."

"No, you can't." Just like that, he'd stepped over a line. It would be easier if it been a wall or he didn't want her so damn much. Not long ago, she'd been just another *Edge* employee, more physically appealing than the majority, but not someone he'd ever thought would hurtle his barriers.

Right now those barriers lay in splinters around him, and he didn't know how it had happened.

She stood up, forcing him to step back to accommodate her. His shirt had never looked so good, flowing over her curves and hanging up a little on her breasts. Her nipples spoke volumes about arousal and sent messages to the part of his anatomy that didn't need any more stimulation.

Then she wrapped her arms around his neck, and his arms circled her waist. She was naked under the soft cotton, much of it flogger-abraded, his doing. More to the point, although her *parents* had done everything within their power to screw her up, she'd survived.

He wasn't going to kiss her, no way did he want that kind of intimacy, and yet he inclined his head as she lifted hers.

They came together gentle, the lightest of touches that kept going, growing deeper by the half moment. Sexual need at its most primitive rolled through him, yet he resisted thrusting his pelvis at her. He wanted something different, not the same old, same old that had always ended with his cock in one of three places.

Maybe for the first time in his life he needed more from a woman than a vehicle for getting off.

Her waist was slimmer than he recalled, her hips smoothly rounded, her body bearing the marks they'd collaborated on.

When he opened his mouth the slightest bit she did the same. Just like that, his mind floated. He was at peace with this woman in his arms and, despite his engorged cock, in no hurry to go beyond the holding on. Her arms around his neck didn't restrain him; rather, he felt her flowing into him and him ceasing to be something separate. Maybe the same was happening to her, a possibility he'd consider another time.

Mindful of what he'd put her through tonight, he leaned over a little so she didn't have to stand on her toes. Rio yawned, making him glad someone was taking this moment lightly. That's what he should do—take Cheyenne's rather crude offering of her pussy followed by rolling over to his side of the bed and falling asleep.

Only no woman had ever spent the night in his bed with him. Knowing that was about to change made it impossible for him to join Rio in yawning.

Determined to stay in the moment, he opened his mouth a

little more. Much as he wanted to bring his tongue into play, simply kissing was safer, tamer. Then his lips started to go numb. Not sure how long they'd been engaged in lip-lock, he broke the connection. Even with his arms around her waist and her breasts brushing him, he felt lonely.

"What?" she whispered. "Maybe you didn't want—"

"The kiss. I started it, I think."

"Thank you."

"For what?"

"I'm not sure," she muttered, resting her head on his chest. "Maybe for putting up with my crazy mind tonight."

He knew how she felt, not that he'd tell her. What was harder to keep under wraps was his need to feel her hair on his chest.

"Where do we go from here, Mace? You don't want me in a spare room or on the couch, and I can't go home unless you drive me."

Reluctantly pushing her back, he waited until she looked up at him, her hands light on his chest. "I don't dance around things," he told her. "Don't know how."

She took a deep, breasts-lifting breath. "Then be direct."

Easier said than done. "I want to have sex with you, but not if you're not up to it."

"Not up to it? You can't be serious."

"But you were rode hard and put away wet."

"I was, and it was fantastic. I'm not made of glass."

"Aren't you?" For reasons he didn't want to examine, he needed her to beg off. He'd have to jerk off to get through the night, but that was nothing compared to the danger of burying his body in hers.

"Try me. You aren't the only one who wants sex." She sighed. "Equal sex, none of that kink stuff this time."

Just like that they'd taken their relationship in a new direction. One that scared the hell out of him.

*　*　*

Watching Mace pull off his pants, it had occurred to Cheyenne that she was going to see him naked for the first time. Instead of waiting for him to handle the task, she'd pulled his shirt over her head and dropped it on the chair in his bedroom. Truth was, she'd been too nervous to simply stand there. Now she sat on the side of the bed swinging her feet and running her hands over the high thread count bottom sheet, wishing she didn't feel so nervous.

"Have you ever worn your hair long?" he asked.

He stood no more than three feet away with his arms at his sides, his breath slow and regular, and his cock reaching for her. Where she had to keep moving because otherwise she'd explode, he seemed to have dismissed his body. Clothed or naked made no difference to him. An erection? No big deal.

Except that in a few minutes that erection would be inside her, filling and maybe completing her.

"Long hair," she belatedly responded. "During my college rebellion stage, but I hate trying to keep it out of my eyes and mouth."

"Point taken. Light on or off?"

"Off." Much more of this clinical approach on his part and she'd slug him.

Watching him reach for the bedside lamp, she changed her mind. He was so damned graceful, no woman could resist, and what did what he said matter? His hips were made for stroking, his buttocks perfect for cupping her hands over, and the hollow place where too many men announced their love affair with food and drink made her mouth water.

The image of trying to suck that taut skin into her mouth loosened something inside, and she went from nervous energy to hunger. She'd checked her body in the bathroom mirror a few minutes ago, surprised and relieved to see that except for a barely detectable flush, her flesh looked untouched. Looking at her, no one would suspect what she'd been through. Her nerves felt alive, blasted out of hibernation alive!

And ready for tonight's next chapter. With Mace.

"This is exciting," she told him. "Granted a little unnerving."

"What are you talking about?"

Wondering why he was keeping those three feet between them, she folded her arms under her breasts, lifting them as she did.

"I had a professor once, a brilliant man who published books on social history and had an office full of diplomas and awards. He intimidated the hell out of me until the day I went in to talk to him about something." She waved her arm, then cupped her breasts to still them. "He was trying to stack playing cards. I tried to pretend I didn't see what he was doing, but he laughed this rich, hearty laugh and said he sucked at it so why did he keep making a fool of himself. From then on we were friends."

"You want us to be friends?"

In some respects, Mace reminded him of the sheep dogs her friend had owned. Like them, he was capable of remaining motionless indefinitely.

"Not friends. We aren't at that point. I don't know if we'll ever be."

When he didn't reply, disappointment knifed through her, but what the hell did she expect, for them to start dressing alike?

"Close relationships take time," she went on, blithering really. "And they're rare. At least that's been true for me. It's a combination of many things, maybe trust most of all."

"I wouldn't know."

24

Because Mace wasn't and never had been close with someone, Cheyenne wondered. Much as she wanted to insist that wasn't true, she knew better. Mace was a lone wolf—and she needed to know why. But not tonight.

Sliding off the bed, she touched her mouth to the base of his throat. Her hands went to his sides. Kissing him repeatedly, she worked her hands down to his hips. When he gripped her buttocks, she debated telling him not to because she wanted to focus on him, but the contact felt too good.

Moistening her lips, she coated his Adam's apple, then moved on to his collarbone. As she did, she caressed his flanks, sometimes getting everything to work together, other times letting her heated cunt distract her. As she threw herself into the action, it dawned on her that he was just standing there, gripping her ass.

What was going on inside his mind? Possibly he wasn't thinking, but she didn't believe that, not if the cadence of his breathing was any indication. She slid her teeth over his collarbone; he arched away a little, then leaned into her, sucking in air as he did. His tremor compelled her to press her breasts against him. He shuddered.

Gathering her thoughts, she struggled to recall what she knew about him. It was so little, nothing about his childhood, not a single word about his education or how and why he'd become a dom. What he wanted from life.

Bending her knees, she glided her tongue down the middle of his breastbone, tasting as she did. His hands moved from her buttocks to her waist, helping her bend. Still, prompted by the strain in her calves, she straightened and wrapped her arms around his neck. Skin touched skin, her breasts flat and full and hard against his ribs. One of his arms remained around her waist. The other went to her back. Gentle, magical fingers stroked her spine.

Sighing, she looked up at him. After a moment he inclined his head, and she covered his mouth with hers. Despite the throbbing in her breasts and sex, she was content.

They weren't animals in heat. There was time for wordless communication and compassion in a touch. His body made hers feel as if it could fly, yet they were floating together, drifting in sensation.

This man was far different from the one who'd restrained and whipped her, not just another side to the same human, but separate.

The press of tears added to her mood. Maybe their staid kiss earlier had brought out the other Mace, the man who understood that sometimes a woman simply needed to be held.

She could do that to him, for him. Kiss his eyelids and forehead, the base of his spine and back of his legs, lightly touching her lips to those places to let him know how precious each one was.

Could she do that tonight? Was there enough patience in her?

The questions went unanswered as he lifted her back onto the bed. Spreading her legs, she took hold of his arms and drew him in. That done, she cupped her hands around his cock, sheltering it as if it was precious.

"I love cock," she admitted. "It intimidates me a bit. Just thinking about one stretching me, skewering me really, gets to me."

"There's nothing mysterious about them."

He started massaging her thighs, making it nearly impossible for her to concentrate on keeping the conversation going. "You've looking at things from a male perspective. Try it from my side."

"No, thanks. I like being a man."

Laughing, she ran a thumb over the top of his cock. "And I like you just the way you are."

Despite the gentle way he ran his fingertips over her thighs, she sensed tension in him. She'd feel the same way if he had both hands on her sex, or would she? Maybe not because she knew what he was capable of, his self-restraint and consideration for her limits. She wanted to demonstrate the same consideration, but until she knew him better ...

"Is the mystery surrounding you deliberate?" she asked. Letting go with one hand, she cradled his weight in her palm. "This isn't part of a scene, is it? I'm seeing the real you?"

"I don't know."

"What do you mean?" So much for floating. Now she was awake, aware, maybe alarmed.

"I don't know what you're seeing, so I can't answer."

She relaxed a little and might have accomplished more if his hands had stilled. Instead, he was creating sweet friction on her thighs.

"That's just it. I don't know what I'm seeing either," she admitted.

"You aren't making sense."

"Who are you? Where did you come from, how did you get here, and what do you want your future to be like?"

"You want to know all that now?"

He was right. Shouldn't she be focusing on getting to the point of intercourse?

Intercourse. Not simply fucking.

"Not now," she conceded. "But later, hopefully." With that, she licked the top of his cock. Her lips went numb, then hummed. "You taste so good."

His only response was a long, low sigh that brought her head up and had her straining to see into the dark.

"I'm serious." She made her point by drawing his tip into her mouth and closing her lips around satin flesh. The floating sensation returned. Holding him, she thought of little. In her mind, they lay side by side on summer-heated sand while gentle waves rocked their united bodies. After awhile the scene changed. Now they stood on a hilltop, arm in arm and naked, looking down at the rest of the world.

"Cheyenne?"

Responding to the tug on her hair as much as her name, she let him go, leaving her saliva on him. "What?"

"I'm not used to this."

"To what?"

"Just being held. Before we go any further, I have to put on protection."

Alone while he dug into his pants' pocket, she pondered what he'd said and why the rubber was in his clothes instead of his nightstand. The possibilities added yet more layers to this secretive man. But as much as she craved answers, she wouldn't push.

"Wait," she said as he tore the wrapper. "I want to . . . you know."

Sliding off the bed for the second time since coming in here, she held out her hand. After too long, he placed the rubber in her palm. She could have accomplished the task standing, but not sure her legs would hold out, she knelt. The urge to house him in her mouth again nearly overwhelmed her.

Wondering at this side to a man accustomed to controlling women, she unrolled the condom over his cock. That done, she stood, not touching him as she did. Not knowing what to do next, she folded her hands together. "Ah, do you have a favorite position?"

Sighing another of those fascinating sighs of his, he ran his hands down her arms. Shivering, she rocked toward him.

"I do," he said. "At least I did before tonight."

"What makes this different?"

"You."

If a single word had ever carried more emotion, she couldn't remember. The scant space between their bodies filled with their shared essence, warm and waiting.

"I love hearing that," she admitted.

Running his hands down her forearms to her wrists, Mace drew her arms behind her. Emotion left over from their bondage session weakened her, and when he walked her backward to the bed, she scooted onto it. Still holding on to her hands, he leaned over her, his chest pushing her off balance.

"I should have left the lights on," he said. "There's not much coming from the bathroom."

"I don't care."

His breath heated her face. She loved having him as her blanket, loved that she trusted him. Although her cunt was alive with need, she willed it to be patient.

One moment her arms were behind her, the next, he pulled them out to the sides and pushed her back. Her head hit the mattress. Gripping her waist, he hauled her further onto the bed until her knees were against the mattress.

Reaching up, she grabbed his shoulders and pulled. If he'd wanted, he could have easily resisted. Instead, he came down on top of her with his upper body braced on his elbows. His cock pressed against her belly, weight and heat seeming to penetrate her.

"Not like this. Mace, please, I need you inside me."

"Already?"

Yes! she wanted to shout. *Touch my sex. You'll have your answer.*

Leaving the admission to rattle around in her, she wrapped her legs around his buttocks.

"You're getting ahead of me." He sounded out of breath. "Unless your belly's going to do the fucking."

"Then do what needs doing."

She'd begun to relax her hold on him when he forced the issue by turning her in a quarter circle so her entire body fit on the bed. Content with the missionary position, she opened herself up to him, knees splayed and hips lifted.

He moved into her, slow and smooth, strong and ready. Inch by inch her pussy filled. When he was there, deep and strong, she again wrapped her legs around him and pressed her heels into his buttocks. Her hands found his shoulders and arms, caressed.

Body straining, he drew back only to come at her once more, withdrew, probed. Her nails dug at him. The pace of his thrusts quickened, rocking her, taking her. Mouth open and head to the side, she tightened her inner muscles around him and fought to match him strength for strength.

"You're making . . . this hard."

"I'm sorry." She tried to relax, but her body had a mind of its own and needs that would be fulfilled.

"Just let me—"

"Do it, damn it!" She scratched his shoulders. "Oh, shit, do it!"

Growling, he drove into her. She was so wet. He slid freely in her, his cock gloriously stroking the weeping tissues. Her belly clenched. When it began relaxing, she tightened it, crying out at the sensation. Her pussy quieted, waited.

Mace pounded at her, his breathing harsh and painful sounding. Listening to him, she envied his lack of restraint. Then, without warning, she was doing the same, sobbing and gasping while raking his shoulders. Her pussy closed down on him, let up, held on. Sweat drenched them. His arms trembled; strain roped his body.

"Yes!" she encouraged, digging her heels into his buttocks. "Yes! Ride me."

If he heard, he let the stupid comment pass. No wonder. Pounding her took his full concentration and all his energy. Her explosion was there, running just under the surface. Somehow she locked on to what he must be experiencing, his release only a breath or thrust away.

"Yes, yes, yes," she chanted.

He responded with a series of harsh grunts. Surely Rio heard.

"It's all right, all right," she said, concerned Mace might injure his throat. The grunts continued; his taut body seemed on the brink of shattering. Wanting to share in his climax, she arched off the mattress and flattened her breasts against his chest, clutching his shoulders as she did.

He strained to bear both their weights, then collapsed, trapping her under him. As the air left her lungs, he rolled over, taking her with him. Now his back was against the sheet, their bodies still together. Resting on top of him, she nibbled his collarbone.

"Shit, woman, shit."

She responded by licking where she'd nibbled, chuckling low when he shuddered. He shuddered again, a shiver really that said he couldn't take much more. Planting her hands first against the bed and then his chest, she carefully sat up. She was in control, on top, his cock trapped inside her. Mindful that she could injure him, she kept her body still while contracting and relaxing her vaginal muscles. Head off the bed, he splayed his hands over her thighs. Reaching behind her with one hand, she stroked his inner thigh.

"Shit," he muttered. "Shit."

Heat ran between her breasts. For the first time in their relationship, she was on top and in control. Granted, he could easily change that. Instead, his hands remained gentle, as he lowered his head. He started breathing again.

"So good," she whispered. "This feels incredible."

Letting her muscles relax, she leaned forward a little. That done, she leaned back until she risked losing her balance. As his cock came with her, she thought of him as her prisoner, helpless like she'd been earlier.

"Ah, shit."

"What is it, Mace? Not used to having the tables turned?"

"Something . . . like that."

Sitting straight again, she lifted herself off him, muscles clenched as she did. His hands abandoned her thighs, waited somewhere in the dark. Then it was time to sink down again and relish the increasing sense of fullness as she swallowed him. She rocked forward, then back, paused, started again. Her cheeks burned, and she panted. Fireflies seemed to have attached themselves to every part of her, miniature feet and wings brushing sensitive skin.

He lightly struck her right breast, the contact quick and exciting.

"Oh, yes, yes!"

He slapped her again, her left breast this time. Laughing, she scratched his chest. Thinking to *punish* him further, she held on to his cock with all her strength and lifted off. She would pull him, stretch him until he begged.

Then his fingers were on her clit, and she lost control. Whimpering and hissing at the same time, she sank onto him. His fingers pressed, circled, stroked her.

Wait! Not yet.

Desperate to hold back, she struggled to focus on him. But it was too late. Shuddering, she rolled into her release. It hit hard and violent, scraping every inch of her. She couldn't stop screaming.

Whether she came once or a series of times was unimportant. Her weightless body danced and her cunt let go, flooding him. Wet heat clung to her inner thighs. The smell of sex seeped into her.

After what seemed like a long time, she began gathering herself together only to cast the effort aside. Mace was shuddering with his back arched and hands gripping her hips. Even with the condom between them, the rush of his offering thrilled her. Smiling, laughing almost, she rode his explosion with him. His cries spoke of a man out of control, lost even.

It's all right. I'll protect you.

From what?

25

Cheyenne lay beside him with her head on his shoulder and a leg draped over his. Hearing Rio stir, Mace wondered if the dog had been in the room the whole time, but mostly he concentrated on Cheyenne's quieting breaths. He didn't want to talk, and he certainly didn't want to think. Sleep tugged at him.

They'd both been shaking when they untangled themselves. Removing the ruined rubber, she set it aside. Then, and this was what had undone him as much as coming, she'd licked the remaining discharge off his fading cock. Her chore completed, she'd stretched out on her side where her breath dampened his skin. He thought about stroking her inner thighs to remind her of what she'd done, but it might start something.

"It's been an incredible night," she whispered. "The most incredible of my life."

"Hmm," was the best he could give her.

"I know. You want to sleep. Me, too, only my mind's whirling. Maybe..."

"What?" He had to force himself to speak.

"I'm not sure I want things to make sense right now." She kissed his shoulder. "That's the plus side to being drunk. Logic doesn't matter. There's no making decisions."

When she didn't explain further, he relaxed. His body had been stripped bare. It felt empty and formless, same as his mind. Strangely, he loved being in this place.

"Mace?"

"What?"

"Have you ever had a woman in this bed?"

Evade. Change the subject. Something. "No."

"Why not?"

Going by the sounds the dog was making, Mace surmised Rio was trying to curl into a ball. Between that and Cheyenne's sweat-stained body against his, he had no other existence.

"I prefer to separate myself from my work," he came up with.

"Turning women on the way you do isn't work. It's an art, a skill. You must have them lined up at the door."

Maybe, only none knew where he lived.

The need for sleep faded, leaving him clear-minded. Why had he erected this barrier between himself and women, and why was Cheyenne the exception?

"You can tell me," she said. "I won't be jealous of your harem, not much."

"There's no harem."

"Right." She sighed. "Fuck them and leave them's your style? Damn, I'm sorry I said that. It's just that you bring out a lot in me I wasn't aware of."

I understand.

"I want to know more about you." Her voice was small and vulnerable. "I have no right. I realize that, but..."

"What?"

"I'm sensing holes in you. Holes and walls. Something's missing, maybe something you were denied at a critical time in your life. It happened to me, so I know what I'm talking about."

"Maybe," he said. "At least you had family, people who wanted you."

"What are you saying?"

More than I should. "You were adopted. I never got that far."

"Your parents abandoned you? Did they lose custody?"

Laying her head on his shoulder, she stroked his chest. Hopefully she knew not to venture lower.

Do it. Just get it out. "Yeah."

"How old were you?"

"A baby."

"My God. What's your first memory?"

"Being in a room with several other boys. Some were crying. A few had blankets over their heads. I kept trying to open the door, but it was locked."

"How, ah, how old were you then?"

She spoke so softly he could barely make out the words. Hopefully she understood he didn't want sympathy. "I'm not sure. Three or four. I eventually got my hands on the file Children's Services kept on me, so I know it was a group home. Eventually it was closed down."

"Because you and the other boys were being warehoused instead of lovingly raised?"

"That wasn't in the file."

"That's how you put your early years together, by reading a file?"

"Pretty much. It's not like I had parents to tell me."

"Oh, Mace. I'm so sorry."

"Don't be."

"Easier said than done," she said after a long silence. "When I was researching my article on parental influence, I talked to a couple of psychiatrists. They said children often block out the negative. It's a way of protecting ourselves."

"I wasn't very good at that."

"You have a lot of memories?"

"More than I wish I did," he told her when he'd been certain he'd keep that to himself his entire life. Maybe having just shot his wad was responsible for the opening floodgates, but he suspected Cheyenne herself had more to do with it. "You're not the only one to change your name. I had mine changed a couple of times—by people who started to adopt me only to let the state take me back. Kind of like a store's return policy."

She again kissed his shoulder, the contact lingering and involving her tongue. When she lowered her head, he felt something hot. Tears? He'd yet to see her cry despite circumstances that did most women in.

"You weren't ever adopted?"

"No, social workers told me I had to trust and open up if I wanted that to happen. To quote you, easier said than done."

"Trust and honesty don't come easily to someone who's been kicked in the teeth enough times."

She'd walked much the same road as he had. She knew what it felt like, so why hold back? "I decided it wasn't worth the risk."

"You're talking about the emotional risk, aren't you? Taking someone's name meant being expected to become part of them."

"And choosing my own said I knew who I was."

"Why Mace?"

"I liked it."

"Just like I like Cheyenne."

Grateful for the light turn in the conversation, he nodded. Then because he couldn't think of a reason not to, he told her about stealing a car at fifteen and getting caught, which led to a juvenile record and being sent to the second group home of his childhood, this one for delinquents. He might have used that time to hone his lawbreaking skills from his fellow inmates if he hadn't been such a loner.

"I had a hell of a chip on my shoulder," he admitted.

"Is it still there?" She nibbled the spot under discussion.

"Hopefully not. Going through life on the defensive's a hell of a way to be."

"It's also protective. It got to where no matter what my folks said, I'd argue the point. I couldn't believe they had my best interests in mind because they'd never bothered to ask my opinion."

"They'd say you were hardheaded?"

"And ungrateful. We play at being civilized, but it's a lot of work."

"I'm sorry." He meant it.

"It is what it is, and I'll be there when and if they need help." She was silent a moment. "I'm trying to put myself in your position, growing up the way you did."

This was a good time to stop. He'd already bled more than he'd ever thought he would. "I know their names," he admitted. "And some of the details of what happened when I was six months old."

"I'd like to hear about it if you feel like it."

He didn't and yet he did. Beyond his comprehension, he needed to open up as never before.

Eyes closed and opened by turn, he handed her everything he'd learned from stealing his thick Children's Services file. It had been winter and night when police had spotted him crying in the backseat of a car with expired tags. The car was parked a block from a bar where his unmarried parents had been drinking. According to the bartender, they'd been there for several hours, arguing. He'd told them he was going kick them out if they didn't quiet down, only to have Mace's father jump him, which led to the police being called. There'd been no mention of a child.

He'd been taken to the hospital and checked for hypothermia followed by an emergency foster home. Police had found drugs in the car and a drug lab in the rundown apartment where his parents were behind in rent. Even before coming to trial, they'd signed away their parental rights. He had no idea where they were or whether they were together, and didn't care.

There'd been something in the record about his mother being pregnant, but if he had a brother or sister, he didn't know. He'd debated hiring a private investigator, but some doors were better left closed. Maybe later.

"I'm so glad police got involved that night," Cheyenne said when he ran down. "Otherwise, who knows how long you would have been exposed to that lifestyle? You spent your childhood being bounced around, but at least you weren't raised in a drug house."

"That's the way I look at it," he said, although it wasn't that simple. "Another positive thing. While locked up, I had to attend school where the focus was on learning a trade. I became interested in computers and from there security systems."

"Did you go to college?"

"For a while, but I didn't see much point in a lot of the classes. The way I look at it, education has to have a specific purpose."

"I know what you're talking about. I signed up for a so-called writing class that turned out to be the instructor's excuse to pontificate about such things as allegory and metaphor."

"I don't know what you're talking about."

"I figured it out, I just didn't care. What was important to me was learning how to thoroughly research a subject and develop organizational skills. Journalism was great for that, a lot of hands-on experience working for the school newspaper. Besides, the running back was the sports' editor. What a hunk."

He'd become weary of his voice and appreciated letting her pick up the conversational ball. Besides, her tone was soothing and now light. While detailing his childhood, there hadn't been enough of him left over for anything else, but with the telling done, his awareness of himself as a man was reasserting itself.

Perhaps mindful that the weight of her head was cutting off the circulation in his shoulder, she'd rolled onto her back during his monologue and lay next to him with her hands on her belly. Instead of quickening the way his threatened to do, her breath was slowing. Knowing he was losing her, he resolved to match her pace. As sleep tugged at him, he reached down for the coverlet and covered both of them.

What the hell have you done, was his last thought.

26

In the morning, Cheyenne offered to fix breakfast so she'd have something to do, but Mace turned her down. She'd awakened believing they'd have sex, but he'd stepped into the shower without so much as a good morning. When he emerged, he'd suggested she do the same, giving her another of his shirts to put on before driving her home.

Once at her own place, she'd changed into her own clothes and, not knowing whether to scream or cry, watched as he went through her house. Now she sat across the kitchen table from him with her stomach growling and the distance between them both welcome and upsetting. The remarkably small camera he'd taken from her spider plant was in a paper bag on the table.

"I don't know whether to feel relieved or more confused," she said after he unnecessarily told her it was the only device he'd found. "At least whoever's responsible wasn't interested in what I do in the bathroom."

"They got what they wanted this way, or at least that was

their intention. What I don't know is whether they came back after planting this."

Pressing her hand to her stomach, she stared at him. His eyes held too many memories of what had taken place between them. "You mean they might have been here more than once?"

"That was their intention. Otherwise, they couldn't get their hands on what's in the memory chip."

"Who would do—that's disgusting."

"It's more than that."

"Dangerous, you mean?"

"That's possible."

Feeling sicker by the moment, she reached for the bag. The impulse to drop it into the garbage disposal nearly overwhelmed her, but Mace held up his hand, stopping her. "It's a long shot, but I'm going to check for fingerprints."

"You can do that? You won't be involving the police, will you?"

"No, not yet."

"I appreciate that." She could hardly think. "I don't want this becoming public if it can be helped. The idea of the police, or anyone, looking at me like that... That's why you're handling it yourself, isn't it? You want to keep *your* name out of it."

"If possible. One step at a time." He fingered the top of the bag. "This is a fairly sophisticated system for its size. It's only been on the market a few months. The price tag is hefty, the technology impressive even to me."

Damn him. If she didn't know better, she'd think he was some technician she'd hired to do repairs around her place. What had happened to the man who'd bared his soul and given her his full attention while she did the same?

"I've dealt with the manufacturer," he continued, "Once I have the serial number, it's possible I can get someone to tell me who bought it."

Fighting the bile in her throat, she gripped the corner of the table. No way was she going to touch him. "And you'll look at the images, won't you?"

"Yes, Cheyenne, there won't be anything I haven't seen."

Of course not. There wasn't anything he didn't know about her—except maybe how she felt at the moment.

"You'll tell me everything you learn, won't you? Advise me on how to proceed."

"It's part of my job."

Your job. Standing, she headed for the living room. "Of course."

"Wait," he said. "We need to discuss your safety. I want you to contact a security company. In the meantime, I'll give you my cell phone number. I'll call you at random times. If you don't answer—"

"I understand," she blurted. "Believe me I'll be careful." *And spooked.* "Look, I've already taken up enough of your morning. I'm sure . . . Mace, I need some time to myself."

Instead of following her, he remained at the table, prompting her to face him. He hadn't taken time to shave. Between that and his faded, threadbare jeans, he looked nothing like an *Edge* employee or Indulgences dom. This was a man who wanted nothing more than to spend the day with his dog, or maybe with a woman equally at home in old jeans.

Much as she wanted to be that woman, she was afraid. They'd gotten too close. It was time to back up, put distance between them.

"You're right," he said, standing and picking up the bag. "Things got out of control last night."

Him, out of control? At a loss for words, she led the way to the front door and opened it. Although he didn't touch her as he stepped outside, his warmth stayed with her. Trying not to think or feel, she watched him drive away. Then she locked her door.

* * *

Instead of going outside when Mace opened his back door, Rio stood, looking up at him.

"Go," Mace said. "I don't have time to play with you. I've got to get working on this." He indicated the bag he'd left on the counter.

Rio sat.

"What is it? You're saying you have a right to know where the lady is and what she was doing here all night?"

Rio's tail started wagging.

"I would tell you if I knew." Kneeling, he scratched behind Rio's ear. "Not the smartest thing I've ever done, that's the one thing I do know."

The explanation, pitiful as it was, seemed to satisfy Rio, who turned his head so Mace didn't have to stretch to reach both places. He hadn't wanted to neuter Rio, but neither had he wanted to deal with an intact and single-minded male or run the risk of being responsible for unwanted puppies. As a result, he couldn't blame Rio for not understanding how complex the whole sex thing was. But even if Rio spent all his waking hours in search of females in heat, he wouldn't understand the whole emotional thing.

Well, neither did he. What he did know was that Cheyenne had touched him as he'd never been touched.

That scared the hell out of him.

He wanted back what he'd had before her.

"She's an amazing creature. The most responsive bitch I've ever seen. I envy you."

Mace sat in Atwood's office watching as a video of Saturday night at Indulgences played. Feeling as if he might crack into countless pieces, he nevertheless kept his hands in his lap. He was flanked by Atwood and Robert, although caught between them might be a more accurate description.

At the moment Cheyenne stood stretched out on the X. Naked and twitching from the lashes he was inflicting on her, she looked nothing like the reporter who at this moment was working in another part of the *Edge* building. Unless things had changed since he'd walked past her cubicle earlier this morning, her fingers were pounding the keyboard, her features intense as she concentrated on what she was writing.

If she knew what he was looking at, she'd never forgive him.

"How did you get your hands on this?" he asked. "My take when I saw the camera in the back room was that it would be for the exclusive use of Indulgences' owners."

"Connections."

"Why are you showing it to me? If you're thinking of blackmailing her—"

"That's not going to be necessary."

What the hell did that mean? "Me then?"

"We pay your salary, Mace. We know how much you're worth."

If he was still the confused and angry teen he'd told Cheyenne about Saturday night, he'd have already started throwing punches, but despite the satisfaction that would bring, he might never get to the why.

"We also know what you'd do with more money if you had it," Robert said. "Buy the woodlot behind your place so you'd have more privacy. However"—Robert grinned a grin Mace longed to wipe from his face—"you might be inclined to cut down some of those trees and build something to rival Indulgences."

On the video, Cheyenne continued to jerk. Although the sound had been silenced, he could hear her grunts and gasps. Studying her, he acknowledged that her reactions weren't any different from the other women he'd *worked* over. Although attractive, she didn't leave the others in her dust. What held her apart from them was his responses to her, responses he was still trying to wrap his mind around.

Bottom line, she scared him when he'd sworn his days of being afraid were behind him.

"The last thing I'd ever do was cut down a tree. What the hell is this about?"

The two men exchanged looks, no easy matter with him between them. He had a permit to carry the gun tucked into the small of his back, not that that's what a civilized man should be thinking about.

"This is about a lot of things," Atwood supplied. "I'm trying to decide what's the best way to approach the bottom line."

"How about the truth?"

"Yes," Robert agreed. "That's our intention. Mace, doing thorough background checks is an important part of what your job entails. Hopefully it comes as no surprise that we've done the same to you."

"I figured you had."

"Going back to your childhood."

Fury threatened to flood Mace. Of course they had. Given his responsibilities at *Edge*, anything less would constitute carelessness on their parts. "Find it interesting, did you?"

"Rather sad, truth be told. We're sorry you had such a rough haul."

"What does it have to do with today?"

"We're getting to that. By the time our investigator finished his job, we had a clear image of a loner, a man who insists on being in control for reasons a psychiatrist would doubtless have a field day with."

Atwood cleared his throat. "You're able to indulge that need for control both at work and via your *private* activities. What we're considering is that dabbling in BDSM might not be enough. It's quite possible, maybe a certainty, that you have an even larger appetite, one you haven't been able to feed."

Robert pointed at the video. "Tell us the truth. Your future here might well hinge on the answer. You'd like nothing better than for that collar to stay on her for the rest of her life, for her to belong to you."

From the moment he'd realized Robert and Atwood had brought him in to view the video still playing, he'd known his suspicions about the two were founded. He couldn't prove it yet, but his gut said they were responsible for what he'd found in Cheyenne's bedroom. There'd always been something a little *dirty* about the magazine because of its focus on life's underbelly. In essence, *Edge* reflected Robert's and Atwood's personalities.

He just hadn't realized how dark their personalities were before now. "Go on."

"We intend to," Atwood said. "But first a clarification. You asked how we got our hands on this arousing demonstration of the BDSM lifestyle. It's more than our having connections. *Edge* has a financial interest in Indulgences. More than just an interest, actually."

"What my partner's trying to say," Robert interjected, "is that he and I are the major Indulgences owners. In fact, the club is why *Edge* operates in the black."

"I should have figured—"

"Don't blame yourself. The IRS has no idea."

"I'm going to come right to the point," Atwood said. He turned his attention to the video. "What does she mean to you?"

"I don't see how that's your business."

"Ah, but it is, or rather it has the potential to be. In some respects, we're at a disadvantage because this session with her is the first time we've studied you at *work*. Prior to this, we've relied on word of mouth because we'd believed it prudent not to be at Indulgences when you were."

"You're sure you got the straight story?" Mace fought to

keep his tone calm. "If I were you, I wouldn't believe a word anyone says in there."

"We appreciate your warning, but those we talked to had no reason to be anything but honest. In fact, they were, how should I put it, encouraged to be so."

He'd spent most of Sunday hiking in the woods with Rio. While the pit followed his nose, he'd concentrated on identifying the various wildlife. If he had his way, he'd be there right now and none of this would be happening. Maybe best scenario, he'd have never met Cheyenne.

Leaning forward, Atwood pressed Pause. The frozen image left no doubt that Mace's hand was on Cheyenne's sex.

"Your talent with regards to this lifestyle"—Atwood pointed— "is highly regarded. To a man, the other doms agree you're a master of the art. To be fair, we put the same question to a number of women, and they all said the same thing."

"Am I up for an award? Dom of the year?"

If his sarcasm bothered Atwood, the man gave no hint. "Potentially much better. But back to our question about her." He pointed again. "How important is she to you?"

The move didn't come easy, yet Mace leaned back in his chair. "If you went to the trouble of having this video made and took the chance of sneaking into her place to plant the camera I found, I'd be a fool not to surmise that you know what happened after she and I left Indulgences."

Pushing to his feet, Robert paced to the closed door. Although he'd locked it earlier, he tested it. "Remind me to never underestimate you."

"That cuts both ways."

Atwood continued to lean forward, the fingers gripping the chair arms turning white. "There's been entirely too much dancing around. You prematurely took her out of Indulgences and drove her to your place where she spent the night. The next morning you returned her to her condo where you remained for the better part of an hour. The two of you haven't connected since then, and when she arrived at work this morning, you didn't acknowledge each other. However, there might have been phone calls we, so far, don't have access to."

"Is there a point to this?" he asked. "Because if I'm not given it, damn fast, I'm out of here."

For a moment no one said anything, yet he sensed his sharp comment had had the desired impact.

"You're a hard bastard," Robert said as he returned to his chair. Instead of sitting, however, he rested his ass against the desk, facing Mace. "Hard enough for the job we intend to offer you."

Knocked off balance by the last thing he expected to hear, Mace studied the backs of his hands, specifically knuckles better suited on a boxer.

"No reaction?" Atwood asked.

"I'm waiting. Besides, I thought we were talking about Cheyenne."

"The two are related. Do you care about her?"

"That depends on your interpretation of care."

"We'd prefer to hear yours."

His guess was he hadn't been in the room over ten minutes, but he could hardly wait to leave. Sitting and talking had never been anywhere on his list of things he wanted to do with his time. Besides, this wasn't just shooting the bull.

"I wouldn't want to hear that she'd been hit by a bus. I gained a certain amount of satisfaction from *helping* her research the piece you assigned her." He stared pointedly at the video. "I got my rocks off Saturday night."

"Do you want a repeat performance?"

Knowing he was being tested, albeit for something he didn't yet understand, he shrugged, then nodded.

"Because you have feelings for her or because she's a good sub?"

"She's practically a virgin to the scene. It's a turn-on."

"Anything else about her turn you on, perhaps whatever it was that led to her spending the night?"

"Let's just say we were insatiable."

"Then why didn't the two of you hook up on Sunday?"

None of your damn business. "I wasn't hungry that day."

Atwood opened and closed his mouth. He then looked over at Robert. For the first time since the bizarre conversation had started, Mace felt as if he had the upper hand.

"I'm a restless man. Horny, but not for the same old, same old. I'm always on the prowl for a new experience."

"You're not interested in playing with her again?"

Making his shrug count, Mace pretended to study Cheyenne's frozen form. "Not particularly. She doesn't have anything more to give."

"Not for you, perhaps, but there are a lot of men who'd love to get their hands on her."

"Have them contact her then."

Atwood's smile was better suited on a ferret. "That's not what the Blind Spot is about."

27

Cheyenne hadn't seen Mace since he'd passed by her cubicle earlier, thank goodness. And he'd ignored her when she arrived this morning. As he'd promised, he'd called several times on Sunday, the conversations brief, which was exactly what she wanted, needed.

However, she had some unfinished business with him that had nothing to do with telling him that she'd made an appointment with a security company.

Both dreading and anticipating her lunch break made concentrating on her article all but impossible. She tried to convince herself she wasn't making progress because she didn't have all the information she needed, but that was a lie. Not only was the time she'd spent in Indulgences' back room burned into her memory and body, there was the matter of the damn collar.

Ordering herself not to touch it didn't stop her fingers from trailing there. Every time she did, heat flowed through her. Much more stimulus and she'd—damn Mace!

After what felt like a good chunk of her life, her coworkers started stirring. Instead of joining them at the adjacent café or nearby restaurants, she headed for the stairs. Fortunately, she had them to herself, which meant not having to hold up her end of a conversation.

Reaching street level, she cautiously opened the door and looked out at the lobby. As he usually was this time of the day, Mace was watching the front door. He wouldn't take his own lunch until everyone was back and accounted for. She waited until the lobby was empty except for him before approaching him. No surprise, he turned before she reached him.

"We need to talk," she said without preliminary. "Now and in private."

"I can't leave, you know that."

Although he was sitting, her senses filled with memories of what it felt like to have him looming over her. His legs were hidden under his desk, not that that helped. A hint of the soap he'd used this morning tantalized.

Damn it, she wasn't going to think about him standing naked under the warm spray. She didn't dare.

"I'm aware of that," she said, then jumped into her canned speech. A storage room containing copies of past magazines given to visitors was off the lobby. They could go in there and keep the door open a crack.

"All right." He started to stand, prompting her to step back. "I'm not going to bite."

"I'm aware of that," she snapped. "It's a matter of my wanting to get this over with as quickly as possible."

Giving weight to her words, she led the way to the storage room. He followed behind, pure sex seeming to radiate out from him to challenge her resolve. But she wasn't going to change her mind. Her sanity depended on it.

The windowless room was small and cramped, and Mace much too close. At least she'd had the sense to turn on the light. Leaning against a floor-to-ceiling shelf filled with musty magazines, she started to fold her arms over her breasts. His eyes followed the movement, and she did what she'd intended back when she'd decided on this meeting. She wrapped her fingers around the collar.

"I want it off. Now."

"You couldn't wait until later?"

"Of course I could." Hoping to keep her voice steady, she spoke slowly and clearly. "But there's no time like the present."

"Why?"

She'd known he'd ask. If only she'd had a hint he would with his arms at his sides while wearing the world's sexiest black knit shirt. The damn thing clung to every muscle.

"The past weekend was a wakeup call for me, Mace." Saying his name wasn't smart, too many nerve endings got involved. "I appreciate your role in it, more than you'll know."

"Get to it, Cheyenne. It's been a hell of a morning for me."

Oh, so she was a nuisance, was she? Well, what did that make him? "I learned I don't like being a sub after all."

"Oh?" He lifted his eyebrows.

Hoping he'd continue to keep his attention on her face and not her too-taut breasts, she nodded. "You know about my childhood. Turns out I was wrong thinking I could put it behind me by having someone boss me around." She gave the collar a tug. "I need to be in control of my body. A big part of that involves getting rid of this."

"I know subs, Cheyenne. You're one."

Another mark in his favor, he wasn't infringing on her personal space. Now if only she could get him out from under her skin. "No, I'm not. Hell, maybe I was until you gave me that demonstration of the real deal."

"I don't believe you."

Imagining popping him in the chops propelled her on. "I'm sorry if I'm deflating your balloon. Maybe you're thinking I found fault with your sexual prowess. Believe me, I didn't. The sex was amazing." Determined to get a grip on the need running through her, she took a deep breath.

"This isn't easy for me, Mace. I'm not going to pretend otherwise. I've never experienced the kind of *intimacy* you and I shared." *Never will again.* "But it isn't healthy for me, and I don't want it to happen again. Can you understand that?"

"I'm trying to."

The bright, bare light overhead stripped his features of definition and made them garish. Hers probably looked no better, but she was grateful for the glare. Otherwise, his dark, intense eyes might be more than she could handle. If only he was simply a body, a sexual object.

"I didn't sleep much last night," she admitted. "And Sunday after you left was damn long. I did a lot of soul searching."

"I imagine you did."

Although she wished he'd admit the same, she wasn't surprised by his response. After all, this was a man who'd learned to keep his emotions to himself. Maybe they'd died in the process.

"What exists between us isn't healthy." There. That's what she'd intended to say all along. "I need and intend for it to stop. Right now I can't deal with how my decision impacts you, but my guess is you'll come out just fine. Maybe the only difference this time is that I pulled the plug instead of the other way around."

"Go on."

Envying his ability to remain motionless for so long, she spun the collar around so the unobtrusive locking device was in front. Then she rammed her hands in the front pockets of her slacks. Her fingers were closer to her crotch than wise, but she was strong and resolute. No way would she touch herself. The fire there would have to burn untended.

"I've said all I intended to. There's no need to spell it out further. We'll continue to run into each other at work, but the personal relationship is over."

He nodded, the first movement from him in she didn't know how long. Such a little thing shouldn't impact her, right? Then why did she want his hands on her, touching everywhere, feeding the fire?

Let me out of here, Mace. Don't make me hurt any more than I am.

No other man handled his body as if it belonged on a sleek-muscled predator. Every move was clean and beautiful and sexy as hell. Guessing he was reaching into his own pocket for the key that would free her made watching even harder. Praying he wouldn't know, she tightened her sex muscles. It didn't help. Nothing would.

As she'd mentally mapped out this conversation, she'd focused entirely on what she'd say and how she thought he'd react. In her stupidity, she hadn't given enough thought to this moment when his fingertips touched her throat.

They'd had sex in the dark at his place, made love really, and she craved those deep shadows where it was just the two of them and their emotions. Instead, she jammed her hands farther into her pockets and kept her feet firmly planted, her head turned to the side to protect her from the full impact of his breath.

When he pulled up on the collar, it alarmed her, but then she realized he was simply getting a better angle on it. Thinking to help, she tilted her head upward. He could easily kiss her this way; if he did, she'd lose it. Her arms would go around him, and she'd widen her stance, draw him into her.

The click signaling her freedom barely penetrated. It wasn't until he drew the collar off her that she faced reality.

"Thank you," she said, determined not to rub her throat.

"You're welcome."

"That's it then," she babbled because he hadn't stepped back. "We're on the, ah, same page. From now on the only thing we have in common is that we work for the same company."

"Sorry. We also share the same memories."

The collar dangled from his fingers, making her question her decision. More than question, she needed to be wearing it again. Needed him owning her.

But if she allowed that to happen, she'd lose herself.

"Memories fade." She could walk past him, but not without their bodies brushing. "I'm sure you'll soon replace me."

He waved the collar in front of her. "What are you going to replace this with?"

Don't do this, please. "Nothing."

"Don't be so sure." He let the collar trail between her breasts, not stopping until it grazed her belly. "The need inside you isn't going to go away that easily."

"Stop it!" She slammed her palms against his chest. He stepped back, which made it possible for her to slide around him. "You don't know me, damn it. You think you can manipulate me by saying those things, but you're wrong."

She was free, standing in the door jam, splitting her attention between his steel-glint gaze and the thankfully still-empty lobby.

"Be careful, Cheyenne. You don't know either of us as well as you think or need to."

Atwood was checking the details of a new advertising contract when his intercom buzzed. He picked it up.

"Her collar's gone," Robert said.

"Shit no."

"Shit yes. You know what that means, don't you?"

"*He* did it. The bastard."

"Maybe, maybe not," Robert corrected. "Here's my thinking. Could be he was just accommodating her, being the considerate bastard he is. If that's the case, I'm thinking it's time for her to undergo an attitude adjustment, a permanent one."

Slapping his hand on the contract, Atwood leaned back. His chair squeaked. "Let's talk about this a minute. The specifics of her becoming a missing person haven't been finalized."

"I'll make sure that happens today. Such a shame that Schulz's stupid and loyal family members became so incensed about her article detailing how he murdered his ex wife—a real bitch, according to them—that they've done something to her. A double shame that her body will never be found."

"You're confident everything can be set in place today?"

"Of course. It isn't as if this is our initial foray into taking a person out of one world and into another."

"True. In that case, I agree we shouldn't put this off. The sooner the *transportation* takes place, the better. How do you think he'll react?"

"You heard me. There's damn little Mace cares about. One thing, despite his protestations to the contrary, I have no doubt he wants her on her knees before him. Hell, he was born for the Blind Spot package. He'll fall right in."

"And disappear from this world, which means we have not one but two *reassignments* to deal with."

"Would you quit obsessing on minor details? The work will be worth the effort."

"I hope you're right."

"I am. Bank on it."

It was nearly nine at night by the time Cheyenne let herself into her condo. Unaccustomed to being out late on a weeknight, she was dragging, but given her state of mind, she hadn't seen a viable alternative. The idea of sitting home mulling over what did no good to mull had left her shaking. Besides, in the wake of the camera in her bedroom, being home spooked her a little. Thursday and a visit from the security company couldn't come soon enough. Her so-called solution had been to go to the mall after work. Feeling isolated from the groups of teens, parents, and children, even the occasional elderly couple ambling around like herself, she'd choked down something called Chinese but didn't taste like it at the food court.

Her stomach had churned as she'd wandered through store after store, avoiding one with its sexily dressed manikins. She'd actually gotten as far as the department store cash register with a pair of shoes, but in the end putting down good money simply because they fit hadn't made sense. Truth was, concentrating on something as complex as shoe styles had been beyond her.

At least, she told herself as she kicked off her flats after checking to make sure her windows were locked, she'd saved herself a charge on her credit card. Hopefully falling asleep wouldn't be as difficult as it had been last night.

In the bathroom, she stripped out of her clothes and washed her face. She grabbed her nightgown from the hook behind the door, but pulling it over her head seemed like a lot of effort. Looking at her reflection in a mirror that needed cleaning, she tried to give her face an objective once-over. Instead, she wound up wondering what Mace had seen when he looked at her.

Too damn much. A band around her neck, restraints on her wrists and ankles, a gag, flogger marks on nearly every inch of her body. There was something else, she acknowledged, specifically sex juices tracking down her inner thighs.

"I did what I had to," she informed the bleary-eyed broad in the mirror. "Got out before I lost me."

She'd done a lousy job of making her bed this morning, which necessitated throwing back the coverlet so she could dig for the top sheet. Finding it wadded near the bottom, she yanked it up. Then came the hard part, contemplating turning off the lights and climbing into bed. Reaching for the lamp wasn't hard, but instead of crawling under the wrinkled sheet, she sat on the side of the bed.

Okay, so she'd sat like this at Mace's house Saturday night. That was no reason for her brain to shut down and her nerves to take over now. She'd assign no more than a minute to indulging a certain itch. Tonight wasn't about climaxing, no way. Granted, a hand was already fingering her pussy. There was no crime in that, nothing that said release had to be part of the scenario. She'd touch a little, stroke what was dangerously sensitive, but she wouldn't pretend Mace was doing the deed, no way.

Sighing, she flopped back on the bed, head landing on her pillow and knees bent, buttocks lifting to aid access. She was already wet, which made it pig simple for a finger to slip past what she really couldn't call a barrier. For a woman who prided herself on staying in shape and away from the dessert table, this part of her anatomy was remarkably soft and puffy.

And responsive.

Another sigh accompanied a roll onto her side. She could do this without Mace either physically or emotionally. Satisfaction had often been a solitary sport for her. She'd made up the necessary rules. All it took was a little imagination, a receptive mindset, experienced fingers.

She was repositioning her arm for greater access when a weight landed on her, pushing her into the mattress. Powerful arms wrenched her onto her belly. A hand pressing against the back of her head kept her face in the pillow and robbed her of air as other hands pulled her arms behind her and handcuffed her. The pressure let up, allowing her to suck in air. As she did, someone forced a gag between her teeth. Moments later, her ankles had been taped together.

"Time to deliver the package," a strange male voice said. "Then we get paid."

* * *

Robert was behind the wheel of a luxury automobile Mace had never seen him driving. He, Robert, and Atwood were heading for the city limits, going the opposite direction from Mace's place.

When Cheyenne hadn't shown up for work on Tuesday, he'd first called her condo and then gone there. He'd used a locksmith's key to get in. Finding her car in the garage, her purse in the living room, and signs of a struggle on the bed had had him on the brink of calling the police. Instead, he'd returned to *Edge* where he'd confronted his employers.

"You work fast," Atwood had said the moment he'd walked into the office. "We didn't think you'd get involved so soon."

In no mood for evasion, he'd demanded to know what the hell they'd done with Cheyenne.

"Let's say she's in a better place. A place we have no doubt you'll approve of once you understand."

Now, the workday and sunlight behind him, he had no choice but to go with the pair. The only good thing about it was that his gun rested in the small of his back.

This end of the valley had never held much interest for him. Known as Industry Row, it was home to many of the area's manufacturing plants. In the wake of the recent recession, several had gone out of business. There were too many "For Sale" signs.

Obviously a deserted building wasn't their destination because Robert kept driving until they reached the foothills. He then turned off the country highway and onto a twisting road where a few hearty souls lived in widely spread houses that clung to the sides of steep slopes. After some five miles, the pavement gave out. From the passenger's seat, Mace noticed that there were no more mailboxes. He'd been here once when he was looking for a place to buy, only to turn around. Isolation was one thing, a nonfunctioning road quite another.

If he could believe the men who'd *enticed* him to accompany them, they were heading to where Cheyenne was. What little white knight was in him said he'd rescue her. An essential question was what, if anything, did she need rescuing from, and did she want him doing it? Another consideration: Robert and Atwood had gone to a lot of trouble getting her to wherever they were going. They'd hardly let him and Cheyenne walk away.

Slowing even more, Robert made a right turn that took them into what at first looked like nothing but forest. However, within a few yards, they were on a paved road that wove up the mountainside.

"As you can see..." Atwood broke the silence. "Considerable effort has gone into making the entrance to the Blind Spot as civilized as possible."

The Blind Spot. Despite his curiosity, Mace kept it tamped down. When necessary, he could be patient.

At length they reached the end of the road and a level turnaround area. When the others got out, he did the same. The air was crisp at this altitude, the night sounds both comforting and disconcerting. He turned his hands into fists, then forced them to relax.

"Up here." Atwood pointed at a path he wouldn't have seen if the car's lights weren't still on. "Not far."

Atwood was right about that. No sooner had they lost the illumination the headlights provided, he found himself looking at a cave entrance. A pale blue light spilled out from it. *The hell!*

"You're quite safe," Robert assured him. "And you're expected, anticipated. We'll allow you to continue to carry your gun, but be assured you won't need it."

As Atwood led the way, the light seemed to reach out to envelop them. As soon as he entered the cave, his skin took on a blue hue. Setting aside disbelief, he followed with Robert bringing up the rear, to keep him from trying to run? The only thing flight would accomplish would be a night on foot in the wilderness, because Robert had pocketed the car key.

They were in a tunnel that looked to be made of blue-white marble. No longer mountain-cold, the air was now warm and fresh, smelling of strawberries and other fruits. Flutes and violins played softly. For someone who'd never believed in anything except the here and now, Mace sensed he was ill-prepared for what lay ahead.

Was Cheyenne here? And if so, why?

28

From her cage, Cheyenne stared out at a beautiful world of massive ferns surrounding a pristine clear pond where exquisite fish swam fed by a thin waterfall. Beyond the ferns were lush iridescent trees the likes of which she'd never seen. White, burgundy, and royal blue birds with sweeping tails and feathers drifted from one tree to another. The setting had a tropical look, but without the humidity she associated with the tropics. The sky was an azure blue without a cloud in it, so clean she longed to stretch her arms to embrace it.

The incomprehensibility beyond her couldn't have been more perfect. Perfect except for the cages. From where she was, she couldn't tell whether the others were occupied. If so, those prisoners were equally silent.

Ten middle-aged men dressed in what she'd call casual professional sat in a circle in padded, comfortable lounge chairs near the pond. She didn't try to reconcile herself to the contrast between what they were enjoying and the marble-like floor she was curled on. Although her hands were tucked between her legs, fingering herself was the last thing she felt inclined to do.

The men were ordinary and studious looking. Although they kept their voices low, she occasionally caught pieces of conversation. They were discussing a cold northern weather system and whether its rapid development represented a significant change from this time last year or was an unexpected anomaly. From what she could tell, they were excited yet cautious about the possibility that this might be the result of something called the Ransan Project.

A low, round table stood in the middle of the circle, and on it were folders and loose papers, reminding her of countless meetings she'd attended. One difference: there'd been no chilled wine bottles and paper-thin wineglasses at her meetings.

The most telling difference between her world and this was the naked, collared, and cowed women tending to the *gentlemen*. They refilled glasses, took notes, circulated folders, talked on cell phones. A few minutes ago, a statuesque blonde had knelt before one of the men and removed his shoes and socks. Now she was massaging his feet, her long hair brushing his instep. Her obviously enhanced breasts looked too large for the rest of her.

There was a woman for each man. They came in various sizes and shapes, although none appeared to be older than mid-thirties. All were attractive. From where she was, she couldn't see into their eyes, but their body language said it all. Afraid, they hated their lots in life.

In part because she had nothing else to do, in part because fear threatened to overwhelm her if she didn't keep it at bay, she wondered at the reason for their apprehension. Granted, they'd been stripped of their clothes and sported gold collars far snugger than the one Mace had put on her, but the men were refined.

She might have believed her assessment of the men, if not for another lounging on the opposite side of the pond. Obviously not involved with the others, his chair reclined to a nearly horizontal position. Dressed in slacks and a button-down dress shirt, he was barefoot and, from the looks of him, asleep or nearly so. He had a *personal* attendant, with the emphasis on the personal.

A curvaceous woman with long, straight black hair knelt beside his chair. If she'd lifted her head, Cheyenne hadn't seen it, but then doing so would interrupt her task. The dozing man's zipper was undone, exposing his erection. The woman held his cock in her cuffed hands and was licking it.

Unable to ignore the reality of what might be her future, she closed her eyes. Although she'd been here since last night, she still couldn't comprehend her new reality. Her captors had said one thing to her when they deposited her near her cage. "Welcome to the Blind Spot." Since then no one had spoken to her, not even the woman who'd removed her bonds and led her into a black-and-white bathroom where she'd been ordered to use the toilet and wash her hands. Twice since then a woman— never the same—had unlocked the cage, helped her out, and taken her back to the bathroom. She'd been given all the water she wanted to drink but hadn't had anything to eat.

The air smelled wonderful, and the music was peaceful. If she'd been looking for the perfect vacation spot, this would be it. She'd dine on strawberries and drink fine wine, swim in the pond, and stand under the waterfall.

Knowing she needed to face reality, she reluctantly opened her eyes. The woman she had no doubt was a slave was still licking the reclining man's cock. He'd turned his head and was looking toward the waterfall.

Two people were emerging from what must be a space behind the water because they weren't wet. The man was tall and stocky, powerfully built. Unlike the others, he wore jeans and short-sleeve brown pullover. He also had on a belt from which dangled rope, cuffs, and a flogger like the one Mace had used on her.

Mace.

The naked woman beyond her was trying to match the man's pace because he had hold of the rope leading from her bound wrists. Her arms reached for him as if entreating him, but her shackled ankles slowed her. She stumbled, caught herself, hurried after him. Although she wasn't wearing a gag, she didn't ask him to wait for her.

By twisting inside her cage, Cheyenne was able to watch as the unlikely pair headed for the men around the meeting table. They looked up, their expressions saying the interruption irritated them. The man being given a foot rub kicked the woman responsible, sending her flying onto her back. Instead of getting up, she remained where she was.

"Bat, you're early," a sitting man said to the one delivering the shackled woman to them. "I thought you understood—"

"I have one of the condemned to deal with," Bat broke in. "Don't have the damn time to dance to your agenda." Jerking the woman to his side, he pressed down on her shoulders, forcing her to kneel. "She's had the necessary attitude adjustment. Not my problem she's worthless."

Another of the sitting men grumbled something Cheyenne couldn't hear. Then he snapped his fingers, indicating he wanted the woman to crawl to his side. She did so with her head low and her body angled so Cheyenne could see whip marks on her pale back.

Bat had already dropped the lead rope and was heading back the way he'd come.

"Wait a minute," yet another man called out. "Where's her documentation? How are we supposed to know where she is in her training without it?"

"Didn't take the time for it," Bat shot back, not bothering to look at who had spoken. "Like I said, she's worthless. She belongs on a farm cleaning stables, maybe."

No one responded to the latest comment. In fact, no one

spoke until Bat, if that's what his name was, was back behind the waterfall.

"Damn him," someone grumbled. "We can't replace him soon enough."

"I couldn't agree more. So when's the new trainer suppose to get here?"

"Anytime. In the meantime, what do we do with this?" The question came from the man who'd ordered the woman to his side. Picking up the loose end of the wrist rope, he wrapped it around his hand and tugged. The woman meekly crawled closer.

"Not much of a flogging," the man holding her announced. "'Cause he's given up on her. What about it, slave? A little more *coaxing* and you'd be eating out of Bat's hand? Eating everything we tell you to more like it."

Everyone except for the woman laughed. Hard as she tried to deny it, Cheyenne had the horrible feeling this would soon be her fate.

She needed answers, some kind of an explanation. Where was she, and why the difference between the sexes here? From what she'd observed, the men were intelligent and educated. No civilized man would condone slavish treatment of women, let alone participate in such behavior.

What did that make them?

And what were their plans for her?

Finally, and maybe most important, did Mace have anything to do with it?

Up until now, traumatized by her experience, she'd managed to keep Mace thoughts at bay. In her mind, Mace represented the real world, the only one she'd ever experienced. Granted, he'd physically, mentally, and emotionally taken her places she'd never been, but through it she'd remained rooted in truth. Now all of that had been taken from her, leaving her with precious little except memories of his hands and more on her.

Was he looking for her? Maybe he'd chalked her disappearance up to a temper tantrum on her part. She'd been unwilling or unable to play by his rules, so what did he want with her?

Her throat dried at the thought that he'd abandoned her. Eventually her absence would send up red flags and people would look for her, but until then—no, she didn't dare let that kind of thinking swamp her. If she did, she might not have the strength and courage to face—what?

The need for answers outweighing her desire for Mace brought her back to reality. The shackled slave was still on her knees while the assembled men seemed to have forgotten about her as they continued their discussion of weather patterns, but the slave's trembling spoke of something dreadful to come.

Finally, as one, the men turned in the direction from which she'd entered this strange world. "Hey, speak of the devils," someone said. "Look who's here."

Although her body ached from the enforced cramped position, she shuffled around. Her throat dried again, but not for the same reason as before. Mace hadn't abandoned her. He was here.

Equally unbelievable, Atwood and Robert were with Mace. Despite her impulse to cry out, she remained silent because going by the greeting she'd just heard, the assembled men had been expecting Mace, Robert, and Atwood. Sick at heart, she blinked back helpless tears.

The men she'd been watching were getting to their feet. Smiling, Robert and Atwood held out their hands and began shaking. Only Mace stood back. Instead of taking in his surroundings, he kept his attention on the men, giving the slaves only the briefest of glances.

Despite the confusion and fear running through her, Cheyenne was in awe of Mace, who now reminded her of a predator. He appeared ready for whatever might happen, taking in everything while keeping his thoughts and impressions to himself. His outfit of well-washed jeans and muscle-defining T-shirt made her body ache. Judging by their intense stares, several of the slaves had taken note of the stallion among geldings.

Stallion? What insanity had her thinking that?

Jerking herself back to reality, she watched as Atwood introduced Mace to everyone. Mace shook each offered hand but said nothing. If he looked around, would he spot her? Maybe not given everything else there was for him to study—unless he'd been here before.

"So," Atwood said when the introductions were over, "what do you think of the Blind Spot? Not what you'd imagined?"

"How could I?" Mace replied. "I'm still trying to put the pieces together."

"It's really quite simple," a short, overweight man said. His tone reminded her of several of her college professors imparting knowledge to the ignorant masses. "For lack of a better definition, the Blind Spot is an alternate universe, a world unto itself existing parallel to and yet on a separate plane from Earth."

Cheyenne's mind spun. Having never been particularly interested in space and disdainful of people's passion for science fiction, she'd prided herself on being grounded in reality. What a fool she'd been.

"Negative versus positive?" Mace asked.

"In some respects, yes. We aren't that different from Earthlings." The *professor* chuckled. "Sorry, I couldn't resist. Truth is, the longer you're here, the more you'll realize there's a vital difference." He tapped himself on the forehead. "Our greater intellect for one and most important."

"We debated explaining that to Mace," Robert broke in, "but decided it would make more of an impact if he saw the proof for himself. So, have we missed anything?"

This wasn't happening! Yes, everything from the moment she'd been kidnapped had been unreal, but seeing her employers and Mace, mostly Mace, was more than she could process. She dimly heard someone explain that it would soon be time to move to the judgment room. Did that mean she'd be left here alone?

29

Again, although she longed to call out Mace's name, Cheyenne held back. Every other woman in here was cowed, the newcomer's back crisscrossed with painful-looking marks. Maybe being caged and silent was better.

"Our timing couldn't be better then," Robert said. "Where is she?"

Almost as one, the men pointed in her direction. Although she desperately wanted not to, she started shaking. Her trembling grew more profound as Robert strode her way. Nothing about hearing the cage door unfasten and then open comforted her. If she could, she'd have slunk away. As it was, she had no choice but to emerge because Robert grabbed her hair and jerked. Pins and needles attacked her legs, forcing her to grit her teeth to keep from moaning.

"Hands behind you," Robert ordered.

If it had been yesterday, she would have told him to go to hell, but back then she'd been dressed, free, and in her own world. Still unable to quiet her trembling, she did as he ordered. Metal bands closed just above her elbows. Obviously Robert had attached something to the bands, because her arms were being forced so close together that they nearly touched. She didn't know what she hated most, the strain in her shoulders or the way her breasts had been thrust forward.

Barely acknowledging her existence, Robert placed a leather collar around her throat and fastened a short lead to the metal ring in front. She didn't care where the restraints had come from, only that she felt even less human than she had in the cage. But she wouldn't cry, damn it! Neither would she beg.

Had Mace been part of this from the beginning? Their sex play had been his way of determining whether she fit into the Blind Spot?

As she and Robert approached him, a stone-faced Mace ran his hands in his back pockets. He'd done that when it was just the two of them, when during one magical night they'd taken turns pulling their dysfunctional childhoods out of closets and shared them. More important, they'd shared their bodies as equals.

"So this is what you meant," Mace said, his comment aimed at Robert, but his emotionless gaze fixed on her. She felt naked and helpless down to her bones. "It's the last thing I expected to see."

"That's understandable." Robert lifted his arm so she was forced onto her toes. "The bitch held out on you, right? What more could a dom want in the way of making her pay for her rebellion?"

This place had been warm enough that even naked she hadn't felt chilled, but with Robert's comment, goose bumps broke out all over her.

"It's what you want," Atwood added. "We understand what makes a man like you tick. Not a bad tradeoff?"

"Why don't you spell out that tradeoff."

In addition to not moving for a long time, Mace could go without blinking almost indefinitely. She couldn't take her eyes off him, but did she want him to touch her? Not if he'd been part of her capture.

"Quite simple," Atwood said, smiling a catlike smile. "There's very shortly going to be a job vacancy in the Blind Spot, one only a very special kind of man can fill. You're that man."

"Go on."

"I intend to. The only concession, although we believe you'll soon agree that the tradeoff is worth it, is that the Blind Spot will become your new home."

"Go on."

"I'm getting there. Bottom line, the world you lived in since birth is behind you. Except when job assignments require you to go there, it's as if Earth never existed. But then, other than the pleasures you participated in at Indulgences and other places, it hasn't been that great for you, has it? Living alone. No parents. Few, if any, friends."

What about Rio, loving him?

Mace shrugged. "I'm the security expert, but you were checking me out."

"We'd be remiss in our duties if we didn't," Robert supplied. "A bit more background. Neither my partner nor I are native to the Blind Spot. Like you, we were recruited. We, how should I say it, changed our nationalities some five years ago. However, unlike you will do, we frequently commute between Earth and here."

"Why?"

"Simple. Earthlings know nothing of the Blind Spot, but the reverse isn't true. To a man here, we concur we must keep our pulse on what transpires on Earth. Being in the communication business serves as the perfect vehicle. Finding you was a plus."

"What about her?" Mace jerked his head at her. "Why is she here?"

With Mace's gaze still on her, Cheyenne was hard put to concentrate on anything else. Even though she remained acutely aware of her nude bondage, she half believed it was just the two of them. At the same time, she knew how dangerous that thinking could be.

"A couple of reasons," Atwood responded. "We believed you'd need an initial inducement to change allegiance from Earth to here, sweetening the pot, so to speak. She fit that role."

"What's the other reason?"

Robert had lowered his arm, but being able to stand flat-footed did little to remind Cheyenne of the freedom she'd always taken for granted. Not long ago, she'd been eager to surrender to Mace, but that had been role-play, a sexual game. Reality was too much to absorb.

"The Blind Spot isn't a democracy," Atwood supplied. "That's a governmental form that doesn't work for us. Much simpler is a dictatorship made up of key senior residents committed to maintaining a highly successful status quo."

The gathered men, who'd all returned to their seats, laughed, but as long as Mace looked at her, she'd look back. If only she could read what, if anything, lay beneath the cool surface. Did the man she'd half believed she was falling in love with exist? If so, where was he?

"Male dictatorship," Atwood went on. "Allowing women to participate in decision making as equals unnecessarily complicates things and is counterproductive. Men are direct. They identify a goal and decide on the simplest and most efficient way of reaching that goal. In contrast, women are distracted and diminished by emotion."

"That's one of Earth's core problems," one of the other men interjected. "They're never going to make the advances we have here as long as emotion is allowed." He pointed at Cheyenne. "Much more rational, and satisfying, is to relegate females to the role of slaves."

Someone else added that the term *slave* encompassed everything from the sex slaves who catered to their masters' every need to those who provided any and all physical tasks the dominant males had no interest in. There were female mechanics, construction workers, farmers, garbage collectors who attended trade schools and lived in segregated housing where yet other females cooked and cleaned for them.

"Who decides which women are assigned what tasks?" Mace asked. How could he ask such a question when she was still trying to absorb what she'd heard?

"That's quite simple to answer," Robert supplied, "especially for you because you spent time in group homes. As soon as children are weaned, they're sent to dormitories separated by sex. The dorms are serviced by child-keeper slaves while certain of our men oversee the upbringing and education that takes place there. Part of the men's duties is to assess the females' suitability for various tasks."

Before she could prepare, Mace grabbed her left nipple. "Let me guess," he said as a film of discomfort and desire enveloped her. "The most attractive females become sex slaves."

Grunting, the heavyset, professor-like man stood. "Right you are. Mace, absorbing the entire concept behind the Blind Spot's success will take time. Unfortunately, further explanation must wait. It's time to move to the judgment room."

"Which is?" Mace asked, not slackening his grip on her.

"Where you will receive the most dramatic demonstration of a key service Blind Spot residents provide for Earthlings. Even your slave will appreciate what's about to happen. If you want to do the honors, you can direct her to where we're going."

Mace released her breast. In the moment that followed, she half believed he would free her. They'd escape together. Instead, he took the lead rope from Robert, slung it over his shoulder, and turned his back to her. Forced to stumble behind him, she contemplated her lack of embarrassment over her nudity. Maybe she was still too shell-shocked to care, but maybe, like the other women here, she was becoming resigned to her fate.

There was another possibility, this one tied into Mace with his powerful, sexy body and her memories of how well hers fit around it.

Don't go there. Not if you want to survive.

30

A silent Cheyenne behind him, Mace paused and took in his surroundings. Everyone, even the other naked women, had gone behind the waterfall. Once there, they'd entered a long, wide, well-lit area he likened to a hall. A number of massive, closed doors led off the *hall*. Despite his desire to explore what lay beyond those doors, he decided not to risk garnering the disapproval of the Blind Spot residents.

Blind Spot? If not for his heart's steady thumping and awareness of Cheyenne's naked body close enough to touch, he would have sworn he was dreaming. Either that or drunk. For someone who insisted on controlling his world, he felt ill-prepared for what he'd been thrust into. At the same time, curiosity kept his head clear. One way or the other, he'd eventually put all the pieces of this puzzle, which included Cheyenne's role in his new reality, together.

Shaking off her impact as best he could, he studied his surroundings. Although the room the entire group had gone into was expensively decorated and furnished, it reminded him of courtrooms he'd been in as a juvenile. Instead of benches for visitors to sit in, there were at least a hundred comfortable chairs arranged in a large semicircle. The majority of the men were already sitting, their slaves kneeling at their sides. Instead of a judge's platform and areas for prosecution and defense attorneys, however, was a solitary chair positioned so whoever was in it faced the audience. Straps were attached to the chair's arms and legs.

At Atwood's and Robert's prompting, he sat between them. Cheyenne stood until Atwood grabbed her collar and forced her to her knees next to Mace. Although her breasts with their hardened nipples were only inches away, he resisted the impulse to touch her. If he ever needed to keep his head about himself, this was the time.

Hoping no one knew of his inner tension, he studied his companions. What held his attention the most was their hands. From what he could tell, they'd all had their nails professionally done. More to the point, if these men had ever done physical labor, it hadn't been for many years. Given the tropical environment they'd just left, shouldn't their exposed skin be tanned? The almost unhealthy pallor told him they didn't spend much time in the sun.

Beyond that, it was obvious they didn't give healthy living much consideration as witness by sagging postures and potbellies under their tailored clothes. If, as he'd been told, they were indeed superior to Earthlings, why didn't they take better care of themselves? A vision of everyone beginning their days by chugging down pills made him shake his head.

Cheyenne shifted position. The here and now was reality, not a dream. Instead of the independent, sexy businesswoman he'd been getting to know, she was now a slave. A sex slave. His if he did whatever it was he'd been brought here to accomplish.

No more need to play according to society's rules. The end to role-playing. Cheyenne would belong to him.

It wouldn't matter what she did or didn't want because he'd

be in charge, he who'd once had to fight to get through each day now had total control over not just another human being, but the one who'd set up residence in his dreams and groin.

Allowing himself a small smile, he ran his fingers into her hair. She looked up at him.

"Guess you won't be telling me you don't want to have anything to do with me after all, will you," he said.

She met him stare for stare. Distracted by her small, helpless body, he nearly missed the sheen in her eyes. Too late for tears.

"It's about time," a man grumbled. "Someone please tell me why we thought Bat could still do the job?"

Mace again pulled his attention off Cheyenne. A muscular man was coming through a side door dragging another man behind him. Naked, the second had on manacles that fastened in front and were attached to leg irons via a thick chain that scraped his flaccid cock. Obviously this was the last place the naked man wanted to be, not that he had any choice in the matter as the larger one forced him over to the chair with the cuffs. Despite his struggles, the stronger man easily secured him via a strap around his neck.

"You're late, Bat," the man who'd just spoken said. "You know what time the trial was supposed to start."

"So sue me. You people think I can be everywhere at once."

Bat folded his arms over a chest Mace had no doubt had gotten that way via uncounted sessions with weights. Studying him, Mace wondered if he'd been brought here to replace Bat.

"That's enough defiance," the speaker continued. "Let's hear your report. What have you observed about the prisoner?"

Cheyenne pressed against Mace, compelling him to look down at her again. Now her eyes were wide and deep, disbelieving and comprehending all at the same time. "That's Carl Schulz," she whispered.

"Who?" he mouthed.

"The wife killer I wrote about. I stared at his picture enough; I have no doubt."

Gone was the hint of tears he'd caught earlier. The mix of understanding and awe confused him until he recalled that Carl Schulz had gone into hiding after brutally killing his ex wife. Everyone believed Schulz had planned his disappearance.

Everyone had been wrong. Schulz was at the Blind Spot, obviously not willingly.

Standing, the man who'd been finding fault with Bat approached Schulz, keeping distance between them. After giving Schulz a look capable of putting him six feet under, the man spoke.

"Mace, I'll bore my companions with what I'm saying, but it's for your benefit. This bastard"—he spat in Schulz's face—"slaughtered his wife in front of her sister. Their children will have to go through life knowing what their father did, hating him."

The man slapped Schulz so hard the prisoner's head snapped back. When, finally, he straightened, Mace saw Schulz had a split lip. Cheyenne, who no longer leaned against him, sucked in a breath.

"Instead of owning up to his crime and taking his punishment like a man, this bastard cleaned out the savings account his son had started for a down payment on a house for his family and moved to Mexico."

The man slapped Schulz again, then a third time when Schulz whimpered. "Shut up, you piece of shit! A piece of advice for you, albeit too late. You should have opted for Earth justice. They're much softer on murderers than we are. There aren't any appeals at the Blind Spot, no years wasted on legal maneuvers."

"What lawyer?" Schulz blubbered. "I didn't get—"

"You got as much consideration as you gave your wife. In

fact, we're giving you something you denied her, a trial. Look around. These gentlemen are judge and jury. You have exactly one minute to try to convince them not to do to you what you did to the woman who gave birth to your children."

Mace didn't need to look at Cheyenne to know they were thinking the same thing: this was eye for an eye, frontier justice.

A sobbing Schulz wasted half of his allotted time trying to compose himself. Finally, he pulled himself together enough to insist that the so-called trial was illegal. Mace thought he might insist on a lawyer or rail against his imprisoners. When he didn't, Mace concluded Schulz had been in custody long enough to know how hopeless things were.

"Enough," the man who seemed to be filling the role of judge interrupted Schulz. "Laws are different at the Blind Spot, and you know it." He turned to the audience. "Have you made up your minds? How do you rule?"

"Guilty," everyone said in unison. Sobbing anew, Schulz sank as deep into his seat as possible. His fingers fluttered helplessly.

"So noted. Now to the punishment phase. Has everyone read the details?"

Several men shook their heads, drawing a disappointed look from the judge. "I realize everyone is busy with other duties, but the Blind Spot prides itself on our proactive approach to Earth failings. Fortunately, our latest slave thoroughly researched the prisoner for her article for *Edge*. Robert, Atwood, do you want to handle this or would you prefer the slave to?"

The two men exchanged looks. Then Robert hauled Cheyenne to her feet. Seeing Robert's hand on her arm tightened Mace's gut and spoke to his cock.

"Do it," Robert ordered Cheyenne. "Tell them everything. Leave out no detail."

Although Cheyenne was now turned from him, he spotted

her clenched fingers. "Before she does," Mace said, "release her arms."

"What?" Robert frowned.

"When and if I accept your offer of employment and residence, she becomes my slave, right?" He made his point by sliding his hand between her legs. Her warmth slipped into him, compelling him to fight down a growl. Yes, the predator lived in him all right. It had begun growing the day he'd heard a juvenile detention door slam behind him. "I don't want damaged merchandise."

Damaged merchandise. Unable to shake off the surreal feeling, Cheyenne locked her legs in place but made no attempt to move away from Mace. His hand rested against her sex, awakening sensations that had no place in her new reality. Just the same, fighting them would accomplish nothing. The Blind Spot surrounded her. Those who lived here were collectively responsible for her nudity and the metal constricting her arms, but that paled next to Mace's presence.

The men who called this place home had investigated Mace and determined he had the necessary skills for fulfilling tasks she couldn't bring herself to think about. Maybe it all came down to their having detected the predator, the dom in him. Although she'd do everything she could regain her freedom, she wouldn't fight Mace. Didn't want to.

Muttering, Robert gripped her arm restraints. A moment later, her arms fell free. They'd soon catch fire; fortunately, they were numb. In telling contrast, her clit burned, and she'd give a great deal, too much, to have Mace slide a finger inside her.

How well he knew her, giving her a taste when she was starving.

"Fine, you happy now?" Robert grumbled. "The ball's in your court, Mace. Get your slave to tell us every disgusting detail."

"Did you hear him?" Mace asked softly, his other hand gliding over her outer thigh and making her stomach knot. "If you were the prosecution, what would you develop your case around?"

Hearing her task described in those terms helped her speak, although maybe the truth was, she needed to forget about herself, and focusing on Carl Schulz might be the only way she could accomplish that.

"His wife's name was Viola," she began. "She was ten years younger than him, a sweet and vivacious woman who adored being a mother. She loved gardening and working at a small plant nursery in the area. Those pursuits helped immensely when it seemed as if her husband disapproved of everything she did. He'd always been controlling, but became even more so once their children left home."

Caught up in her determination to speak for Viola, she started to step toward Schulz only to stop because doing so would take her away from Mace.

"Both children told me they moved out as soon as they could support themselves," she said with Mace's hand dangerously back on her sex and her senses spinning. "They begged their mother to come with them, but she didn't want to be a burden on them."

Schulz's face contorted. If he started crying, she'd slap him herself. In the meantime, she'd continue to take her strength from Mace's presence.

"You already know she'd gone to live with her sister. She'd asked for and received a restraining order, but her sister guessed he followed her home from work. He broke into the house." Already sick knowing what she had to say next, she rubbed her arms. Mace did the same to her right thigh, massaging it until she thought she'd scream.

At length, her voice tight and gaze hard on the white-faced Schulz, she detailed the attack. When Schulz kicked in the flimsy back screen, his former sister-in-law's little dog had attacked him. Schulz had kicked the dog with enough force that it flew across the room and slammed into a wall, killing it. As her sister dialed 911, Viola had tried to escape out front, but he'd overtaken her, knocking her facedown in the entryway and slashing her repeatedly. Police recovered a severed finger. Viola had fought for her life, but she hadn't stood a chance as witnessed by the twenty-two wounds in her back, sides, and front. The fatal cut had been the one to her throat.

"Anything you'd like to dispute?" the "judge" demanded of Schulz. "Something detectives and sister got wrong? Maybe you didn't mean to kill the dog, it just happened to be in the wrong place?"

"Yes!" Schulz fairly screamed. "That's it. And my stabbing Viola, I had to defend myself."

Any other time Cheyenne would have thrown the god-awful lie back in Schulz's face, but her place in the world had changed. She might be punished for saying more than necessary.

"Is that so?" The "judge" leaned close. "Care to show us your scars? Oh wait, that isn't necessary because we can see your body. Your unmarked body." Looking as if he'd come face-to-face with a mound of crap, the "judge" straightened and faced the assembled men. His gaze skimmed over her, but she couldn't give him her attention because Mace's hand had returned to the heated valley between her legs. How she wanted to believe the gesture was his private way of reassuring her, but she didn't dare.

"Gentlemen, we've been through this phase numerous times in the past, so I don't need to spell out the details," the "judge" continued. "You have two options to consider. One, the condemned will be put to death in a manner consistent with what he would face on Earth. Two, his punishment will be a duplicate of what he subjected his victim to."

Fighting Mace's impact on her nearly shattered body, she concentrated on what she'd just heard and her role in the proclamation. She'd told the "jury" that Viola had been stabbed twenty-two times.

"Option number two," the men said as one. Hearing that, she gasped, but the sound was buried under Schulz's inhuman scream. Grabbing her hand, Mace pulled her back down on her knees. She couldn't guess whether he was concerned she'd faint or was exerting his command over her.

"Silence!" the "judge" ordered a sobbing Schulz. "Listen to me, you bastard. You forfeited your right to live when you took your wife's life. Punishment will be carried out tomorrow. Tonight"—he smiled—"is for contemplation, perhaps praying to whatever God you do or don't believe in, or losing bowel control. There'll be no last meal. We don't believe in wasting good food on someone who won't be around long enough to digest it. Take him away," he ordered Bat. "And once he's in his cage, I want you to join several of us in my chambers."

In turmoil, Cheyenne put her hands over her face and lowered her head, stopping when the collar pressed against the underside of her chin.

"Hold your head high," Mace commanded, grabbing her hair. "I don't ever want to see that hangdog look on you."

"But he's going to be stab—"

A jerk on her hair accompanied by a light slap to the side of her face silenced her. "You heard the sentence. Accept it just as you must accept that you're my slave."

31

The so-called judge's chambers put Cheyenne in mind of several of her college professors' offices, except that this room was much larger and thus not cramped. It, too, had floor-to-ceiling bookshelves filled with legal texts. An oblong cherry desk stood in the middle, and a half-dozen high-backed black leather chairs had been placed around it. Music that reminded her of a funeral dirge came from unseen speakers.

While Robert, the judge, and Mace took their seats, Atwood commanded her to stand in a corner opposite the closed door. There were no windows in the room. Between that, the hundreds of leather-bound books, depressing music, and dark paneling, she wondered if a cave could be any worse. Even if she managed to make it through the door, where would she run to? Doubtless, she'd be recaptured and punished. A wave of light-headedness forced her to lean against the wall.

This was no dream.

"Bat will join us shortly," the judge told Mace, who'd positioned himself so she couldn't see his features. "In the meantime, we want to bring you up to speed. First, any questions?"

Mace's laugh lacked warmth, and yet she let it into her. Her thigh and sex remembered his touch. "I hardly know where to begin," Mace said, leaning forward and placing his elbows on the desk. "My understanding is that I've been selected to fulfill a specific task here. Based on what I've been doing on Earth and what appears to be your dissatisfaction with Bat, am I right to assume I'll be taking over for him—if I agree?"

"Oh," Robert said, "you'll agree. You've barely scratched the surface of what the Blind Spot has to offer. We brought you first to the lagoon because it's a favorite."

"With the men perhaps," Mace said, and handed her a glance that didn't last long enough. "But do the women agree?"

"They're slaves. Who cares what they think?"

"Look at it this way, Mace," the judge broke in. "It's male instinct to dominate. Look at nature. With few exceptions, the males of the species are the leaders. They're aggressive, larger, stronger. Unfortunately, Earth's humans have been corrupted in large part because of female emotion. That unfortunate component has watered down civilization. Instead of pure power, which is necessary for ultimate survival, Earthlings have been weakened by democracy."

An unexpected sound turned her toward the front door. Bat, his eyes lighting on each of the four men in turn, entered.

"The sniveling coward's back in his cell," Bat announced. "One second he's sobbing like a spoiled brat, the next he curses. I might gag him later. For now, however, he needs to listen to the sound of his voice while knowing no one cares."

Images of Schulz shackled in his cell while waiting to be executed made her shudder. No one had commanded her not to try to cover herself, but it was too late for modesty. Besides, her arms felt so heavy she wasn't sure she could lift them.

"Sit down, Bat," the judge ordered. "This won't take long."

"Fine." Bat pulled back the nearest chair and dropped into

it. "I can make it even shorter. You're not happy with my recent job performance. Hell, no one is. I could apologize, but it wouldn't be sincere."

"Why is that?" Robert's question left Cheyenne with a vivid impression of how much power he and Atwood wielded here.

"I'm burned out. Tired. The rewards aren't part of the problem; I couldn't ask for more." He winked at Mace. "Give yourself a few days on the job; you'll see what I'm talking about."

Bat faced the judge. "He's my replacement, right? Recruited and brought here without anyone bothering to inform me."

"Your knowing wouldn't have made any difference," the judge said. "Our minds are made up."

"I'm certain they are." Bat turned his attention to her, eyebrows lifting in what she took to be approval. "What's this, two for the price of one? You figured your new jailer would be more likely to accept the offer if he's allowed to keep his sex slave?"

"I'm not—" Cheyenne started.

"Shut up," Atwood barked. "Another word out of you and you'll be gagged."

"You hear that?" Bat addressed Mace, who so far had been a silent observer. "See how easy it is to dominate a slave here. Like you, I came from Earth, where my desires and inclinations were severely curtailed by the laws there. It's way different here. You'll love it."

"That's for me to decide," Mace said. Hearing his voice caused her cunt to heat. Juice leaked from her.

"Won't take long." As Cheyenne tried to concentrate, Bat described the opulent apartment he lived in. Whatever he wanted in the way of food or entertainment was granted him. A just-released movie, no problem. Front row seat to a concert, done. An endless succession of sex slaves delivered to his door, done and done.

"It's been a great gig in that respect," Bat explained. "And working with recalcitrant slaves has its rewards, but there's a downside." He said the last looking at the judge.

"Tell me about the downside," Mace said.

"Having everything I do scrutinized and criticized. Think about working for hundreds of bosses, each with their personal opinion about how things should be done."

Try as she did, Cheyenne couldn't keep her mind on the rest of the conversation. She caught enough to realize that the judge, Robert, and Atwood didn't agree with Bat's assessment, saying that if Bat were competent, there'd be no need for scrutiny. All that truly mattered to her was that Mace was being offered the job of overseeing slave training and responsibility for criminals brought to the Blind Spot from Earth. In exchange for the opportunity that he was well-qualified for, he'd live rent free in a fine apartment and never have to pay a restaurant bill.

In addition, she'd become his personal sex slave.

"That's not all," Atwood added, giving her a demeaning look. "You're free to bring home any and all slaves you want to, and for them to remain as long as they amuse you."

"Yeah." Bat smiled the first real smile she'd seen on him. "That doesn't get old." He jabbed a finger in her direction. "Get tired of her and you can swap her out for the new. Believe me, that'll happen. Variety's the name of the game here."

"You never became attached to one slave?"

"Hell no. They're damn interchangeable once the spark's out of them."

Mace, don't let that happen to me!

"What about him?" Mace asked the judge, indicating Bat. If he knew what she was thinking, he gave no indication.

The judge shrugged. "He retires. Yes, he'll have to move to lesser surroundings, but the retirement package includes a steady stream of female entertainment, just not in the same abundance as before."

"Try getting that kind of severance pay on Earth," Bat said. "I ain't complaining, not that it would do any good. Pretty clear this is no democracy. By the way, when you get tired of her"—he grinned at Cheyenne—"I'll teach her a few tricks of the trade."

"So"—the judge leaned toward Mace—"this brings us to the final part of this interview. We require a demonstration of your domination skills. A public one."

"When?" Mace asked.

"No time like the present."

32

Back in the grotto area, Cheyenne stood with her legs nearly a foot apart and her hands bound behind her. Although she still had on the collar, Bat had removed her leash before commanding her to follow him out of the judge's chambers. His explanation had been that he wanted to see how submissive she was. If not for the warning look from Mace, she would have bolted.

Patio chairs at one end of the pond were filled with men, but whether these were the same she'd seen earlier didn't matter. Expressionless women serviced them, only occasionally looking at her. When Bat turned her over to him, Mace had positioned her in front of the pond so she was forced to face the audience. Then he'd taken a rope from Bat's belt, but instead of immediately restraining her, he'd run his hands over her arms and then down her sides until she squirmed.

"Hold still!" He'd punctuated his command by slapping her buttocks.

Although he went back to caressing her sides, she'd forced herself not to move. Only then did he cross her wrists one over the other and tie them in place. That done, he turned his attention to her belly and hips, his fingers gentle and possessive at the same time. Unable to fill her lungs with enough air, she rocked from side to side, nearly oblivious to male laughter.

"There's more than one way of gaining control over a woman." Mace sounded as if he was delivering a lecture. "I'm an advocate of mixed messages when it comes to breaking down a submissive's barriers. Mixing the good with the bad keeps her off balance."

Turning her so her back was to the men, he ran his knuckles down her spine. He did so slowly, pressing firmly and then barely touching her by turn. When he reached the small of her back, he planted a hand over her belly to keep her in place. Gone were his knuckles, replaced by nails laying light furrows over the tops of her buttocks.

No matter how she fought to remain silent, moan after moan broke free. Spreading her legs even, she begged with her body. The moment she did, she acknowledged that she'd demeaned herself. The hand over her belly remained resolutely in place while the other left first horizontal and then vertical tracks on her ass.

"My God, my God," she cried, trying to pull away. "Mace, please."

She'd barely gotten the words out when he slapped her buttock with such force she nearly fell.

"What's my name?" He spanked her again.

"Master. Master!"

"That's the last time you'll ever make that mistake, understand," he ordered with his mouth against her ear. "To make sure you learn your lesson—Bat, if I may, a flogger please."

This wasn't happening! Once again she couldn't believe her life had turned into this. And yet it had.

Lifting her bound arms, Mace forced her to lean forward. Shamefully aware of how much of her sex showed, she longed to close her legs, but she'd lose her balance if she did.

"She's interesting." Mace continued his educational tone. "A true submissive. I've worked with enough women to know when I have the real deal." Still holding on to her arms, he slid the flogger along an inner thigh. An involuntary shudder raced through her. If she dropped to her knees and rubbed her cheek against his cock, would he let her out of her *misery?*

"There, did you see that?" The flogger slid over her other thigh. "Most women in this position would be too aware of their surroundings to respond fully, but she's a prisoner of her body's instinct."

"Is there a point to this?" Cheyenne recognized Atwood's voice. "So far all I see is the bitch getting turned on."

"That's exactly the point. It's honey and vinegar technology." The strands continued their sensual journey over her thighs, making her rise onto her toes while trying to dig them into the ground. Nothing helped. She still ached. Longed.

"My belief," Mace continued, "is that all women have the potential to become slaves to their carnal needs. It takes the approach I'm demonstrating. Over time, frequent and prolonged sexual stimulation reprograms their bodies. They'll do whatever they're ordered to, endure every discomfort their master or masters deem appropriate. That's not to say they like what's happening to them, quite the contrary. But their pussies don't care."

The flogger was gone. Tense, she tried to look back at him only to sigh and sag as his fingers brushed her labia. His touch was light, promise and potential. Too few seconds later he stopped, and she ground her teeth together to keep from begging.

After what felt like forever, he caressed her again, the pressure stronger than the first time and reaching deeper. Her knees buckled, and she stumbled about in her effort to regain her balance. Throughout her struggle, Mace stayed with her, holding on to her arms while his fingers continued to kiss the heart and soul of her pleasure.

"Granted, your view of the slave's sex could be clearer," he went on, "but there's no way you didn't notice what just happened. Whether she likes it or not, she craves this attention, don't you, slave?"

"Yes, Master."

"But my pleasuring your sex isn't enough, is it? You want more."

Don't do this to me! "Yes, Master."

"To further the demonstration, I need to make an adjustment." Lifting up on her arms, Mace forced her so far forward she now looked at her hanging labia and his dark, invading hand. If she could, she'd lick his knuckles in gratitude and surrender. "Now I'm increasing her sense of helplessness by ratcheting up the *insult* on her sexual organs. Done properly, this technique so disorients a slave that she loses touch with who she is or, should I say, used to be."

Hating Mace's words, and maybe him as well, she struggled to keep her legs under her as he backed her closer to the audience. When he had her where he wanted, he released some of the tension on her arms so her shoulders no longer felt as if they might snap. However, he refused to let her straighten.

"I realize I'm preaching to the choir." He chuckled. "Because I gather all of you are experienced in proper slave treatment. But if my assessment of operations at the Blind Spot is correct, I will soon be fully responsible for all training aspects. Much as a dog trainer shows the pet's actual owner how to work with the animal, Bat instructed you in certain techniques, correct?"

Although she heard mutters of agreement, only two things mattered. First, Mace stood so close that his leg pressed against hers in a blatant message of power. Second, even though the finger now on her clit wasn't moving, the wild thing raging through her remained at full force.

"I've only begun work on this subject," he continued, "so I would be remiss if I turned her over to anyone now. That said, I want to demonstrate the progress I've made. If you see the potential in her and agree that I have the necessary skills to bring out the best in a slave, I'd be honored to accept the position."

"So demonstrate already," someone grumbled. "Talk's cheap."

"True." Mace rubbed her clit, then abandoned it. "Bat," she barely heard him say, "if I may, I'd like to borrow your nipple clamps."

Nipple clamps!

To her surprise, instead of torturing her breasts as soon as Bat complied with his request, Mace ran a finger into the crack between her ass cheeks until he reached her puckered opening. His finger, well-lubricated thanks to the juices she had no control over, glided like silk over her bun hole. Her anal muscles tightened repeatedly; reality again faded. The faint sound of the waterfall quieted her nerves, making it possible for her to ignore the strain in her shoulders and the men who might one day claim her.

Mace's strokes on that most personal of places warmed and soothed even as he moved closer and closer to her pussy. She gave up trying to keep her mouth closed. Her breath hissed in time with his gliding caresses, and her hips rocked without her knowing how that was happening.

Being drunk had felt like this. When buzzed, she felt as if she was floating. Everything was right then, with the world painted in pastels even as her awareness of her sexuality grew. After a glass of wine, she wanted a man, simple as that. Inhibitions were relaxed, so why not do what felt good?

This moment was good, all floating warmth and trust. She

was a fool for trusting Mace, but that mattered little. He'd taken over her body and was laying claim to everything.

"When things are done right," Mace was saying, "a kind of hypnosis takes place. Pain and pleasure mesh into one. As example..."

The hand she was falling in love with pressed more firmly against her rear entrance, a finger pushing past the tight muscles. He'd released her wrists, but until he gave her permission to stand upright—

A sharp burning sensation ripped her attention from her ass to her right breast. Gasping, she tried to turn away only to be pulled back in place via the clamp gripping her nipple. Despite her resolve, she cried out when he closed another clamp around her left nipple. A chain dangled between her breasts.

"Take it," Mace said so softly she doubted anyone else heard. "Show them what you're made of."

Staring at the chain made what he'd just done even more real. The slender links appeared to be made of gold, same as the clamps. Hadn't she read that gold was a relatively soft metal? Not soft enough.

But Mace, her master, had ordered—or was it encouraged— her to accept the discomfort. If nothing else, she'd do that.

She gasped again when he took hold of the chain and lifted it, but praying this was what he wanted, she straightened. As the blood flowed back into her body, she silently thanked Mace for positioning her so her back was still to the men. Using the chain to guide her, he turned her around. Her gaze lit on Atwood and Robert, whose grins put her in mind of cats staring at a cornered mouse. Had everything they'd said about admiring her writing been lies?

Taking note of the naked blonde on her knees between her bosses, the last of her former life slipped away. The blonde had unzipped the men's pants and held an erect cock in each hand.

"How much input will I have in the equipment I'll be

using?" Mace asked, seemingly oblivious to what the kneeling slave was doing.

"You'll have a budget." Atwood sounded slightly out of breath. "But it's generous. Why?"

Mace's hold on the chain had been so light she'd nearly dismissed it. Now he shook the chain, causing her to suck in her stomach.

"Because I'm interested in refining this little toy, making it more substantial for starters. For now, however, I believe I can make do."

Several men nodded encouragement. Mace's essence seemed to be reaching her through the chain, either that or her apprehension was responsible.

Lifting the chain again, Mace brought it to her mouth. "Take and hold it," he ordered. "So far you've had all the fun. Now it's my turn."

Closing her teeth around the links drew her breasts up, but as long as she kept her head down, the strain was manageable. She doubted that would continue.

"Head up," he commanded. "Let's show some pride, slave."

Despite the need to beg him to take pity on her, she remembered what he'd said about demonstrating what she was made of. She'd never again work for *Edge*, but her former employers would remember her courage. Even more vital, she'd prove herself to Mace somehow.

As she lifted her head, her vision blurred. The pull on her nipples hurt. Hot tension radiated out from them and into her belly. The burning reached her pussy, compelling her to press her legs together.

"There it is," Mace announced, "the conduit between pleasure and pain." He kicked the flogger he must have dropped when she wasn't paying attention, sending it sliding toward the audience. "I don't need that after all, at least not now. That's because I've already primed her pump with a little flogger teasing, then with the clamps. Legs open, slave. Push your hips forward."

Mindless, she obeyed. No thoughts reached her mind when he grasped her labial lips and lightly rolled them about. Her muscles were being reamed out and left vacant.

"Head straight. No matter what I do, you are to keep the pose. Otherwise, you'll be punished."

Carefully motionless, she tried to spot him out of the corners of her eyes, but what did connecting with him matter? Mace was touching her in the only part of her body she cared about.

Thanks to the fluids flowing from her, his fingers roamed freely. She repeatedly struggled to control her breathing, only to suck desperately for air every time a rough finger pad traveled the length of her sex. She rose onto her toes, giving him easy access to her anus. Pressure there deliciously knotted her belly. His finger pressed against her rear opening until it took everything she had not to beg him to fill her there.

Long after she'd gone mad, he abruptly withdrew. A second later, his hands were on her flanks, nails doubtlessly leaving white furrows as he teasingly raked them.

"I've always wanted to do something," he said. "Unfortunately, Earth's liberated women would have me arrested. Here, however, that won't be a concern, will it, gentlemen?"

Mutters of agreement penetrated her pleasure/pain fog, but with his fingers working her flanks, she was hard put to recall what he'd just asked.

"As for the specifics of the something," he continued, "I intend to pierce a large number of nipples, maybe every slave's, and place rings in the holes, starting with this one."

Switching his attack, he scratched her belly. Light-headed, she shivered. "Once the body modification has been applied, controlling a slave will be a simple matter. No more need to concern ourselves with how long blood flow to a breast can be compromised."

All ten fingers now marched over her ribs, moving closer and closer to her captured breasts. Her mind swam, then sank. "I'm all for simplifying work here," Mace continued, "streamlining the process so the focus is on pleasure for all of us, the men that is."

Did any part of her not feel on the brink of exploding? The erotic scratching had driven her crazy. The heels of his hands pressed against her ribs.

"Looks like she's getting her kicks." Bat sounded irritated. "Hell, I thought you were going to whip her. I was looking forward to seeing that."

"I'm sure you were, but I believe I've clarified my intention." Mace kneaded her breasts, making her cry out. "You do your training your way. Me, I'm committed to making sure a slave isn't overloaded with pain. Otherwise, she winds up like the broken creatures you've created."

"Whatever," Bat spluttered. "We'll see how well this damn stupid so-called technique of yours works."

"Oh, it does. As I'm about to demonstrate."

Despite everything her breasts were being subjected to, Cheyenne struggled to regain control over her responses. She wasn't sure why she'd gasped when he massaged her breasts when there'd been no pain.

Her jaw had started to ache, but Mace hadn't given her permission to release the chain. While applying the clamps, he'd stood so close she wasn't certain where he left off and she began. It wouldn't be this way if she was free, if he hadn't made it clear he controlled her.

Would it?

She hated his hands—and loved them. Feared his strength as

much as she worshipped it. She wanted her mind and body back, yet didn't.

"I've been handcuffed," Mace said from behind her—how had he gotten there without her knowing? "Hated it." He massaged her shoulders with fingers that effortlessly found every strained muscle. "But my circumstance was different. Damn different."

Running his arms around her waist from behind, he drew her against him. Even with his clothes between them, his insistent erection ignited her.

"Feels damn good," he announced, repeatedly thrusting his cock at her. "But not quite good enough, and I'm a man who gets what he wants."

Backing away a few inches, he again took hold of her bound wrists and lifted them, forcing her to lean forward. She opened her mouth, releasing the chain. The links dropped, pulling on her breasts and forcing a moan past her lips.

If he heard, or cared, Mace gave no indication. A telltale sound told her he'd unfastened his zipper. Starved for him, she spread her legs as wide as she could, stood on her toes, and thrust her buttocks back at him.

"Take notice," Mace announced with his cock gliding over her sex. "No objection on her part, no holding back because she's ready. Primed. I not so humbly take credit."

Eyes closed and pussy dripping, Cheyenne wondered at his ability to bring their bodies together. He had to deeply bend his knees, but with his hands gripping her hips, she wouldn't fall. In this one thing she could trust him.

He was taking her from behind, doggy style, her hair over her eyes and head low, useless hands now against her back, the nipple chain swaying.

On a sigh, she let him in. Welcomed him fully and without reservation. He entered rough and fast, power barely controlled. Pure male, he was at his sexual peak. He'd denied himself while teasing and priming her, but obviously that was behind him.

Strange hands clamped onto her shoulders, bringing her out of herself long enough to realize that Bat had anchored her in place. Grateful for his support, she braced her legs and readied herself for Mace's thrusts.

His urgent strength caught and surrounded her. Standing in the middle of the waterfall would feel like this. The sound of rushing water was missing, but his quick, deep breaths completed her. Big and hard, his cock burned every inch of her channel. His balls slapped her. Heat circled her breasts; her nipples throbbed. Her pussy pulsed.

"Shit, shit," she gasped. Before she could draw breath to continue, Mace dug his fingertips into her, warning her to remain silent.

She was caught between the two men, Mace fucking her and Bat standing between her and the others. She was being used, her pussy anyway. Undoubtedly that was the fate of all Blind Spot slaves; whatever pleasure they might get from sex was unintended.

What about now? Had Mace considered her pleasure in the moments leading up to this?

His cock dove deeper, stayed longer. Then he pulled back, searing her. Her cheeks, throat, even her ribs burned. Mouth open, she held herself ready for his next thrust, but it came so fast and strong it caught her unprepared. The top of her head collided with Bat.

Looking down, she stared at the chain. Loving the pull on her breasts, she forgot everything else. She was a slave; Mace had made her his. Her lot was to wear whatever he placed on her, to submit to have her nipples pierced if that's what he wished.

Right now he was fucking her.

Finding his pace, she lost her thoughts.

"Jesus fuck!" Mace cried. "Ah, hell, fuck."

He strained against her, his cum washing her. She welcomed the heat with spasms that gripped her entire body. Panting, she dove into her own climax. Even with her eyes open, she didn't see Bat and no longer felt his grip. A hot, wild waterfall rushed over her, and she screamed.

Mace remained fastened to her, his cock twitching and body trembling. Hands that could be rough and kind by turns glided over her sides. His breathing was ragged.

"You fucking done? Damn it, Mace, this is getting boring."

Atwood's voice penetrated her mind by degrees, cold slowly replacing the glorious heat. She became aware of the strain in her body, particularly the pulling in her breasts, and Mace's sweaty body wrapped around and in hers. Then his cock slipped away and along with it her insane and dangerous fantasy that things were right and good between them.

33

Marks colored Cheyenne's nipples, but other than that, her wildly tangled hair, and the blotches on her cheeks and throat, she looked much as she had the first time he'd seen her—except for being naked. If it wasn't for the chance of damaging her nipples, Mace would love to see the clamps back in place. As for the collar he'd ordered removed, that, too, had enhanced her appearance. However, as he'd just explained, the collar hadn't been his idea. From now on everything she did or didn't wear was his decision.

At the moment, he, Robert, Atwood, the man who'd represented himself as judge during Carl Schulz's sham of a trial, Bat, and Cheyenne were the only people still at the grotto. The others had left for dinner, or rather he assumed the men would eat. He didn't know about the women.

Except for Cheyenne, every member of the small group was sitting to the right of the grotto and so close to the waterfall that an occasional spray reached them. Still feeling the effects of a climax that had rattled his teeth, he appreciated the cool drops.

The others, undoubtedly familiar with getting damp here, ignored it.

As for Cheyenne, she stood to his side, her fingers laced together and hands low on her belly. She seemed oblivious to her surroundings, and her eyes were glazed and mouth slack. Much as he wanted to take credit, he suspected the truth was she couldn't comprehend the turn her life had taken.

Damn but she was exquisite, the perfect sex slave with her soft yet strong thighs, neatly rounded belly, and full, receptive breasts. A man, him at least, could lose himself in that lush body. What made her even more appealing was the way she responded to being handled like his possession.

Maybe she was a natural, maybe not. Whatever the truth didn't matter because circumstances had made her his. He could and would do everything he wanted to her, and she'd grovel before him in gratitude or at least acceptance. As long as she was his, he'd see himself as a dom—one with his own living, breathing sex object.

If anyone asked, he'd tell them life couldn't get any better.

"We're hungry, Mace," the judge grumbled, "so let's get to this. I for one was impressed with your performance." He gave Cheyenne a dismissive glance. "Your little puppet did everything right. Your lecture was tiresome, but I understand your determination to make your point. If you have another point to gnaw over, which I assume you do, get to it. Now."

Cheyenne seemed to draw into herself as the judge spoke. He frowned at her, then turned his attention back to his audience.

"It's quite simple, a matter of timing. I'm eager to begin my new duties. In truth, thinking about the latitude I'll have to do what I've only been able to imagine is a hell of a turn-on. However, before I can assume those duties, there are some loose ends I must tie up on Earth."

"What?" Robert grumbled. "We'll take care of everything at *Edge,* explain away both your and her absence. We're disappointed in you two, taking off together like that, stealing from the company. Not only did you make off with expensive security equipment, she took her laptop containing sensitive material and interview notes for several hard-hitting political pieces. Obviously the two of you plan to profit from our loss, but until you surface, we can't prosecute."

Robert and Atwood exchanged superior grins, then Atwood spoke. "Time will pass, people forget. Concerned with our image, we'll decide not to take our suspicions to law enforcement. They won't get involved. You have no family and her parents will disown her once we speak to them. A year or so and it'll be as if you never existed on Earth."

Mace had to hand it to the two, they knew their business. If he bought into the party line, it would be as if he'd never existed on Earth. He had a place here, a job he'd love.

"I applaud your planning. I'm certain what I just heard is the overview. I hope to eventually learn the details of our disappearances. What about my house and her condo?"

Atwood shrugged. "So many places are going into foreclosure these days. You know how it is, people can't pay the mortgage or have defrauded those they work for. They pack up in the middle of the night and slip away. The banks step in, everything takes a long time, but eventually new owners move in."

Mace leaned forward. "What about Rio?"

"Who?"

"My dog."

"That damn ugly pit bull," Robert muttered. "I saw that picture you have of him. Get real, Mace. The humane society won't want him, he's unadoptable. People take one look at those fighting scars and they run the other way."

"Exactly." Although his legs were still post-fuck weak, Mace stood and walked over to the edge of the pond. He'd never seen such beautiful fish or pristine water. He'd always wanted to take up fishing. Maybe the Blind Spot included rivers filled with salmon and trout and expert guides, free of course. "I'm the only one who wants him."

"Are you thinking what I believe you are?" the judge asked. "If so, stop right now. That dog isn't welcome here."

"Why not?"

"You'll understand once you meet the members of the kennel club. All Blind Spot dogs are bred along champion bloodlines. They're magnificent. A scarred former fighting dog—believe me, he'd be ordered destroyed."

"No." Mace breathed the word.

"Yes, indeed. Actually, I'm speaking hypothetically because he wouldn't be allowed in in the first place."

"Then—"

"Bat," the judge interrupted, "tomorrow morning you are to go to Mace's place and dispose of the mutt."

"No." Mace kept his voice low and didn't look at Cheyenne. Just the same, he sensed her tension. "I have to do it."

"What's wrong?" Bat demanded. "Don't think I can slit some damn mutt's throat?"

"You won't be able to get close enough for that. He'll rip out your throat first."

First disbelief and then acceptance transformed Bat's features. Based on the way they leaned forward, the others were interested in the outcome.

"Then I'll shoot him," Bat said.

"Maybe you'll get a bullet in the right place before he takes you down, but hitting a moving target isn't easy. Another thing, I have a couple of neighbors. They'll hear."

Shaking his head, Bat settled back in his seat. Mace noted how weary his eyes looked, how deep the lines around them.

"Look." Mace stepped toward Bat, then stopped. Out of the corner of his eye he caught Cheyenne's horrified expression.

"I've had the hell investigated out of me by whomever does those things here. It's no secret I grew up being passed around. The shrinks are right when they say a person can't love if they haven't experienced it as a child, can't commit when it's never happened to them. That dog bonded to me, I don't know why, maybe because he saw some of himself in me."

"And you bonded to him."

Ignoring Bat, Mace split his attention among the other men. "Bond? Me? You want the truth? Coming home to that ugly, dangerous beast meant not having to sweat break-ins. It also meant having to go home every night instead of spending it in some broad's bed, hair all over the damn place, accidents on the carpet, insane barking at nothing, vet bills, and lugging in dog food only to have him reject most of it."

"Your point is?" the judge asked.

"Point is, there's only one thing to do and I'm the only one who can do it, tomorrow."

"Not by yourself," the judge insisted. "Bat, you're going with him, make sure it happens."

"Hell," Bat muttered.

"Fine. Whatever," Mace muttered back. For the first time since the discussion had begun, he faced Cheyenne. The color had drained from her face, and she looked sick. So that's what hate looked like coming from her. "And she's tagging along."

"What?" Atwood vigorously shook his head. "Hell no, she belongs here."

"I couldn't agree more. But making her watch the mutt bleed out will leave her with no doubt of what her owner's capable of."

34

Not long ago, seeing Mace's house would have jump-started her libido, but now Cheyenne would give anything not to be here. However, being locked in the backseat of a car with Mace and Bat in front left her with no choice.

Dreading what was coming, she glanced down at her bound hands, but the sense of helplessness was more than she could handle, prompting her to again stare at the back of Mace's head. Who was this man? Certainly not who she'd once believed he was.

At least she hadn't had to spend the night in his presence. Bat had locked her in a cell with a single bed, toilet, and sink. He'd even given her a blanket. The light had gone out as soon as he'd locked the door behind him, leaving her with a vague impression of an area consisting of a double row of cells separated by a corridor that resembled the jails and prisons she'd seen on TV. She'd heard both male and female voices, but other than giving her name when she was asked, she'd said nothing. From the overheard conversations, she gathered this was where anyone who ran afoul of Blind Spot standards was imprisoned.

Bat came for her at dawn. He'd directed her to go into a community shower, and although two men and a collared women were already in there, she'd been so grateful for the chance to clean up, she'd barely noticed them. Next had come a rough towel followed by a gray, shapeless, sleeveless dresslike garment that came to her knees. Bat had taken her back to her cell where she'd found a bowl of semiwarm oatmeal on her bed, which she'd gulped down. Shortly after, Bat had returned, tied her hands, and led her outside the Blind Spot.

Mace was waiting near the vehicle. He hadn't acknowledged her, thank goodness, because there was nothing she wanted to say to him.

Kill Rio. How heartless could he be?

"Not bad," Bat said, parking close to Mace's front door. "One thing you're going to have to get used to at the Blind Spot is lack of privacy. The powers that be are Big Brother." Bat glanced back at her. "But there's the trade-off."

"Hmm," Mace muttered. "I left him out back when Robert and Atwood gave me my marching orders. Otherwise, there'd be crap and piss all over the place."

"I don't hear anything," Bat said. "Shouldn't he be barking?"

Mace shook his head. "He doesn't recognize the sound of this car so he's waiting to see what's going to happen."

"No wonder you don't trust him."

But Mace did trust Rio just as the dog trusted the one human to show him kindness and love. Staring at Mace's shoulders, she struggled to reconcile what was about to happen with the relationship she'd observed between man and animal.

"How's this going to go down?" Bat sounded unsure.

"I owe Rio one thing, a quick, painless death."

"How humane of you!" Cheyenne snapped. "I'm sure you won't look into his eyes. I wish to hell you had to so you'd have to live with that the rest of your life."

"Shut up," Mace ordered. "You're so dead set to see his expression, I'll make sure you aren't disappointed."

That said, he got out, opened her door, unfastened her seat belt, and grabbed her arm. Praying for numbness, she got out without waiting for him to haul her. Instead of stepping back and making room for her, he remained close so she had no choice but to press her body to his side. He ran a hand down her back, ending with pressing his knuckles against her spine. Just like that she wanted him.

Hated both of them.

"What are you doing?" she muttered, unable to move.

"Getting your attention," he whispered back and spread his fingers over her left ass cheek.

He'd done that all right, but why? Didn't he know how much she loathed him?

"We're going together," Bat said as he joined them. His gaze lit on what Mace was doing, but he didn't say anything. Reaching behind him, he pulled a pistol out of his waistband in back. "Mace, I don't trust you."

"You'd be a fool if you did."

Bat frowned, then nodded and held up his pistol. "I've shown you mine. Time for you to do the same."

Mace's hand had been on her hip during the exchange. Now he pushed her away and repeated what Bat had just done. The two weapons were nearly twins of each other.

"You've known I was armed all along," Mace said. "What about the others?"

"Same with them. Let's call it part of the test they put you through. They figured that if you weren't willing to come on board, you'd have started shooting."

"Doesn't sound like the smartest decision they could make."

Bat chuckled. His expression left no doubt of his awareness of the scant inches between her and Mace. "That's what I told them. They figured they had the bases covered when they told me to aim for your gut the moment you made a move I didn't like."

"Interesting."

"Not, in my opinion, nearly as interesting as what I'm seeing right now." Bat nodded at Mace, then at her, finally back at Mace again. "Not the kind of relationship I've ever seen at the Blind Spot. You want to explain?"

Both pistols hung at the men's sides. She might be wrong but thought she sensed mutual respect between them. Instead of the revulsion she'd felt when Mace first touched her, her body started to warm. The things they'd both admitted the night they'd spent together ran through her. Mace had grown up a stranger to love. What did that make him now? What needs remained unfulfilled?

"Explain Cheyenne's and my relationship," Mace said. "I don't think I have to."

"Fuck. Whatever. Look, let's get this over with."

Saying nothing, Mace stepped away from her and started around the side of his house. She could run. Even barefoot, she might make it to a neighbor before Mace or Bat brought her down.

No, she couldn't.

Shaking, she followed Mace with Bat by her side. She went numb as Mace unlashed the gate leading to Rio's domain. Whatever was going to happen had been set in motion, and she was part of it.

"Nice," Bat said as he reached the backyard. He now held the gun with both hands, a man ready for a four-legged ambush. "Hell of a lot of room back here. Where's the—"

Rio stepped out of the shadows. He seemed to grin as he acknowledged first Mace and then her, but his hackles rose when he settled his gaze on Bat. "He isn't going to attack unless I tell him to," Mace said.

"I see." Bat didn't move. Cheyenne had to give him credit for not acting scared, but maybe he believed his gun evened the score. "You've got knives in your kitchen, right? Get one. Let's get this over with."

"No."

At the single word from Mace, her world tipped. Instead of loping over to Mace for a greeting, Rio didn't move. The instinct for survival screamed at her to watch Bat's every move. Instead, she studied the silent interplay between Mace and his dog. They loved each other; she'd never again doubt that.

"So you were lying, weren't you?" Bat said. He aimed his weapon at her. Despite what the pistol was capable of, it didn't seem real to her. "I thought about telling the others I didn't believe you."

"Why didn't you?" Mace's gun remained at his side.

"Lots of reasons."

Mace acknowledged Bat's pistol with a nod. "I need to know what they are."

"Yeah, I guess you do. She means as much to you as the mutt does, doesn't she?"

"You tell me. And for the record, I know you aren't going to fire that thing."

Sighing, Bat lowered the pistol so it dangled from his fingers. "You read me as well as I do you, maybe better."

"You tell me." Still looking at Bat, Mace walked over to her and began untying her hands. "Here's my thinking. You're so burned out, you really don't care how today plays out."

"Not burned out." Bat extended the back of his free hand toward Rio. The pit took a step toward him. "Okay, that's some of it, but keying into the relationship between you and her got me thinking about what I've missed."

Maybe it was having her hands free that loosened Cheyenne's throat. Maybe Mace's fingers gliding over her wrists was responsible. Either way, she'd never felt more alive.

"Keying in?" she asked Bat. "What did you sense?"

"Caring. Same as what's going on between him and his dog." Bat smiled, drawing her attention to Rio's tongue still washing Bat's hand. "I thought everything had died in me, that the ability to care had been killed over the years. Guess I was wrong." Sinking to his knees, he lay his weapon on the ground and cradled Rio's head in his hands.

"Yeah," Mace said and pulled her into his embrace. "You were."

"You sensed—" Bat started.

"I wasn't sure." Mace pressed his lips to the top of her head, and she went weak and soft. "You threw up a lot of angry crap, but I kept thinking there was more to the way you acted than being fed up with everyone telling you what to do."

Bat looked up. "You're right about that. I've had it with those so-called human beings assuming I'm frozen inside. So..." He signed. "What are we going to do?"

A moment ago, Cheyenne believed she was incapable of thinking, but the rest of her life—and Mace's—depended on what happened right now.

"Mace overpowered you," she said, her thoughts barely ahead of her words and Mace's warmth spreading through her. "It wouldn't have happened if I hadn't tried to run. You took off after me. That's when he ... hit you on the back of your head?"

"He knocked me out with his gun?"

"I don't know." She looked up at Mace, seeing little more than a blur. "Maybe."

"We could make it work," Mace said to Bat, "if that's what you want?"

"Why the hell do you think I was quiet all the way here? I was trying to figure out—the last thing I expected was cooperation from the two of you. Or this." After hugging Rio, Bat got to his feet. "I thought he didn't like people."

"Just those he doesn't understand."

"I'm that transparent?" Bat's features sobered. "Isn't that something. The only ones who can see through me are you and a piss ugly dog."

"Maybe you let your defenses down around them," Cheyenne offered. "I know I was blind to Mace's love for Rio. I should have known he'd never kill him."

"You didn't because you had other things on your mind." Mace ran his fingers down her spine. "We don't have much time. They're expecting us back."

"All they're going to get is me," Bat said. "With a raging headache and bleeding scalp. Damn, let's get this over with."

Forcing herself, Cheyenne stepped away from Mace. She scratched behind Rio's ears, then held her hand out toward Bat. It would take time for her to fully comprehend what was taking place, but the essence was Mace's dog trusted Bat. She would too.

"Are you going to be all right?" she asked Bat as he covered her fingers with his.

"Yeah, they need me too much not to buy into my story."

"And then?" Mace asked.

She stepped aside so the two men could shake. Watching them, she blinked back tears.

"They'll eventually find someone to replace me. I'll retire. Hell, maybe I'll get a dog."

"You'd be good at it," Mace said.

"I hope so. The two of you can't stay here. You're not going to be safe in this state, maybe not in this part of the country."

"I know," Mace said. "We're leaving, the three of us." Taking her in his arms, he nodded at Rio.

35

Six months later

"You're sweaty."

"So are you."

"You have more body mass; therefore, your sweat index is greater than mine."

"Body mass has never been identified as the sole criteria for any kind of index. However, I have a suggestion that should demonstrate without a doubt which of us gets an A for effort. I do want to point out that you've been out here soaking up the rays. Might I suggest a shower."

Cheyenne, who'd been sitting in a reclining lawn chair on their back deck going over interview notes since coming home an hour ago, lifted her sunglasses so she could give Mace the glare he deserved. "Are you saying I stink?" she asked the familiar shadow looming over her.

"I would never say such a thing about a lady." He cupped a protective hand over his crotch. "Not if I wanted to keep my manhood."

"At least you understand the danger you're in. What was

your first suggestion, the one having to do with measuring sweat?"

Instead of answering, Mace took her notebook and placed it on the ground. He then covered her waiting and eager mouth with his practiced toe-curling kiss.

"I thought we might take turns licking sweat from each other's bodies. See who gets full first."

"That's gross." She playfully slapped his chest. Damn the loose cotton shirt worn by so many Floridians. Granted, it made sense given the state's humidity, but it got in the way of what she wanted to touch. "There's a pitcher of iced tea in the refrigerator." Reaching for the small wooden table at her elbow, she picked up her nearly empty glass. "While you're getting yourself some." She extended it toward him.

"Wait a minute. Who's the dom and who's the sub around here?"

"I forgot." When he took the glass from her, she rewarded his effort by unbuttoning a button on his shirt and sliding her fingers into the space she'd created. "At least I made the tea. Give me some credit."

Sliding the fingers of his free hand into her lengthening hair, he pulled her head back so she stared at the sky. "I'll give you something all right, but it won't be credit. First, though, my throat's parched."

Leaving her, he headed for the back door that led to the kitchen of the two-bedroom house they'd signed the papers on last month. The place wasn't upscale by any stretch of anyone's imagination, but it had a fenced backyard. The fact that a canal formed the rear boundary was a plus, but most important, Rio was safe here. Safe and endlessly entertained by the birds, turtles, lizards, snakes, and other critters drawn to the slow-moving water. Wildlife Mace had already spent hours photographing.

At the moment, Rio was sleeping in the shade provided by a

nearby palm tree. As long as the large overhead patio fan stirred the air, he wouldn't stir, not even to greet his master.

"You're absolutely spoiled," Cheyenne informed the snoring pit. "Nothing but the best for you. Just wait until July. Then I won't be able to drag you away from the AC."

Her either, she admitted. Sitting outside in shorts and a sleeveless top a little before nightfall in April made moving across the country worth it. However, from what she understood, it wouldn't be long before she'd be clinging to the air-conditioning.

Speaking of clinging to something, or should she say someone, Mace was back. He'd shed his shirt and shoes. The faded shorts he'd replaced his slacks with reminded her of how he'd looked last weekend when they'd gone fishing in the gulf.

Holding his glass, Mace toed the other reclining chair next to hers and stretched out on it. He took a long swallow, then put down the glass. Turning toward her, he unceremoniously pulled up her top so her unrestrained breasts were on display.

"So how did it go?" he asked, looking at her breasts as if they were only mildly interesting.

"Good. She's remembering things she thought she'd forgotten. What a nightmare. If I'd experienced what she had, I wouldn't want to remember either."

"You went through a lot when we were in the Blind Spot. Maybe she senses you're kindred souls."

Not exactly, but then Mace didn't need that pointed out. Twenty-four-year-old Angela Staples had decided she could no longer remain silent about what she'd seen and experienced living with a drug-addicted and dealing husband. Although her ex was in federal prison, she was concerned, and probably rightfully so, that certain drug kingpins would want to silence her. As a result, it had taken her awhile to find a writer she trusted. In the end, they'd found each other when Angela decided to take a journalism class Cheyenne was teaching at the local community college.

Neither author nor narrator would use their real names, but based on clips of her previous work and an outline of the proposed book, Cheyenne had found an agent who had quickly sold the project to a major publishing company. Only the agent, editor, and publisher knew who she and Crystal really were. The advance had been enough for the down payment on the house, while Mace's security consulting under an assumed name was making the mortgage payments.

"Any idea how many more sessions between the two of you before you have everything you need?" he asked.

"Not many." Thank goodness for shade. Otherwise, she'd have a sunburn on her nipples. She tweaked one. "Is there a point to this?"

"Point?" Mace grinned and turned onto his side so he faced her. "Well, as a matter of fact, yes."

"You know what I'm talking about." She pretended to slap him. "I'm trying to see where this falls under the foreplay umbrella."

"I'm thinking more in terms of eye candy." Tilting his head, he made a show of studying one breast at a time. "I picked up the mail. Two bills. A clothing store ad I threw away so you wouldn't be tempted. The news is on in case you care what's happening in the world."

"Hmm." Turning onto her own side, she licked her fingers and ran them down his chest. "What clothing store? I need a bathing suit."

"Nope, I want my woman naked."

She licked again, depositing more moisture on her fingers. "Which you get a hell of a lot." Watching him breathe, in particular the way his nonexistent belly disappeared, nearly chased away the thoughts that had been plaguing her. "How was your day?"

"Same old, same old." Licking his lip, he began circling her right breast. "Did a little alligator wrestling. What do you think of opening a bait shop? You'd have to get up early to be ready for first-light fishermen. I'm a little unclear on how you'd get the bait, but you'd meet a lot of interesting people. Old salts and tourists."

Between his handling of her breast and her attempt to meet him sensation for sensation, she was hard put to concentrate on anything else.

"What's this *me* business? Your idea, your bait shop."

"No can do." Looking too bored for her to believe, he stared in on her other breast. He'd have to be dead not to notice he'd hardened her nipples. "You're the one with the flexible hours. Lie down. I want to try something."

She did as he ordered, shivering in anticipation as he knelt beside her. "I thought we were going to watch the news."

"It'll be there later." He licked the tip of one nipple, then the other. "Damn but you have perky knockers."

Breathe. Keep it calm, somehow. "Wow, you sure know how to sweet talk a woman."

Closing in on her, he sucked a nipple into his mouth. If not for the recliner, she would have flowed out all over the patio. Her lids drooped. She couldn't summon the strength to lift her arms.

"That feel good?" he asked, coming up for air. He took hold of her breast again, drawing it deep. Her stomach lurched. Whipping her head from side to side helped, a little.

"Good," she managed. "Damn good for an old man."

"Not old, experienced."

Most days they didn't speak about the first chapter in their lives together, but there was no pretending it hadn't happened. Mace was incredibly experienced when it came to what a woman's body needed, and she loved being the recipient of that knowledge, most of the time. Sighing, she tried to lose herself in sensation. His warm, insistent mouth owned not just her breast, but her entire body. All except for a small part of her mind.

Long before she was ready for him to do so, Mace released her. Air from the fan dried her breast.

"What is it?" he asked.

"What is what?"

"Don't do that, Cheyenne." Shifting position, he placed his arms on either side of her and leaned down so his breath washed her forehead. "I saw it in your body language the moment I spotted you."

Of course he did. There wasn't a single thing he didn't know about her just as there wasn't anything she didn't love about him.

"I can't stop thinking about it," she admitted, wrapping her arms around his neck.

"The Blind Spot you mean."

"And the people there, mostly the women. I keep thinking there must be something we can—"

"There isn't."

He was right. They'd discussed the way things were at the Blind Spot numerous times, taking turns trying to come up with a way to free the females. The lawbreakers from Earth were another matter. They couldn't go back. Talking to law enforcement wouldn't change anything. The FBI, CIA, Secret Service, all those agencies would declare them insane. There was no such place as the Blind Spot.

Only there was.

"Cheyenne," Mace whispered. "I want to change things there as much as you do, but for now that's not going to happen."

"I know, but—"

"I think I know why it's bothering you today. You admire what Angela has made of her life. You want to do the same."

Her system felt soft and alive, a combination of sexual tension and love. Mace, her life, was responsible.

"I guess I do." She might have said more if Rio hadn't chosen that moment to yawn, loudly.

"That's one of the things I love about you," Mace went on with his breath brushing her sensitive nipples. "You care, deeply."

"Maybe too much."

"There's no such thing. Honey, for now the Blind Spot is beyond our ability to do anything about. Like Bat said, the entrance disappears when it isn't being used. But you can help those living with addicts by making sure Angela's voice is heard. I know what kind of job you do. The writing will be powerful."

Loving him as she'd never believed it was possible to love, she increased her hold on him. His weight settled on hers. She was cursing their respective shorts when the recliner collapsed under them. At the last moment, he ran his hand between the back of her head and the concrete.

"You okay?" he asked, making no move to get off.

"I guess. There's this oaf on me."

"An oaf who very much likes where he is, so what the hell are you going to do about it?"

Just like that, she lost the thoughts that had mentally taken her back to the Blind Spot. Mace was right. They'd fight the battles they could.

Only battles weren't their only option. Right now she'd rake her nails over her man's back, and he'd lift his head and nibble her chin. Right now they'd tear off each other's clothes and fuck on what remained of a lounge chair.

Later they'd take their naked, satiated bodies inside so they could feed their dog and stare at the news with her head on his still-naked lap and his hand stroking her equally naked buttocks.

There'd be no talk of bait shops, only that of photo-taking trips into the Everglades and the pros and cons of nipple rings.

Turn the page for a special excerpt of Katana Collins's

SOUL STRIPPER

It's called Sin City for a reason. Nowhere else are the temptations so great, the sex so good, and the demons so bad. . . .

By day, Monica is a barista in a local café. It doesn't pay a lot, but it puts her up close and personal with her sexy boss, Drew. Unfortunately, that's as far as a succubus can go unless she wants to take his soul. Monica needs mind-blowing sex to sustain her, and she finds her victims every night at a local strip club where she's an exotic dancer. But when her powers begin to diminish and her fellow succubi start turning up dead, all bets are off. Monica realizes she's the one immortal who has a chance in hell of making things right . . .

An Aphrodisia trade paperback on sale now.

PROLOGUE

She lay on top of his body, her bare breasts pressed against his tight muscles. His breathing was steady against her chest. She lifted herself up quietly so as not to wake him. She hadn't known her date for long, but he seemed nice enough.

She walked to her bathroom, not bothering to turn on the light. A candle glowed on the sink, and she ran the faucet to splash some water on her face. A tendril of red, curly hair fell over one shoulder, and she could taste something bad in her mouth—what was that? Morning breath? She grabbed her toothbrush, which hadn't been used in ages. Every now and then to spruce up before a date, but really—she had no need for one other than keeping up appearances. She scrubbed the bristles against her teeth, the action feeling foreign, and stared at her reflection.

It was dark, but her succubus vision was sharp.

There was something next to her mouth—a crease? It couldn't be. Succubi don't *get* wrinkles. She closed her eyes and shifted, thinking about what areas she wanted to change. Where there would normally be a tingle—some shiver of magic running through her body—she felt hardly anything. A few goose bumps rose on her arms. When she opened her eyes, the crease was still there, though slightly less visible. She spit the minty foam into the sink and tossed her toothbrush down, bringing her face in closer to the mirror to investigate.

She was naked with the exception of the beautiful anklet dangling just above her foot—a gift from the man lying in her bed, fast asleep. Her breasts brushed the cold porcelain of her sink, making her jump back slightly. She closed her eyes and shifted into clothes. The power was still there, though barely. She looked down, now wearing a sheer camisole and panties. It wasn't what she had in mind, but at least it was something. Her head was spinning and she was dizzy, faint from the energy spent.

The light behind her clicked on and she jumped, turning to find her date standing behind her. His eyes, which had been so kind only hours before, now seemed like empty, bottomless holes. "Trouble sleeping?"

She shook her head, fiery hair tickling her collarbone. A pull came from deep in her gut, feeling his aura's shift from earlier in the night. It was red—a purplish red. She sent him the sweetest smile she could muster and casually tossed her hair behind her shoulder. "Not at all. Just wanted to freshen up before round two." She reached for the sink, grabbing her porcelain hand mirror from the vanity and slowly brought it to her face. She kept one eye on him and managed to act as though she were looking at her reflection.

His chiseled jaw clenched, and his face twisted into a sadistic smile. "Come now, Savannah. We both know there's not going to be a round two. I can smell your fear." From behind his back, he pulled out a knife with a serrated blade. He moved quickly, lunging at the succubus, but even in her exhausted state she moved faster.

She smashed the porcelain mirror against the counter, the

glass shattering, leaving her with the pointed shard of the handle. She swung the shiv toward him, just barely missing his arm. They each stood in a crouched position, ready to strike.

He laughed at her. His head tipped back, the low chuckle escaping his throat like the soft rattle of a dangerous snake. With no warning, he threw his knife, the blade slicing through her bare foot, staking it to the hardwood floor.

She screamed, her body crumpling into a heap, and yanked the knife away. She sat there, blade in one hand, shiv in the other, waiting for her foot to heal itself. Waiting for regeneration that didn't come. He cackled above her. She looked up to find him standing over her, another knife in his hand.

He knelt, eyes cold like stone. "You're waiting for something that's not going to happen, hun. You are practically human. Nothing's going to heal itself this time."

Her breath became shorter—panic. She had not felt true fear in such a long time. Not since she was human. She forced her breathing to slow down. Forced herself to stop the tunnel vision from closing around her. She still held two weapons, his knife in one hand and her shiv in the other. She would not go down without a fight. The small tingle of power coursed through her veins, reminding her she still had a touch of magic left—she would find the right time to use it.

She swiped the knife across his bare chest, and the blade slid into his tender flesh. He fell back, a scream echoing in the bathroom. In the moment it took him to gather his composure, she leaped over his body, running to the bedroom. Her leap was not high enough and he raised his knife, cutting her deeply behind the knee.

Both legs were damaged. She could hardly stand; most of her weight rested on her hands, leaning on the dresser. She had lost the knife somewhere along the jump, but the shiv was still clenched so tightly in her fist that her palm was bleeding. The blood from her knee traveled down her leg, over her calf, and as it dripped across her beautiful anklet, steam rose with a sizzle, as though the anklet were absorbing the blood. The blood that hit the anklet dropped to the floor, still steaming and sizzling, creating burn marks like a chemical spill.

He walked slowly toward her, knives dripping with blood. His, hers—did it matter? "It's over, Savannah."

She shook her head, eyes wide and wet. "Why?"

His eyes creased, and he smiled in that evil way again. He shuddered with pleasure as her body trembled in fear before him. "You kill for a living. And now, so do I."

Adjusting her body, she forced herself to stand so that she was leaning only against one arm—the shiv stretched out in front of her. "Then come and get me, fucker." Despite her tough exterior, her heart hammered against her ribs.

He ran toward her. As he did, she shifted into a serpent with her last remaining power. Her fangs sunk into his abdomen just before his knives slit her throat. A handful of scales fluttered to the floor and a fang ripped out of her mouth as she choked on her own blood. She fell to the ground, transforming back into her human form. A bloody goddess with lifeless eyes.

He chuckled softly and licked the blood from his knife, his body radiating with the power of fresh blood and a new kill. Her magic entered his body with her blood, slithering down his throat like a fine cognac. He bent down and ran his hand down the length of her lifeless body. Using the edge of the knife, he gathered a pool of blood on the blade and scraped it across two small test tubes. "I'd fuck you one last time, but I fear it would somehow wake you," he whispered to himself. "Such a waste." His fingers trailed down her hips, across her ass, and down her thighs until he reached the anklet. He ripped it swiftly from her body, pocketing it before taking off.

1

The smell of coffee always turns me on.

Well, it might not be the coffee as much as it is my manager *at* the coffee shop. Drew. I liked to repeat his name in my head. Drew. *Drew. An*drew Sullivan—one of the best men I've ever met. Which might not be saying much for him considering the degenerates I hang out with. I wiped down a table with a few stains, thinking about those dimples of his. He always had the faint aroma of coffee on his clothes. And under his cotton T-shirts, I could see the slightest ripple of muscles. Long and lean. The muscles of a soccer player.

I stood there wiping the same spot over and over, my nails scraping against the tabletop. I imagined Drew's lips gently brushing against the dip in my neck. His growing erection pressing into me as he tenderly nibbled the soft skin above my collarbone. *Monica, Monica,* he'd moan. . . .

"Monica?" His smooth voice snapped me out of my dream. "I think that table's clean." His lips curled into a playful smile, eyes sparkling with mischief. He turned his attention back to the faucet, wrench in hand, fixing the constant drip that had been annoying all the baristas over the past week.

"Oh. Right, of course. Sorry, Drew. I'm sort of lost in my own thoughts today." My eyes traveled to his tight ass; his signature dirty towel was hanging from the back pocket of his jeans. Disoriented, I turned to move on to my next task and slammed into a customer closing in on the table I just cleaned. His iced coffee spilled onto my chest. Ice dribbled down my white T-shirt, and cold coffee covered my now-tight nipples.

"Oh shit." I looked up at the regular customer whose caffeinated beverage I was now wearing. He looked angry—which for anyone else might have been a problem. But for me? This was an easy fix for any succubus over a century old. That's what I am—a succubus. And whatever notions you have in your head about succubi are probably wrong. Just because I am a minion of Hell doesn't necessarily make me an "evil" being.

I used to be an angel and am apparently the *only* angel-turned-succubus known within the demon realm. I guess this sort of makes me a celebrity. They call me the golden succubus—the nickname makes me cringe. It's a bit too reminiscent of a particular "golden" sex act.

I looked up at the angry man standing over me and felt the tingles as my succubus magic handled the situation. My bottom lip pouted naturally when I spoke. "I am just *so* sorry." As I took a deep breath, his eyes fixed on my nipples pushing out my wet T-shirt. "I'm such a klutz!" Running my fingernail along his forearm, his face softened.

"It's really no problem." He flashed a smile after licking his lips. "We should really get you out of that shirt." He lifted a hand to his mouth, and I noticed a wedding band on that ring finger of his.

Fucking men.

I opened my mouth to answer, but before I could, Drew

stepped between us, his eyebrows low over his eyes. "You can go have a seat—we'll bring you another coffee."

"*Iced* coffee." The married man smirked and looked past Drew, meeting my eyes.

"Iced coffee? What's the matter—can't take the heat?"

"It's Vegas, man. Who drinks hot coffee in the middle of the desert?"

Drew's mouth tipped into a barely visible smile. "*I* do."

The customer ran a hand through his dark brown hair. "Fine, whatever man."

Drew was still standing protectively in front of me, and I touched his arm lightly, an attempt to break him from his aggressive stance. As he rocked back on his heels, Drew's face cracked into a friendlier smile—one that was much more appropriate as the owner of the coffee shop. He clapped the man on the bicep in that weird way men do to each other. "Just messin' with you, man. Have a seat. I'll get your iced coffee."

Once the customer was out of earshot, Drew swiveled around, his smile entirely gone, replaced again with the anger I had seen a moment ago. He leaned down, his face suddenly close to mine. "Do you have to come on to every friggin' customer?" He grunted and pushed past my shoulder, heading back behind the counter.

"*Me?* I don't know if you saw the whole thing, Drew—but that guy came on to *me*. Not the other way around." I was whispering so not to create a scene in the crowded café.

"You don't even realize how much you flirt."

I paused, taking in his vibe. "We're not talking about *him* anymore, are we?"

He snorted and slammed some of his tools around, not answering right away. After a few seconds of silence, he stood with his hands on his hips, not meeting my eyes. "That was a long time ago, Mon. Trust me, I'm not exactly sitting at home pining away over you."

"Six months is not that long ago." Ever since I started working for him here at the coffee shop, I knew he was bound to ask me out at some point. He managed to hold out longer than most men—almost two years after we first met, he invited me to dinner. And I for some stupid reason still have a conscience—that little bit of angel left in me—and had to say no. I couldn't take that risk with Drew's soul.

He sighed. "It is in the dating world. You should know that."

I resisted the urge to roll my eyes. "Whatever. I'm happy you've moved on." I swallowed. His lips pressed together and one eyebrow twitched into an arch. Maybe he knew I was bluffing, maybe he didn't. It didn't exactly matter anymore. We held each other's gaze for seconds too long. I broke the eye contact first and joined him behind the counter, pulling out a new cup of ice for the customer's replacement coffee.

Drew cut me off, taking the cup from me. "Why don't I refill this for you? You're still a little bit—eh—indecent." His eyes flicked toward my breasts.

"Oh. Right." I glanced down at my shirt. Brown stains covered my hard nipples. "And—I really am sorry. About spilling the coffee," I clarified quickly. "I feel off my game today. Spilling stuff, drifting off, daydreaming..."

Drew smiled at me, turning back into his normal self. "It's fine, Monica. Really." He tossed me the hand towel that was hanging in his back pocket.

I smiled back. "Well, feel free to take the refill out of my hips—oops, I mean, *tips.*" I smirked, exaggerating the flirting.

He rolled his eyes. "There you go again." He smiled, lines creasing around his mouth. "I have an extra shirt in my office, if you need it."

I headed to the bathroom. "No, it's fine. I think I have one in my bag."

I shut the bathroom door and slid the lock to the left. Can't have anyone walking in while I'm shapeshifting. In actuality, my shapeshifting is just a mind-trick on mortals and immortals. A mirage of sorts. I took a look at the reflection in the mirror. My dark blond hair still looked in place, parted on the side with a slight curl at the ends. But my shirt was a mess. I focused—closed my eyes. A familiar prickle surrounding my body as I shifted into another clean, white shirt.

The idea of stealing souls for Hell makes my stomach twist. Even though I am technically a demon, you could say I sort of play for both teams whenever possible. Ethical souls are the nutrition. They're like eating fresh vegetables and free-range chicken. The bad souls, well, they're the fast-food equivalent. I'm essentially sustaining my existence on this mortal plane on a diet of chocolate and potato chips. My body certainly craves something better, but I allow the indulgence only when absolutely necessary.

I looked away from the mirror. I wasn't always such an immortal vigilante. There was a time I accepted my fate as a succubus. A time in my existence I wasn't exactly proud of.

Maybe I should try a new hair color—go blonder—surfer bleach blond . . . like Drew's new girlfriend, Adrienne. Ugh. I couldn't even bear the thought of it—Drew with a girlfriend. A *blond* girlfriend. It was just so . . . so . . . obvious. I mean, okay, my hair was blond, too, but mine was natural. I hadn't changed my looks much since my angel days, partially because I liked my cherub features but also because the art of shifting takes a lot of power. It simply takes less energy to adjust the looks I already have in people's minds rather than create a new vision entirely.

I thought again of Adrienne and her platinum blond hair. The sort of white blond that looked as though it had been singed at the bottom—brittle and crisp. It just screamed Pamela Anderson. Sighing, I walked out of the bathroom to finish up my closing shift duties.

I finished cleaning the tables and restocked the sugar, and as

I carried another bag of arabica coffee beans to the front, I inhaled their scent and thought of Drew. That sweet smell that hits you at the back of the throat. That scent will get me through the end of my night job. The strip club doesn't always have the nicest men . . . or the nicest smells, for that matter.

"Aren't you going to be late for the club?" Once again, Drew snapped me out of my thoughts.

Nine p.m. Which meant yes . . . I was going to be late. I flashed him a smile. "Yes, probably. With any luck, I'll be fired." I laughed to myself at the thought. Lucien would never dream of firing me. I'm his best dancer and the closest thing to a sister that he's got. As my ArchDemon, Lucien is in charge of Nevada and the entire Southwest region. He may seem threatening to most, but when he pitches his fits, I only ever see a petulant teenager stomping his feet and raising his voice.

Drew took a few steps closer to me and placed his rough hand on my elbow. They were the hands of a carpenter. A hard worker—rough and masculine. "Maybe you should quit. I could give you a raise here." His green eyes grew wider with hope—and perhaps a slight hint of desire.

My mouth tipped into a sad smile. "You can offer me a thousand dollars per night?" *Not to mention the easy access to men's souls.* The strip club is the best way to meet bad boys and avoid the good ones. The degenerates that come into that club give me just enough energy to keep running. I glanced back up at his green eyes, his warm breath tickling my lips. Drew's soul was clean. Pure and totally Heaven-bound. Sure, he was quite the flirt—even with a girlfriend. But that alone doesn't warrant a one-way ticket to Hell. He deserved better than me. Even still, when he was this close to my body, my ethical stance became fogged.

Drew chuckled, and his laugh reminded me of water bubbling over a fountain. "No, I definitely can't offer you that."

His hand was still on my elbow, and his fingers moved in gentle circles over my skin. "But I can give you unlimited coffee and an extra two dollars an hour."

"That's a *tempting* offer," I teased, "but somehow I'm not so sure I can sustain my life on coffee."

"I could find other ways to keep you happy here." His breathing became more shallow and his face lowered closer to mine. I knew he was just reacting to my succubus pheromones. It wasn't Drew talking—it was simply his carnal desire coming through. No man can resist a succubus in heat. And though I rationally knew this, I still couldn't pull my gaze away from his. I could feel the need from deep within my body, an itch to have sex with someone so deliciously pure and good. I looked down at my nails and they were glossier, with a sheen most women paid good money to get. My powers were running low, which meant only one thing—I needed to sleep with someone tonight. Everything about me was designed to draw in humans. I'm like a shiny, intricate spiderweb, waiting to catch my prey. As my body requires a recharge, my hair gets shinier, my eyes become more vibrant, and I emit a pheromone unlike any a human has ever produced.

We stayed there, eyes locked, as the bell above the door chimed. I sensed Adrienne's aura before even hearing her acrylic heels clacking against the floor—another succubus perk. Being able to sense most auras—human and demon. I quickly broke away from Drew's grasp and grabbed my bag.

"Well, hey there, handsome!" Adrienne came up behind Drew and wrapped her orange, faux-tanned arms around his shoulders. Her platinum hair fell into her eyes, making her black roots even more painfully obvious. *Ugh, a typical Vegas girl,* I thought. Which was admittedly ironic, since *I* was the stripper out of the two of us. Her aura shone as a bright red. That usually meant one thing—adultery. I'd seen her aura just the other day and it had been green. She must have recently finished the deed. I inhaled, and though I couldn't smell the stench of sex on her, there was something different about her scent.

Drew's face faltered and he withdrew his hand from me as if my touch burned. His eyelids drooped in that way that a man's does after watching golf for a few hours.

"Hey, back at you, gorgeous." His voice sounded genuine, for the most part. It strained a little bit on the word *gorgeous,* but that also might have just been my imagination.

Without thinking, I groaned. Adrienne darted an agitated look in my direction and Drew's head dropped to the side, his eyes rolling at me in a chastising way that made me feel like a teenager.

"Oh, um, sorry. I can't find my costume for tonight. I thought I had it in my bag." Adrienne narrowed her eyes at me, obviously not buying my story. Maybe I'm not as smooth as I thought.

Drew sighed. "Don't mind Monica, babe. She's our resident cynic here at the café."

I shrugged at Adrienne. "Well, I'd better get going. See you tomorrow, Drew." I rushed past them, bumping her shoulder in the process.

But before exiting through the door, I saw the married man from earlier. The one whose coffee I spilled. His eyes went directly toward my tits, acting as though if he just stared hard enough he'd develop X-ray vision. I ran up to him, grabbing my card from the bottom of my bag. "Here," I said, handing him the card. "If you're interested, I'll be dancing there tonight." It simply had my stage name, *Mirage,* listed with the strip club's name and information.

His eyes sparkled and he licked his lips as he glanced down at my card. "Oh, I know this place," he said.

I looked back again at Drew to find him staring at me. His

lips were pressed into a thin line, eyebrows knitted in the center. *Good*, I thought, *be jealous*. I turned and headed for the exit, glancing over my shoulder one last time to look at Drew. Instead, I found the married man staring at my ass. Sometimes it was just too easy being a succubus.

The itch between my legs simply would not go away. As I drove down Las Vegas's dusty roads, I knew I had to take care of my desire, and soon. I hoped the married coffee shop guy would show up, or I'd be forced to sleep with one of the other regular assholes who frequented Hell's Lair. That's the name of the strip club—real original, huh? I shifted myself into my stripper look while driving, which was becoming increasingly hard to do as my powers lessened. I made my hair a dark brown— almost black—as I tried to decide which costume to wear tonight. Schoolgirl seemed too obvious. Cowgirl was *so* overdone here in Nevada. And dressing like an angel hit a little too close to home for me. Maybe a 1950s housewife character tonight? Or even better—I'll go vintage chic. Classy but naughty. I shifted into a tight black dress that was backless but left some for the imagination. Underneath, I put on lacy black underwear that was styled in a retro fashion, with thigh-high stockings that had a seam running up the back of my leg and a garter belt. As the finishing touches, I added a pillbox hat, black elbow-length gloves, and a long cigarette holder. Like the one Audrey Hepburn had in *Breakfast at Tiffany's*. I had to make my shift gradually so that the other drivers on the road didn't notice anything funny. Luckily, Lucien's club isn't in the heart of Vegas. Being off the beaten path, makes it a little easier to not only attract the scum of the earth but it is also perfect for bringing in the immortal crowd.

I parked and ran inside, feeling completely out of place. The costume didn't even look like a stripper's costume. Grabbing one last look at myself in the full-sized mirror at the entrance, I had to admit it was unusual for a dirty strip club but still incredibly sexy.

I walked into the dark, smoky club and saw a few of the girls dancing on the stage. Hell's Lair was frequented by both mortals and demon-folk, and the seats around the stage reflected the lowest of low from both worlds. The floor was slick with oil, grease, and probably bodily fluids that I didn't let myself think too hard about. To the right and left of the stage were two bars. I crossed next to the crowd of men who were circling around the stage, each turning to look at me as I made my way past them, the smell of my sex hitting their noses—among their other regions. I nodded at T, our bartender and bouncer, and he winked in my direction. T got his name because he wears jewelry like Mr. T, and although he has a similar coloring and height, that's where the resemblance ends. Where Mr. T had muscles, T simply has fat.

Standing in front of the stage entrance blocking my way was Lenny, the annoying new manager Lucien had hired to run the place. He stood there, arms crossed over his man boobs, tapping his foot with his eyebrows knitted together. I inwardly rolled my eyes. He's shorter than me, probably somewhere around five foot four, and his greasy black hair combed over his balding scalp resulted in a zebra striping pattern along the top of his head. His belt was cinched tightly around his hips, and his belly spilled out over top. I could guarantee that at some point during the night, his shirt would come untucked, revealing his dimpled belly fat.

"You are late! Again!" He pulled out his clipboard and scribbled something down.

This time I rolled my eyes so that he saw me and brushed past him to go backstage.

He followed at my heels like some sort of balding, ugly

puppy. "Monica! *Monica!* Are you even listening to me? I'll fire you if you continue this pattern."

At that threat, I twirled around to face him. A slow smile spread across my face. I spoke quietly and calmly—and continued to give him a biting smile through my gritted teeth. "No. You won't fire me, Lenny. You can't and you *know* it. Now get the fuck out of my dressing room." I sat down at my mirror and dabbed on some lip gloss.

His chin dropped to his chest, creating even more jowls. "You're on in fifteen minutes," he muttered, dragging his feet behind him.

For tonight's music, I chose an old jazz tune with a lot of bass. The curtain opened and the spotlight warmed me. I started center stage, and as the first beat began, I smoked my cigarette from the long holder, taking the time to inhale deeply and slowly. The smoke streamed from my lips and swirled around the top of my head. After slipping the gloves off one at a time, I tossed them into the audience. As I slowly pulsated my hips to the rhythm, the dollar bills shot high into the air like statues in my honor. Starting with an older gentleman to my left, I allowed him to unzip my dress and peel it down over my body. His knuckles shook nervously as they brushed the smooth flesh on my back. When it reached my ankles, I opened my legs to him and stuck my hip in his face. Giving me a shy smile, he tucked a twenty into the garter belt. I danced away, moving on to the next man in the crowd, but not before I let my fingernail travel down the older man's cheek.

I stood at the edge of the stage, moving my hips in rhythm to the music. At the back of the crowd, I met eyes with a sexy man. Despite the dark bar and bright spotlight, I could see him clearly. Thank you, succubus vision. He had dark brown hair that tickled the tops of his ears and thick eyebrows that sat low over his eyes. I held his gaze for a few moments. He broke eye contact first and turned to leave the club. Some men just can't handle a forward woman.

Pivoting, I found my next tip, and that's when I noticed him against the edge of the stage. There, in the front row, was my married man from the coffee shop. His knuckle was raised to his lips, and low and behold—he had no wedding ring on his finger. Tsk, tsk. My lacy panties grew even wetter. He was no Drew, but he was definitely hotter than most of the men in this joint. Not to mention the most nervous. The beat wore on, the neon lights hit his eyes, and I sauntered over to him, crouching down so that my breasts were in his face. I was sure he could smell my sex from where he stood below me. I took another drag from the cigarette and blew it into his face. He drank in the smoke—and his eyes flashed with lust. I was his cocaine— his drug of choice, sweeter than any alcohol, more addictive than nicotine, and far more dangerous than any hallucinogen. I passed him the cigarette and he took a drag as I unhooked my corset, letting the straps drag over my arms and fall to the floor. My nipples puckered as the men around me gasped.

Through my peripherals, I saw more dollars fly into the air. I winked at my married man and continued on to collect the rest of the money. I moved fluently around the stage and fin- ished my dance in nothing except heels, thigh-highs, and the pillbox hat.

After my set, I quickly shifted into my original dress, sans the panties and corset, and headed back out to the club. Every man I passed called out to get my attention. Propositioning voices circled around me as I walked straight for my married man. I was done waiting. I needed my fix now. The needy feeling was not one I ever got used to—an itch that is so uncomfortable, if we wait too long, it actually becomes painful. With the types of men I sleep with, I'm lucky to make it forty-eight hours before I need to find my next fix.

Ignoring everyone else, I plopped myself down on his lap.

His eyes darted around the club. "My name is Erik." I smiled to myself watching him glance nervously about.

"Really?" It was less of a question and more of a bored statement. No need to feign any interest. "Well, Erik, I don't give a fuck what your name is." I took another drag of my cigarette and looked into his mundane brown eyes. "Buy a private dance."

"Oh, um, well . . . I-I don't know about that. You see, I'm a newlywed and I was just curious about this place . . ."

"Erik, please." I rolled my eyes. "You knew what you were getting into by coming here. Especially after a personal invitation from me." I lowered my face so that my lips brushed his as I spoke. "So . . . buy a fucking private dance. Now." I paused once more, giving a second thought to how forceful my voice was. "Unless, that is, your wife satisfies you fully."

If the stress lines around his face were any indication, I'd bet that he was sexually frustrated. But for a moment, his face softened at the mention of his wife. I thought he was going to push me off his lap. Go running back to his wife for some plain old meat-and-potatoes missionary sex.

Instead, he simply nodded, drool practically dripping from his lips. "She's a prude. Only ever cares about her work."

I sighed. Men are such shits. In the couple of centuries that I've been around, that's never changed. I guess I couldn't be too annoyed by him though—it was that lack of morality that would give me enough energy to survive the next couple of days up here on Earth. I grabbed his hand, leading him to the back room. I yelled to Lenny as I passed the pot-bellied manager. "Gotta private one here, Lenny." He marked something on his clipboard.

I shut the door behind me. "Money first, *Erik*."

"Right. Uh, how much again?"

"Four hundred dollars. Plus tip."

"Four hundred? Dollars?"

"Plus tip."

He gulped. "Wow, I don't know that I have that much . . ."

I slipped my tongue in his ear. "Trust me. I'm worth it. What I'm about to do to you would typically cost much, *much* more." I pressed my breasts into his back.

"You're killing me. . . ." He groaned and exhaled between barely open lips. It was unclear whether he was referencing his wallet or his libido.

Ha. "Oh, sweetie. If you only knew." I nibbled his earlobe.

He reached into his back pocket, opening up an expensive-looking leather wallet. A few wallet pictures of a baby fell to the floor. I bent to pick them up and studied the beautiful child smiling back at me. She couldn't have been more than six months old. A knot formed in my throat, and I instinctively placed a hand on my stomach. "Is this your daughter?"

Erik grabbed the photograph and tucked it into the folds of his wallet. "Nah. It's my brother's kid."

My eyes narrowed as I studied his aura. No shift in color—he was telling the truth. I sighed, my tense shoulders relaxing.

He handed me the cash without any more debate, plus an extra twenty. Cheap-ass. You don't come to a strip club with several hundred dollars in your wallet and plan on leaving here innocently. It definitely made me feel better about what was to happen. Nevertheless, I always marvel at how easy it is to get men to cheat on their wives.

He sat in a chair in the middle of the room. I slowly undid the buttons of his shirt and slid it down over his shoulders. Surprisingly, he had an amazing body. Much more fit than I thought he would be. Grabbing his bottom lip between my teeth, I sucked on it while undoing his belt and lowered his pants. They dropped to the floor with a clunk.

"What do you have in those pockets? Rocks?" I smirked, tilting my head to the side. He was already hard, standing at full attention.

I left him in the chair, his pants pooled around his ankles, and danced around him, lifting my leg over his shoulder. It offered him close-up view of my sex peeking out from under the black fabric of my dress. "You want to taste me, don't you, *Erik?*"

He cleared his throat, allowing his eyes to travel up my thigh and land on the glistening flesh between my legs. "Uh-huh." His eyes were wide and dazed.

"So? Go ahead. Give me your best tongue."

He flicked his tongue out, lightly brushing over my skin. The contact made me moan softly, yearning for more. He slowly ran his tongue along my lips and into my folds until finally covering my clit with his mouth, sucking. I grabbed his hair and pulled him into me harder. Two fingers entered me. I was so wet, I begged for a third. He quickly obliged, pulsating them in and out with a "come hither" sort of movement. My muscles tightened around him. It wouldn't take long for me to come.

"Just your tongue...." My voice was hoarse and breathy. He followed my orders, removing his fingers and delving his tongue deep within me. In seconds, I was coming on his face.

As my tremors finished, I grabbed his hair and pulled his face back so that he could see mine. "How'd I taste?"

"Amazing." His voice was gruff. The shy stutter was completely gone, replaced with lust.

"Tell me I taste better than your wife," I demanded.

"You taste so much better than my wife. She's nothing compared to you."

I turned around and had him unzip my dress, slipping the soft fabric off my body. The movement made my already-hard nipples even tighter. Naked, with the exception of my thigh-high stockings and heels, I straddled him.

"Wait." Concern suddenly filled his eyes. For a moment, there was hope for his soul. "Don't we need ... protection?"

I laughed a sultry, throaty chuckle. "Not with me, baby.

That's not an issue. Relax...." I dropped to my knees and lowered my mouth to his cock, running my lips along his shaft and twisting my tongue around his tip. I loved the feel of a cock slamming into the back of my throat. I increased my pressure and speed until he was ready for me.

I sat up, facing away from him in the reverse cowgirl position, and lowered myself down. It felt incredible having him fill me entirely. He sat there, not moving at all. And it figured. For four hundred dollars, of course he expected me to do the work. I lifted myself up, enjoying the sensation of his dick pulling away from me, and just before I lifted up entirely, I came back down hard. He groaned and grabbed my breasts, tweaking my nipples. I continued bouncing on him, feeling his size grow larger as he got more and more excited.

"You like that?" I asked, much louder than before. "You like being fucked by someone other than your wife?"

"God, yes," he cried out.

"Tell me!" I turned so that I could face him and grabbed his face roughly with one hand. "Say it again." I continued fucking him hard, squeezing my muscles as I reached his tip. My wetness grew with each thrust—so much so that I could feel it dripping out over my lips.

I slapped him across the cheek, perhaps harder than I intended to. "I *said*, tell me!"

"I love being fucked by you. You're so much better than my wife."

My itch raged on, worse than before, almost unbearably so. It wouldn't be relieved until he came—my release would come when he did. I could tell by his suddenly larger girth stretching my insides that he wasn't going to last much longer. I rolled my hips in circles over him, and his velvety tip rubbed just the right areas. The swelling felt amazing. He grabbed my ass and pulled me down onto him hard. His body trembled and his juices filled me. I groaned in delight at both his release and the life I was sucking from him. The orgasm was good, but the high from his soul was even better.

In a flash, I saw a movie reel of his life. Like a flipbook, I caught a quick glimpse of what was to come in Erik's life and what the world would lack by my stealing a portion of it. I saw him playing catch with a little boy, signing divorce papers, and finally . . . I saw him sitting quietly in a rocking chair, eyes closed. I exhaled, and it wasn't until that second that I realized I had been holding my breath. You just never know until that moment what exactly you're taking from your conquest. Knowing he was going to die peacefully in his rocking chair allowed my stress to melt away.

Seconds later, my human form radiated with life—*his* life. Muscles deep inside me tensed, and the sweet release of my own orgasm squeezed every last drop from him. With a forefinger, he flicked my clit and I screamed as the tremors rolled through my body again.

Pulling away from his body, I could feel his cum dripping down my thighs. I put my other leg back up on his shoulder. "Lick me," I demanded.

"But, I-I—" he stammered, staring nervously at his juices combined with my own.

"Shut the fuck up and *lick* me." I spoke through clenched teeth.

More hesitantly than before, he brought his tongue to the dripping area between my legs, tentatively licking.

"Harder!"

His tongue stiffened, and the tension built inside me once again. My muscles pulsed, squeezing the cum out of me and onto his tongue.

"How do I taste *now?*"

"Still amazing," he said. He slapped my ass, squeezing my cheek with one hand.

His sudden force caught me off guard, and I moaned as my

body convulsed in yet another orgasm. After, I leaned down and licked the juices from his lips.

We finished dressing and he came up behind me, kissing my neck. "That was amazing." He reached in front and caressed my breast through the material of my dress. "*You* are amazing. I had no idea it could be that great." He tucked another hundred dollar bill between my cleavage. "Can I see you again?" He was speaking fast, and I could see the effects of succubus sex affecting him already. It acts as a sort of high, making my victims more manic and stronger than they normally are. One of the many ways we succubi keep them addicted, coming back for more.

I rolled my eyes, and even though he couldn't see me, he probably sensed my annoyance. "Well, of course we'll *see* each other again. You're in the coffee shop every fucking day."

He turned me around so I was face-to-face with him. I didn't realize before how tall he was. My eyes were about level with his pecs. "That's not what I meant." He brushed a piece of hair from my face.

"I-I know." I stammered slightly, feeling uncharacteristically bad for the man. "But I try to keep my two lives separate. My dancing life and the café life. Inviting you here was a . . . a momentary lapse in judgment."

He tilted my chin toward his and gave a small tug on my almost black locks. "I like this look. Is it a wig?" Then with the same hand, he cupped my jaw. For a second there, I really thought he was going to kiss me.

"Something like that," I replied.

"So, I can visit you here at the club?"

I nodded, sadness washing over me. Leaning in, he brushed his lips against mine. It was so intimate. So atypical for me. Intimacy was not something I experienced on a sexual level. It had been decades since I had felt that sort of sexual affection and actually acted on it. My stomach clenched; a rush of sorrow flooded me for . . . everything. For his wife. His deceit. Because of me, he would die a week sooner than he should have; I stole part of this man's soul and suckered him into cheating on his wife. Okay, well, maybe I didn't sucker him, but I certainly offered temptation. He may have gone his entire marriage without any infidelity if it hadn't been for me. Maybe I was the reason he'd be signing those divorce papers in the future. I needed to get away from him—away from this club.

I broke free from his kiss and headed toward the door. "I'll see you around, Erik." It was the first time I said his name without dripping sarcasm.

As the door clicked shut behind me, I instantaneously felt Lucien's presence. Seconds later, he stood before me. And he did not look happy.

"My office, Monica. Now."

GREAT BOOKS,
GREAT SAVINGS!

When You Visit Our Website:
www.kensingtonbooks.com
You Can Save Money Off The Retail Price
Of Any Book You Purchase!

- **All Your Favorite Kensington Authors**
- **New Releases & Timeless Classics**
- **Overnight Shipping Available**
- **eBooks Available For Many Titles**
- **All Major Credit Cards Accepted**

Visit Us Today To Start Saving!
www.kensingtonbooks.com

All Orders Are Subject To Availability.
Shipping and Handling Charges Apply.
Offers and Prices Subject To Change Without Notice.